His Dark
and Phi

WITHDRAWN

No longer the property of the
Boston Public Library.
Sale of this material benefits the Library.

Popular Culture and Philosophy®   Series Editor: George A. Reisch

For full details of all Popular Culture and Philosophy® books, visit www.opencourtbooks.com.

Popular Culture and Philosophy®

His Dark Materials and Philosophy

Paradox Lost

EDITED BY

RICHARD GREENE AND

RACHEL ROBISON-GREENE

OPEN COURT
Chicago

Volume 132 in the series, Popular Culture and Philosophy®, edited by George A. Reisch

To find out more about Open Court books, visit our website at www.opencourtbooks.com.

Open Court Publishing Company is a division of Carus Publishing Company, dba Cricket Media.

Copyright © 2020 by Carus Publishing Company, dba Cricket Media

First printing 2020

All rights reserved. No part of this publication may be reproduced, stored in a retrieval system, or transmitted, in any form or by any means, electronic, mechanical, photocopying, recording, or otherwise, without the prior written permission of the publisher, Open Court Publishing Company, 70 East Lake Street, Suite 800, Chicago, Illinois 60601.

Printed and bound in the United States of America.

His Dark Materials and Philosophy: Paradox Lost

This book has not been prepared, authorized, or endorsed by the creators or producers of *His Dark Materials*.

ISBN: 978-0-8126-9486-4

Library of Congress Control Number: 2020937776

This book is also available as an e-book (ISBN 978-0-8126-9488-8)

For Patrick Croskery

Contents

Contents

Thanks

Working on this project has been a pleasure, in no small part because of the many fine folks who have assisted us along the way. In particular, a debt of gratitude is owed to David Ramsay Steele and George Reisch at Open Court, the contributors to this volume, and our respective academic departments at Utah State University and Weber State University. Chapters 1, 2, 3, 5, 8, 10, and 13 appeared in *The Golden Compass and Philosophy: God Bites the Dust* (2009), and were revised and updated for this volume. Finally, we'd like to thank those family members, students, friends, and colleagues with whom we've had fruitful and rewarding conversations on various aspects of all things *His Dark Materials* as it relates to philosophical themes.

Lyra, a Spyglass, and Bears, Oh My!

His Dark Materials is as ripe for philosophical discussion and analysis as any work of fiction ever. Yes, that's a pretty bold statement, but it's true. A quick look at the table of contents of this volume reveals that Pullman's trilogy (and its subsequent additions) covers big philosophical issues, such as the nature and existence of God, death, a number of topics in metaphysics and epistemology, feminism, political philosophy, aesthetics, and, perhaps, most importantly, truth (and many others).

While more than one chapter discusses Lyra Belaqua's often tenuous relation to the truth, there are good reasons for highlighting here the relevance of *His Dark Materials* for young readers today. Lyra's journey begins with her plainly disregarding the truth whenever it suits her. In simple terms, Lyra lies a lot. She lies to avoid trouble, she lies to get people to do her bidding, and she seems to lie just for the fun of it. As the story progresses, lying becomes essential for Lyra to complete her heroic journey. Lying is a means to a very important end. In fact, by the end of *The Northern Lights* (the first book in the trilogy, which was released in the North America as *The Golden Compass*) Lyra's lying actually restores Iorek Byrnison to his rightful place as king of the Panserbjørne, by (falsely) telling his rival, Iofur Raknison, that she is Iorek Byrnison's dæmon, and that all the Panserbjørne can have human dæmons, as well. The reader is meant to applaud this lie, which comes at one of the most pivotal points in the story. Iorek Byrnison commemorates the lie by renaming Lyra Belacqua, "Lyra Silvertongue," a moniker that Lyra proudly adopts.

This raises an interesting question. Since *His Dark Materials* is taken to be primarily directed at a young adult audience (although we highly recommend it to adults, as well), is this the sort of message that we ought to be sending to our children? (While most people familiar with *His Dark Materials* consider that it is written for young adults, Pullman is on record as saying that he did not write it with any particular age group in mind.)

The first installment of the *His Dark Materials* collection of novels and follow-ups was published in 1995. And though it garnered a ton of critical praise and a whole slew of awards for children's literature (including the prestigious Carnegie Medal for children's literature!), it was no stranger to controversy. It is not difficult to see why. *His Dark Materials* involves a scathing attack on a very powerful religious institution (one that bears more than a passing resemblance to the Catholic Church), responses to both Milton's *Paradise Lost* and C.S. Lewis's *The Chronicles of Narnia*, and the literal killing of God. Needless to say, hackles were raised and calls to have the book banned were issued.

Here is five cents' worth of free advice for aspiring writers and filmmakers. There is no better publicity for a new book, play, or movie than having large religious organizations call for your work to be banned or boycotted. For prominent examples see The *Harry Potter* book series, Monty Python's *Life of Brian*, and *The Da Vinci Code*.

While most of the outrage came from Catholic groups, other prominent Christians, such as the Archbishop of Canterbury, came to the work's defense. (The Archbishop of Canterbury is popularly regarded as head of the Church of England, though technically he is second in command to the English monarch.) Some took the line that *His Dark Materials* was critical of neither organized religion nor religious views, but, rather, only of religious dogmatism, as divorced from actual religious practice.

It's worth noting that literally none of the controversy centered around Lyra's lies (although much scholarly attention has been paid to the topic). Back in 1995 no one was worried that the message being sent to children regarding the value of being truthful was a bad one. There are a couple of reasons for this.

First, as the trilogy progresses, the message regarding the permissibility of lying and the value of being truthful changes substantially. By the latter parts of the third book of the trilogy, *The Amber Spyglass*, Lyra's attitude toward the truth has changed. The prophecy regarding Lyra is that she will kill death itself. When she gets to the world of the dead, she finds that the harpies who guard the people there are desperate for entertainment, but they aren't interested in Lyra's lies. They want to hear *true* stories. She strikes a deal with them. The harpies will lead the dead through the hole that Roger cut if and only if the dead tell the harpies true stories about their lives. From this point forward, Lyra's silver tongue is put to use telling truths—her storytelling ability is upgraded by her recognition that the truth is valuable.

The payoff appears to be that, since over the course of her journey Lyra learns a valuable lesson about the nature and value of truth, the message being sent to children reading the trilogy is ultimately a good one. There is redemption along the way.

And yet, things are not quite that simple with *His Dark Materials*. Take a typical story of redemption—*A Christmas Carol*—for example. In that story, Ebenezer Scrooge is shown as miserly and uncaring about the welfare of others, even those closest to him. He is shown the error of his ways, and eventually comes to realize that he has lived life very badly. This sort of narrative is fairly common. We see this in television shows like *All in the Family* and *The Good Place*, where main characters Archie Bunker and Eleanor Shellstrop, respectively, over time see the error of their ways. Countless movies follow this pattern, as well (Perhaps the best example of this being *Groundhog Day*).

This, however, is not the case with Lyra's lying. While she eventually comes to have a proper understanding of the value of truth, it's not true that leading up to that realization, the reader is supposed to view her lying as a bad thing. If anything, it's presented as a fortuitous and virtuous thing—a force for good, so to speak. Nevertheless, it's not unreasonable to suppose that Lyra's final word on the topic is the one the audience is supposed to believe is the correct word, and that the message to the children reading *His Dark Materials* is ultimately a positive one.

The second reason that in 1995 we were not worried about the message *His Dark Materials* was sending (especially to young adult readers) is that back then the truth was on considerably firmer footing that is on today. In that sense, we need to be considerably more protective of truth as a societal good, than we used to.

To elaborate, in recent decades the very idea of truth has come under attack. This attack has come on a number of fronts. Certain segments of academia have been casting doubt on the idea of objective truth for several generations. The arguments proffered typically conclude that some sort of relativism is the case. Recently academic relativism has begun to gain a foothold outside the academy.

At the same time, we've seen confidence in our most cherished journalistic institutions erode. It was not that long ago that what we saw on the nightly news or read in the daily news was considered beyond reproach. The rise of the twenty-four-hour news cycles, and the sensationalistic reporting required to fill twenty-four hours, along with the increased amount of partisan political programming found on most news networks, has provided readers and viewers with reason to be more skeptical of what they are being told. Of course, a healthy skepticism can be a very good thing, but on a societal level, we don't seem to have a healthy skepticism. Instead we just have doubt, or worse, many people suffer from severe confirmation bias.

More recently, we've seen an increase in the number of politicians willing to lie for personal gain. While there have always been politicians willing to lie, the instances of it were considerably less frequent. Political lies stood out, and when they were exposed, the liars where shamed, shunned, and publicly called out. Now politicians use euphemisms, such as "spinning," to justify lying. It's part of the job. One often finds oneself amazed at the kind of mental gymnastics used to spin certain actions and yet, completely unfazed by the occurrence of the spin. We've come to expect it.

To make matters worse some politicians, such as our current Commander in Chief, have worked hard to actually discredit the news agencies. A sizeable portion of society believes that the news is fake, and that "alternative facts" are somehow legitimate. People are being asked to not believe what is right in front of their eyes, even when what they are seeing is backed-up with ample and compelling evidence. These same politicians trade in conspiracy theories about how the seemingly compelling evidence must be false.

Finally, there have been attacks on academic freedom from both the political left and the political right. A number of philosophical positions have come be considered not politically correct, such that one wonders whether certain philosophers actually hold the positions that they espouse, or whether they just feel compelled to publicly adopt those positions. The unfettered pursuit of any and all ideas in the academy is facing a grave threat.

The bottom line is that we're rapidly chipping away at the idea of truth. That is not to say that there is no such thing as objective truth or facts of the matter, but respect for truth is dwindling, and we are in danger of not having truth drive our decision-making. It's not a good state of affairs that we find ourselves in.

So, how does this bear on *His Dark Materials*? The worry is that given Lyra's blatant disregard for the truth throughout most of the trilogy, and its subsequent glorification, *His Dark Materials* doesn't play as well in 2020 as it did in 1995. The question then is: is *His Dark Materials* tone deaf in 2020? Should lying for personal gain or pleasure make us more uncomfortable now, given our present relationship with the truth, than it did twenty or thirty years ago?

There's no shortage of works of entertainment that, no matter how great they seemed in their day, serve to make viewers uncomfortable now. Take for example, the movie *Animal House*. When it came out audiences absolutely loved it. While many of the bits still work, certain scenes, such as the one where Bluto climbs a ladder to look through a window as sorority girls get undressed, or the one where the Pinto deliberates about whether to have sex with a thirteen-year-old who has passed out from drinking too much, make audiences extremely uncomfortable, and are just not funny. *Blazing Saddles*, which generally has a positive message about the evils of racism and racist language, leaves audiences uncomfortable, by being, perhaps, too flippant in its approach. The television comedy *The Honeymooners* was groundbreaking and featured wonderful performances by Jackie Gleason and Art Carney but doesn't play well with today's audiences, given its frequent lighthearted threats of domestic violence ("one of these days, Alice, bang, straight to the moon!").

Lyra's lies certainly don't rise to the same level as the above examples regarding the extent to which they make readers uncomfortable. Viewers of the recent BBC/HBO adaption of the trilogy still cheer Lyra's tricking Iofur Raknison into fighting Iorek Byrnison. The question is, should viewers react strongly to the lying (again, given our present circumstances)? One reason for thinking that they should not be bothered by Lyra's lies is that they are (usually) not told just for personal gain, but also for good. She is lying to save her friend Roger, she is lying to help Iorek, she is lying to escape Mrs. Coulter, and so forth. The problem with this response, however, is that it opens the door for our lying politicians to say the same thing. Recall Lyndon B. Johnson's famous lie to the effect that he would not go to war with Vietnam if elected, even though he full intended to the whole time. When pressed on it, he said it was justified because his being elected was better for the country than Goldwater's being elected. Every politician believes that their lies are for the greater good.

Perhaps the payoff is that we should be made to feel uncomfortable by Lyra's lies. To the extent that Lyra's realization about the value of truth shines a light on her years as Lyra Silvertongue, reading *His Dark Materials* in our current circumstances not only shines a light on Lyra's lies, it also does so on lies told in the public sphere. Our contention is that this particular moral of *His Dark Materials* plays better now than it did when it came out. The analogy with the aforementioned "uncomfortable" works of entertainment is not apt. A better analogy exists between *His Dark Materials* and works such as *The Adventures of Huckleberry Finn*. Certainly, the racist language of *Huck Finn* makes readers un-comfortable, but it ought to. It is highlighting something true, that ought to be brought to light. For similar reasons, *His Dark Materials* is precisely the sort of thing we should be having our children read.

Part I

---

*"That's what you are.
Argue with anything else,
but don't argue with
your own nature."*

1
One of These Gods Is Not Like the Other

RACHEL ROBISON-GREENE

There's no shortage of controversy over Philip Pullman's *His Dark Materials* trilogy. The novels take a dim view of organized religion, portraying it as an institution which has power as its goal and is willing to tear the souls away from children in order to maintain that power. Even more dramatically, Lord Asriel, one of the key characters in the trilogy, embarks on a quest to kill God in order to reclaim freedom for all the persons under the deity's tyrannical rule.

Critics of the series object that the novels are directed toward children; at this impressionable age, the content of the novels may cause them to reject religion and form the belief that faith in God is dangerous.

The Authority and the Christian God

What is it that leads those thinkers who believe in God to the conclusion that such a being is worthy of praise and worship? It's not just the fact that he is our creator. One can imagine a malevolent being creating a universe for the sole purpose of inflicting pain and suffering on its inhabitants. Such a creator would be the proper object of fear and possibly anger, but not worship and praise.

Similarly, we could imagine a wiser being creating life in a universe in much the same way that a scientist cultivates bacteria in a petri dish. Once the life is created, this being pays little attention to it and is completely apathetic when it comes to the well-being of the creatures he has created. Such a creator doesn't seem deserving of worship either. We might be grateful to the entity, but could not be criticized for failing to be awe-inspired in a way that properly motivates worship.

The reason that religious thinkers believe that God is worthy of our worship and praise is that he is a being who possesses all perfections appropriate to a God. What would such perfections be? There are certain role-based perfections that we can rule out. A perfect piece of chocolate may have a taste that is the best possible balance of bitterness and sweetness. This is not a perfection that we would expect God to have, because God is not a piece of chocolate. The perfections we would expect God to have are those perfections that are thought by philosophers and theologians to be appropriate to a God. These perfections are being all-good (omnibenevolent), all-knowing (omniscient), and all-powerful (omnipotent).

Omnibenevolence

We have seen why, in virtue of his attributes, the Christian God, if he exists, is worthy of worship and praise. But what of the God that Pullman has created? Does he have attributes that are equally worthy of worship?

Let's first consider the issue of omnibenevolence. If a being is omnibenevolent, then that being has a desire to bring about the best possible state of affairs and, if possible, the being acts on this desire (as we will see, for an omnipotent being, acting on this desire will always be possible). The best possible state of affairs will be the state of affairs that is best not just for God, but for all of his creatures. If this is the case then a world without suffering in it will presumably be better than a world in which suffering occurs.

On the face of it, it seems that if a God who either created or rules over a universe is both all good and all powerful, then there should not be suffering in that universe. At first blush, one might think that a world with suffering in it is logically inconsistent with an omnibenevolent God. This problem is known by philosophers and theologians as the Problem of Evil, and it's a problem for any God who is thought to be omnibenevolent, omniscient, and omnipotent.

If suffering exists in the world, then either God desires that his creatures suffer (in which case he is not omnibenevolent), he does not have the power to prevent the suffering (in which case he is not omnipotent), or he does not know that the suffering is occurring (in which case he is not omniscient).

Let's see whether the God of the *His Dark Materials* trilogy is resistant to the problem of evil. To do this, one need only look to see whether suffering exists in Pullman's universe. We need not even finish the first chapter of the first book in the series to find what we're looking for:

> The Master took from his pocket a folded paper and laid it on the table beside the wine. He took the stopper out of a decanter containing a rich golden wine, unfolded the paper, and poured a thin stream of white powder into the decanter before crumpling the paper and throwing it into the fire. Then he took a pencil from his pocket stirred the wine until the powder had dissolved, and replaced the stopper. (*The Golden Compass*, p. 6)

Right out of the gate, we see a trusted official of a prestigious university attempting to poison a man to prevent him from relaying information that is dangerous to the church. And he would have gotten away with it too if it weren't for that blasted kid!

But, you might think, the master didn't succeed in his plot to kill Lord Asriel. The Authority survives the first chapter unscathed by the Problem of Evil. Perhaps. But we don't need to look very much further to see parents grieving because their children have been kidnapped, an armored bear reduced to a shadow of his former glory because his armor has been taken from him, and, perhaps the greatest suffering seen in the series, the cutting of a child from their dæmon. Doctor Cooper, who is in charge of the cutting process, describes the procedure in the following way:

> So we've developed a kind of guillotine, I suppose you could say. The blade is made of manganese and titanium alloy, and the child is placed in a compartment—like a small cabin—of alloy mesh, with the dæmon in a similar compartment connecting with it. While there is a connection, or course, the link remains. Then the blade is brought down between them, severing the link at once. (p. 273)

This description would sound grotesque enough if what Dr. Cooper and his cohorts were doing was cutting off body parts, but what he is describing is actually cutting a child away from their soul. This is an extremely painful process which ruins the lives of the children it is performed on. The suffering of poor Tony Costa is unparalleled:

> He couldn't settle, he couldn't stay in one place; he kept asking after his dæmon, where she was, was she a coming soon, and all; and he kept such a tight hold on that bare old piece of fish as if . . . Oh, I can't speak of it, child; but he closed his eyes and finally fell still, and that was the first time he looked peaceful, for he was like any other dead person then, with their dæmon gone in the course of nature. (p. 218)

If the Authority knows of this immense suffering that the people in his universe are experiencing and does nothing, then it seems he is either not omnibenevolent, not omnipotent, or not omniscient.

You might be thinking that it may be true that Pullman's Authority is subject to the Problem of Evil, but that in this respect the Authority and the Christian God in our non-fictional universe stand or fall together. For surely there is immense suffering in this world. People go hungry every day. Innocent people are brutally killed. Painful diseases ravage massive numbers of the populace. All of this is true. But, as we'll see, a difference remains between the trouble the Problem of Evil poses for Pullman's Authority and the trouble the problem creates for the Christian God.

There is a way to reject the conclusion that the existence of suffering in the world is logically inconsistent with God's omnibenevolence. In order to show this, thinkers construct what they call theodicies—apologies or explanations for God's actions that show that the actions in question are not inconsistent with his divine attributes. In response to the problem of evil, such theodicies suggest that there is something God desires to put in the world that is so good that a world which contains this thing and all of the suffering that comes with it is, in fact, the best possible world. A common suggestion for this special something is free will.

Free will is so good that, even though it produces suffering, the world with free will and all its resultant suffering is the best possible world. This kind of a response carves out a place for it to be the case both that evil exists in the world and God is all-good. This kind of a response is not available to save the God of Pullman's universe. Why? Because we actually know what the Authority's intentions are. We know that even if the Authority had the power to change the fact the people are suffering in the world, he does not have the desire to end it. In fact, through the years he has allowed clouds to gather around his citadel on the Clouded Mountain and has even delegated much of his Authority to another angel—Metatron, who he certainly would have known did not have the best interests of others at heart. We see even Metatron attempt to kill a number of characters in the book, including Balthamos, Baruch, and perhaps Will. He sends a large, fierce angel to attack the party:

> The clouds were parting, and through the dark gap a figure was speeding down: small at first, but as it came closer second by second, the form became bigger and more imposing. He was making straight for them, with unmistakable malevolence. (*The Amber Spyglass*, p. 29)

Pullman describes Metatron and his followers as beings that often have sinister intentions. An omniscient, omnibenevolent God would certainly not delegate his authority to such a malevolent being.

Unlike in our own world, we really do know these facts about the Authority. There are beings who actually interact with him and are aware that he has weaknesses. These facts about the Authority bar an attempt to save him from the trouble raised by the Problem of Evil. For though it may be true that a theodicy shows that an omnibenevolent God is not logically inconsistent with the existence of evil, we know that in the case of the Authority, it actually turns out to be the case that God is simply ambivalent to the suffering of the creatures over which he claims authority. We have conclusive evidence that at least part of the reason that the Authority does not intervene to stop suffering is that he simply doesn't care.

We do not have the same access to the actual actions and desires of the Christian God. Theodicies show that it is at least possible that, in order to create the best possible world, it was necessary for God to create a world with some evil in it. This story allows us, at least for the time being, to hold on to God's divine attributes, including omnibenevolence.

Omniscience

Is the God of Pullman's universe omniscient? I will provide at least one reason to think he is not. One puzzle that gets raised in philosophy of religion is the following: if God is omniscient, then he knows everything that can be known. This would include facts about the future. Some facts about the future are facts about the actions that agents will perform. If this is the case, then God knew before we ever performed an action that we would perform that very action. If this is the case, then we do not act freely. We cannot do other than what God knew we would do.

Consider the case of Lyra. Lyra has a destiny and all sorts of entities in the book seem to know about it. The witches certainly do. The Oblation Board tortures one of them to learn what she knows about Lyra's destiny. In her agony, she confesses:

> She is the one who came before, and you have hated her and feared her ever since! Well now, she has come again, and you failed to find her . . . She was there on Svalbard—she was with Lord Asriel, and you lost her. She escaped and she will be—(*The Subtle Knife*, p. 39)

The witch is here referring to the "name of Lyra's destiny." The girl is destined to play Eve, to free all living creatures. This confession motivates Mrs. Coulter to find Lyra and coax her into a deep sleep so she can hide with her safely in a remote cave.

Not long after the Oblation Board learns the news about Lyra, the Consistorial Court of Discipline learns it as well from an alethiometer reader:

> It says that if it comes about that the child is tempted, as Eve was, then she is likely to fall. On the outcome will depend . . . everything.

> And if this temptation does take place, and if the child gives in, then Dust and sin will triumph. (The Amber Spyglass, p. 68)

After learning this news, the Consistorial Court sends out an assassin, Father Gomez, to kill Lyra so that the temptation does not occur.

Of all of the entities who should take an interest in Lyra's destiny and who should act to preserve their interests in this matter, the one who seems to have the most to lose is the Authority. All the other entities learn about Lyra's destiny with very little time left to do anything about it. Lyra's destiny, if fulfilled, will bring an end to the Authority's reign. If the Authority were omniscient, he would have known long before Lyra was ever born that she would be the one to bring about the events that led to his destruction, yet he does nothing to prepare for it, let alone stop it. When she encounters him just before he disintegrates, he seems surprised by her presence.

Omnipotence

If a being is omnipotent, they have the power to do all things that are logically possible. We only have to read the description that Pullman provides of the Authority right before he disintegrates to see that he is not all powerful. Lyra and Will find the old angel inside a crystal litter, and Pullman describes their encounter with him in the following way:

> Will cut through the crystal in one movement and reached in to help the angel out. Demented and powerless, the aged being could only weep and mumble in fear and pain and misery, and he shrank away from what seemed like yet another threat. (*The Amber Spyglass*, p. 410)

As soon as Will and Lyra release him from the crystal, he vanishes completely, powerless in the face of the open air. It's hard to envisage a creature farther removed from being omnipotent.

Not only does the Authority fail to possess any of the divine attributes that the Christian God possesses, Pullman's God isn't even worthy of any gratitude. As we saw above, being a creator may be enough to warrant such gratitude.

The God of Pullman's universe is not even worthy of the gratitude we might feel for its creator for, as Will learns from Balthamos, the Authority was not a creator.

> The Authority, God, the Creator, the Lord, Yahweh, Adonai, the King, the Father, the Almighty—those were all names he gave himself. He was never the creator. He was an angel like ourselves— the first angel, true, the most powerful, but he was formed of dust as we are, and Dust is only a name for what happens to matter when it begins to understand itself. Matter loves matter. It seeks to know more about itself, and Dust is formed. The first angels condensed out of dust and the Authority was the first of all. He told those that came after him that he had created them, but it was a lie. (*The Amber Spyglass*, p. 32)

Let's consider the picture we now have of the Authority. He is not omnibenevolent, so he is not worthy of worship or even respect on the basis of his goodness. He allows bad things to happen and does nothing to stop them. In fact, he even participates in them, teaming up with Metatron to create a long-term inquisition. He lies to the creatures he claims authority over, telling them he created them when he didn't. Far from being worthy of worship for his goodness, the behavior of the Authority is morally reprehensible.

The Authority is also not worthy of worship on the basis of his omniscience. He possesses no special powers aside from being one of the strongest angels to exist early in the history of conscious matter. He must send his regents out to discover information for him, information which, if he were omniscient, he would already know. He doesn't even seem to be aware of Lyra and her destiny, though creatures far younger and less advanced than he knew about it and acted to either help Lyra or stop her. The Authority is certainly not worthy of worship on the basis of the power he possesses. All it takes is mere open air to destroy him.

We can conclude that the Authority possesses none of the attributes that make the Christian God worthy of worship. Are there other qualities he possesses that would rightly motivate worship? The only quality that seems noteworthy about him is that he was the first conscious thing. This might make him interesting and it may even make him inherently valuable. This value would be similar to the value we might find in, for example, the bones of the earliest dinosaur. We value it for the place it occupies in our history. But though we might find value in the bones, we don't worship them for being the first. The fact that the Authority was the first conscious being should not motivate worship either, unless the length of his life has given him traits that make him worthy. There is no evidence that it did. In fact, it seems that, instead of becoming wiser and more honorable, he became weaker and more corrupt.

Pullman provides us with all of the relevant information about the Authority, and at the end of the trilogy, we can see that the God of the *His Dark Materials* universe is not the proper object of worship. The belief or faith that we might have in the Authority would boil down to believing in or having faith in some guy with no admirable qualities who played no part in creation. To give our religious devotion to such a being would be strange and even dangerous.

If we had similar intelligence related to the Christian God, it would be morally wrong for us to continue to worship him. As evidenced in *His Dark Materials,* belief in such a being could lead us to do terrible things to our fellow creatures. What would be interesting about this situation, however, is that in our world God is defined in terms of his attributes—if we learned that God was weak or corrupt or that there were things that he failed to know, that being would not be God. If at some time in the future the person we referred to as God committed a bad act, it wouldn't be the case that that being, at that moment stopped being God. The being in question was *never* God. God, by definition is incapable of such behavior. It is not possible to worship the Christian God while mistakenly worshipping some being with the attributes that the Authority has. Because of his failings, a being like the Authority could not be God.

His Dark Materials succeeds in showing that worshipping a God with the attributes of the Authority may be bad. But the Authority is a different type of being altogether from the God that philosophers and theologians discuss in our own world. Pullman has not shown that believing in or worshipping the Christian God is a bad thing.

The Magisterium

As we've seen, the scope of Pullman's attack in the *Dark Materials* trilogy does not extend to belief in a Christian God. Let's now consider whether Pullman's attack on organized religion is more successful.

The religion practiced in Lyra's world seems to be quite similar to the Christian religion. Its holy text is quite similar to the Bible, only with modifications relevant to the existence of dæmons. The Magisterium, like most religious institutions in our own world, is structured in such a way that the authority figures have quite a bit of power over the way the church is run, which also gives them quite a bit of power over the lives of the members of the church.

It may not be bad to believe in an all-good, all-knowing, all-powerful God. It is hard to find evidence, however, that such a being actually exists. Many people long for such evidence because they find the idea that such a being exists very comforting, and in many cases it gives meaning to their lives. If a religious institution purports to have such evidence, they have substantial power over those people who believe them. Religious officials may themselves actually believe they have such evidence, and, for the sake of argument, let's assume that it's even possible that in some cases they *do,* in fact, have the evidence. What is important for Pullman's critique to be successful, however, is what these institutions are willing to do with the power that this evidence gives them.

There are least two things that the Magisterium is willing to do with their power that are morally objectionable. First, they use it to suppress information that would be useful to society. They prevent society from gaining scientific knowledge that would help people understand how the universe really works because they are afraid that it might make people turn from the church, which would diminish its power. In its private dealings, the Magisterium acknowledges the existence of Dust and of other worlds, even using this information to perform experiments on children. In its public dealings, however, the Magisterium strives to keep information about Dust and other worlds suppressed.

Do religious institutions in our world engage in the same kind of behavior? History shows us that they certainly do. The church punished heretics who suggested that the Earth moves around the sun rather than the other way around. Religious institutions continue to ignore substantial evidence in favor of evolution because such a theory undermines the story the Church wants to tell about the beginning of life in this universe.

Second, the Magisterium is willing to harm innocent people in order to advance its agenda. It is willing to cut children from their souls because they have a vague idea that the settling of Dust *might* have something to do with original sin. They're willing to kill people for information or kill people in order to prevent classified information from becoming accessible to the public. They are even willing to kill an innocent child to keep her from fulfilling her destiny.

Do religious institutions in our own world engage in this kind of behavior? Again, it seems clear that they do. Religious institutions have been willing to kill people and destroy entire cultures in an attempt to make the whole world believe as they do. They have been willing to suggest that entire groups of peaceful people are enemies in an attempt to maintain political power. Like the religious institutions in the *Dark Materials* universe, religious institutions in our world have historically been willing to harm innocent people in an attempt to maintain their power.

Many of the moral failings that the Magisterium has are also failings that religious institutions in our own world have. So it seems that Pullman's description of the Magisterium in the trilogy is successful as an attack on religious institutions in our own world.

Pullman and His Project

His Dark Materials doesn't succeed (and perhaps Pullman didn't intend it to succeed) in showing that belief in an all-good, all-knowing, all-powerful God is bad. Pullman's Authority is not sufficiently similar to the Christian God for Pullman to be successful in making that point. The Authority is an interesting character in a very well written series, but he is nothing like the God that philosophers and theologians discuss. He is a fictional character. Though the Christian God may possibly be a work of fiction as well, he would be a very different fictional character.

Where Pullman's critique is successful, however, is in providing an imaginative and powerful illustration of the dangers of organized religion. Unlike the comparison between God and the Authority, the comparison between the religious institutions in Pullman's world and those in our own reveals a number of morally relevant similarities.

Does the fact that Pullman's work brings to light these similarities make his book series dangerous for children? I don't think so. If approached in the right way, the books can be used to teach children valuable lessons. If the God we claim to believe in is an all-good, all-knowing, all-powerful God, and the religious institution we're affiliated with condones actions that reason tells us such a being would never advise us to engage in, that gives us good reason to question the motivations of the religious institution. Far from being dangerous, it's good to teach children to critically evaluate the actions of governing bodies rather than suggesting that they follow those bodies blindly.

If God really is all-knowing, then he knew from eternity that Pullman would write *His Dark Materials*. If you believe God is all powerful, and if he found the series objectionable or did not think it fit into his greater plan, then he could have done something to prevent the series from being published. He didn't. Perhaps these facts should lead the religious person to look for the good in Pullman's series. God did.

2
Cuts Like a Knife

RANDALL E. AUXIER

I don't like that knife.

—IOREK BYRNISON in *The Amber Spyglass*, p. 160

Wearily Lyra sighed; she had forgotten how roundabout scholars could be. It was difficult to tell them the truth when a lie would have been so much easier for them to understand.

—*The Golden Compass*, p. 85

Methinks Master Pullman has known a scholar or two. Tiresomely roundabout. We ask the most annoyingly precise questions, and we insist that everything make genuine sense, so if you don't want to watch your own story melt away into contradictions and paradoxes, you'd best avoid us.

But in this case, it's too late, Philip. We found you. And not only scholars, but the most tiresome lot of them . . . philosophers. No one has more patience with hair-splitting than we do, and no, we won't settle for lies. Fortunately, we're only having some fun at the moment, so we (or at least I) ought to be able to loosen up a little for the space of one chapter.

What in the Worlds Is He Talking About?

His Dark Materials is brimming with philosophical themes and ideas. One friend of mine, himself a novelist, remarked that Book III (*The Amber Spyglass*) is so long because Pull-

15

man was more interested in developing the philosophical ideas than he was in moving the plot along. Probably so. But even allowing this, I don't think it's quite right to think of Pullman as a philosopher, even secondarily. He wisely does not even try to solve all of the problems he explores, and indeed, he doesn't make any serious effort to be logically consistent in presenting them.

For example, in Book I Pullman has Lord Asriel describe the splitting of worlds this way:

> Now that world [in the Aurora], and every other universe, came about as a result of possibility. Take the example of tossing a coin: it can come down heads or tails, and we don't know before it lands which way it's going to fall. If it comes down heads, that means the possibility of its coming down tails has collapsed. Until that moment the two possibilities were equal. But on another world, it does come down tails. And when that happens, the two worlds split apart. I'm using the example of tossing a coin to make it clearer. In fact, these possibility collapses happen at the level of elementary particles, but they happen in just the same way: one moment, several things are possible, the next moment only one happens, and the rest don't exist. Except that other worlds have sprung into being, on which they did happen. (*The Golden Compass*, pp. 376–77)

But in Book III, Pullman, narrating a tough decision to be made by Will Parry, says:

> Will considered what to do. When you choose one way out of many, all the ways you don't take are snuffed out like candles, as if they'd never existed. At the moment, all Will's choices existed at once. But to keep them all in existence meant doing nothing. He had to choose after all. (*The Amber Spyglass*, p. 12)

That's it. No mention of other worlds springing into being in which each alternative was respectively taken. Looking at the two passages, anybody can see that we can't have it both ways. At least sometimes (or maybe even always), making a choice either creates a new parallel world (first quote), or it doesn't (second quote). If our choices only sometimes create new worlds, it would be nice to know when that happens and why. Pullman is unhelpfully silent on the matter.

Yet, looking at the second passage, if there really is no other world in which Will's various other choices are acted on, then it undermines the premise of the whole trilogy, because there wouldn't be other worlds for Will to cut into. On the other hand, I'm sure you can see what a mess it would be to try to tell a story where each choice by every character resulted in a new alternative narrative thread, describing the events in which each genuine option really happened in some world. In fact—unless you're Stephen King—telling any story requires that you exclude all the stories that you're not telling at that moment, right?

That's all well and good. We're telling the story we're telling, and not telling the story we aren't telling, and that is both wiser and necessary. We may tell a story about many worlds without trying to tell about every single one. So, actually things don't get too tedious or paradoxical until one supposes that we might travel between these contrary worlds that (at least sometimes) get created when we make a choice, or when a coin comes down heads. Lord Asriel says, in the same conversation as above:

> No one thought it would ever be possible to cross from one universe to another. That would violate fundamental laws, we thought. Well, we were wrong; we learned to see the world up there. If light can cross, so can we. . . . And I'm going to that world beyond the Aurora, because I think that's where all the Dust in this universe comes from. (*The Golden Compass*, pp. 376–77)

The issue is really "travel." Such travel, philosophically speaking, requires four ideas:

1. **something that remains identifiable while**

2. **moving through some arrangement of**

3. **space, in some**

4. **duration of time.**

We can generate all sorts of paradoxes regarding any of these four ideas, once we have that subtle knife. And you've seen plenty of movies where these problems come up.

Just as a teaser, consider this: Whenever Will and Lyra make a bad choice, why don't they just use the knife to cut right over into the nearby world (that recently sprang into being) in which they made a better choice? Well, part of the problem is that they would, I assume, encounter the doubles of themselves, and that would get complicated in a hurry. Pretty soon we'd have a whole herd of Wills and Lyras, making better choices for sure but increasingly bothersome to feed and clothe. This paradox calls into question 1 above, since we now do not know how to identify the "thing" (Will or Lyra) that has moved through space and time. Who is the real Will or Lyra? The hungriest? The best dressed?

Pullman briefly considers this prospect in Book II, when he has Lyra contemplate whether there might be "another Lyra" in Will's Oxford. "A chill ran down her back, and mouse-shaped Pantalaimon shivered in her pocket. She shook herself; there were mysteries enough without imagining more" (*The Subtle Knife*, p. 74). So Pullman leaves the question open, and proceeds to tell a story in which "transworld identity" is unique—only one Lyra, one Will, one Mrs. Coulter, and so on. He evades the question rather than answering it. That's fine for a novelist.

Similarly, one could wonder why Pullman decides to keep day and night constant across the various worlds—nighttime in Cittàgazze corresponds with night-time in both Oxfords, and similarly with the seasons, and so forth. I see no reason why this has to be a constant, but it does avoid troublesome questions. So when I picture the Earth hurtling through space, I suppose that I need to imagine billions more right on top of it, in other dimensions of possibility, but all of them are in the same place as far as their turning and orbiting goes. So, that is one way of handling 3 above, space.

But if we imagine that there's just one world that, for some reason, falls a little behind in its rotations or its orbit, could Will still cut into it? How? Does the knife do space travel? And if so, what time would it be when we stepped through there? I have trouble enough understanding what happens when I cross the International Date Line in this world.

I would also point out that Pullman likes to keep spaces constant, so that whatever world exists on top of another world shares the same constant space in a different dimension of possibility. He assumes that when Will and Lyra sit on the "same bench" in their different Oxfords, they remain "close." That's how Pullman wants us to imagine it.

But don't think about this too much, even on Pullman's terms. It may begin to dawn on you that somehow Lyra walks into the hills above Cittàgazze from the far north of her world, over Asriel's bridge, while Will finds a window into the same city from his Oxford, which is supposed to be right on top of Lyra's Oxford, which is a thousand miles from where she walked over Lord Asriel's bridge. My advice is not to expect consistency in these matters. It will simply frustrate your mind and spoil your enjoyment of the story. It's best to evade, as Pullman does. There are mysteries enough without imagining more, as he puts it.

The Barnard-Stokes Business

Such evasions may serve a novelist well enough, but they won't do for a physicist or a philosopher. We are wearisome and roundabout. In Lyra's world, a pair of trouble-makers, "renegade experimental theologians" named Barnard and Stokes, suggested a theory that Pullman clearly likes. He calls it the "Barnard-Stokes business." In our world, the physicist Hugh Everett (1930–1982) proposed this same hypothesis of the "plurality of worlds" in 1957. He was no renegade—he actually did top-secret work for the US Department of Defense—but he was trying to provide an interpretation for some unsettling implications about the collapse of wave functions in quantum physics. He wasn't at all interested in the possibility of travel among complementary worlds, or even whether such worlds are "actual places." That is a question for metaphysics, not physics.

And some metaphysician was eventually bound to try to defend the idea that such possible worlds really do exist. Most notoriously, a philosopher named David K. Lewis (1941–2001) tried to argue for it in a book called *On the Plurality of Worlds*. I have no reason to think Pullman read this book or even knows about it, but it was widely discussed by philosophers, and it still is. But Pullman constantly violates Lewis's restrictions on the idea of many worlds. And Pullman makes arguments of the sort that Lewis happily destroys. In particular, Lewis insists that even though the many worlds actually exist, they are "causally independent" of one another—the very view of which Lord Asriel says "we were wrong." What Lewis means is that the worlds have no effect on one another. Thus, travel among them is impossible. It is unlikely enough to defend the actuality of all (or some) possible worlds, but it is simply crazy to suggest viable travel among them, Lewis thinks. In this instance, I'll have to side with the common sense of the despised Church in Asriel's world. It's not that Barnard and Stokes are heretics, it's that they aren't talking sense. Anyway, in our world, the "Barnard-Stokes business" might be called the "Everett-Lewis business." It's out there, and you can learn about it if you want to.

A Shout-out

Church and Everett-Lewis be damned, for Pullman there are lots of ways to get from one world to another. Consider some. Witches "know" about the other worlds, but do not traditionally visit them. How they "know" isn't clarified (I have a theory about that in Chapter 5 of this volume). Yet, even just "knowing" requires that something permits exchange or communication of some sort among the worlds. And remember that the Gallivespian lodestone resonator also communicates across worlds by quantum entanglement, and the alethiometer somehow reads across worlds. Add to that: a single hair of Lyra's remains vitally connected to its owner, even if she's wandering around the world of the Dead.

Then there's Dust. Assuming that Dust

1. **moves the alethiometer needles,**

2. **interacts with Mary Malone's computer apparatus, and**

3. **moves the sticks of the I Ching (whether in Will's world or in that of the mulefa),**

then Dust also somehow communicates across worlds or exists in many at the same time. These happenings indicate that the many worlds may be causally connected. Whether things like quantum entanglement and the non-localized exchange of information require "causation" remains a hot topic among philosophers and physicists, but it's enough to be aware that some intelligible connection (whether causal or not) is involved in communication. These worlds can affect one another.

A Pause for the Cause

Communication isn't the only effect of one world on another. For Pullman, angels can travel among the worlds, both physically and using imagination, and affect things. And someone can open a huge doorway by harnessing the energy of Dust released in intercision. One can also make a bomb so powerful as to detonate it in one world and blow a hole through another world, a hole so big that it opens onto the Abyss. And apparently there are "cracks" everywhere after that, in which all the worlds are bleeding vital force into the Abyss. These connections among worlds seem pretty "causal" to me.

And finally, there's the knife—our particular point of interest, if you'll tolerate my pun. So not only does Pullman allow us to remain who-we-are as we move among worlds, he devises a bunch of different ways that such travel might be carried out. We could spend all our time thinking about any one of these—for example, the use of imagination for traveling among worlds, described by the Angel Xaphania near the end of Book III, could easily occupy us for a whole chapter. I want to cut to the quick. I want to be the bearer of my own subtle knife (and keep all my fingers), and use it to reveal a "cosmos" in Pullman's ponderings, because I think that his knife helps us see how it all fits together.

Cosmos

I've already said a few words about physics and metaphysics, but philosophers and physicists also share another word: cosmology. Obviously, physics is concerned with the physical world, and metaphysics includes all the problems of physics and also questions about whether (and how) nonphysical entities or energies might or might not exist, and how they might affect or influence physical things. For example, is an "idea" a physical thing? It's not obvious. Metaphysics concerns itself with questions such as whether the "mind" is just the same thing as the "brain," with no remainder, on the one hand, or whether I might have an idea in my mind that can be correlated with some sort of physical process in my brain, but the two are not the same thing, on the other hand.

But in addition to all this, philosophers and physicists also discuss cosmology, which is the science (or study) of order (*kosmos* is just the Greek word for order). In modern times, this has meant the study of the order of nature. Most scientists and philosophers believe that "nature" is an ultimate category—nothing beyond nature really exists. So studying the order of nature is the same as studying all order. Anyone can see that nature is complex, so the study of cosmology has to do with grasping how the various forms of order we find in nature are best explained. Cosmology is neither quite the same as physics or metaphysics, but it uses both, just as far as they reveal patterns of order.

For example, time has a characteristic "order," a "before and after," a sort of durational arrow of cumulative flow. And space has a characteristic order, in which everything must be somewhere, a sort of localizability that can be measured with instruments or modeled with geometries. And perhaps consciousness has an order as well—it's one type of temporal process that is spontaneous and intentional, directed toward objects in space and time other than itself. And so on. There are three examples of types of order, and cosmology tries to say how they fit together into one order. Our popular Big Bang theory is a bit of cosmology. When we speak of cosmology, then, we're concerned with how all the things that really exist are ordered in relation to each other, how the fundamental forces we discover combine to create all that we see, feel, and experience. Needless to say, it's not rocket science or brain surgery—it's far worse. Rocket science and brain surgery are pretty clear and simple by comparison.

And Chaos

The ancients had lots of different cosmologies, so you would find many different answers to questions about what is the sky, where did the earth come from, what is a person, what is a soul, what are the stars, how were people created, and what are the gods. The ancients also usually had an idea like "chaos," which was either an absence of order, or more commonly the power of disorder or the destruction of order. These ancient cosmologies are expressed in stories and myths that say what sorts of things exist by telling how they came into being. Sometimes also there are stories about how and when things pass out of being.

In the book of Genesis, when God is intent on whipping up a cosmos, "the Earth is without form and void." That's Hebrew chaos. The Greeks thought of the primal waters around the whole world as chaos—they called these waters okeanos. Pretty much everyone seems to agree that chaos is "deep" and very much to be avoided, so it's a relief when God or Cronos tells the Abyss to behave itself and stay over there where it belongs, away from us and our order.

A Menagerie

Philip Pullman's cosmology is, frankly, a mish-mash of ancient and modern ideas about what types of things exist and in what order. But let me offer just the simplest list to give you a sense of what we are dealing with. According to Pullman, at least the following types of conscious entities exist:

1. humans (this may or may not include witches),

2. ordinary animals (like Moxie, Will's cat),

3. talking Animals (like armored bears and arctic foxes),

4. night-ghasts (a type of spirit who haunt Lyra in Book I; may include Nälkäinens, Breathless Ones, the old ghost at Godstow, and the bad spirits pinned to the clockwork of the buzzing spies),

5. cliff-ghasts (ancient dragon-like noxious beings),

6. ghosts (such as are found in the world of the Dead),

7. daemons (this may or may not include "souls"),

8. angels (apparently a different kind of spirit than the various ghasts),

9. Dust, or matter (which "loves Dust").

There are also some beings that may be peculiar to the world of the dead, such as 10. harpies, 11. deaths, and 12. that unco-operative Boatman. And there are the mulefa, whom we are told are "people," so one assumes that they are, in the relevant sense, the same sort of thing as humans, but we are not told whether they have daemons inside them, or ghosts, or deaths. Then we have to add 13. the specters (also apparently the same as "Windsuckers").

We learn near the end of the trilogy that specters are little pieces of the Abyss, set loose in the world by the unwise (sinful? forbidden?) act of cutting through from one world to another. The specters are conscious (Pullman calls them "malevolent"—which literally means having a bad will) and they can be commanded (by Mrs. Coulter, who also teaches them they can fly). So here the suggestion is that 14. the Abyss as a whole may also be conscious in some sense, since the parts of it are conscious. As you can see, I've been tiresomely scholarly in listing Pullman's entities. There are probably some I've missed, of course, but this will be enough for a sketch of a cosmology.

Panpsychism

There you have at least fourteen types of conscious beings that can exist more or less independently, or separate conscious modes of existing. It would take a good while to sort them all out. As a list, this is not a cosmology, it's an "ontology," which is to say, it's an account of what exists without much regard for how they exist, and their levels of being and their origins and relations and dependencies upon one another. I have listed only the conscious beings because, as far as I can tell, Pullman intends to occupy a position philosophers call "panpsychism," which is the view that everything that really exists is conscious. So the idea that "dead matter" exists is an idea Pullman rejects. That is also part of the reason I am inclined to say that the Abyss is in some way conscious (and malevolent).

Panpsychism is not a popular view among philosophers these days. But some very famous ones in the past have defended panpsychism. These days there are simply oceans of philosophers who believe that some things are conscious and some just aren't. This conviction provides them with endless swimming (and treading and drowning) as they marvel at how anything can be conscious, since they think most things aren't, but a few things (like philosophers), clearly are. These ocean swimmers are called dualists. I don't like them. Pullman skips over these vast and tedious waters and just dives into the small pond of current philosophers who think that everything is conscious, and who just smile at the idea of "dead matter."

I think we can safely say that all of Pullman's worlds are conscious, and they all rest delicately above the Abyss, and the Abyss doesn't like it, which is why all those worlds are in danger of falling back into a sort of chaos. In the Abyss these tiny drops of awareness are powerless to connect, communicate, build, create, even though they still "exist." This is chaos for Pullman: a kind of awareness that is isolated and alone, which is to say, awareness trapped and powerless amid the complete absence of beauty.

Lost in Space(time)

So, given the list of conscious beings above, all kinds of questions arise. For example, why do ghosts hold together in the world of the dead (whether they like it or not), but dissolve in the "open air"? Why can some ghosts resist dissolving in Asriel's Republic, and why can they "fight" with specters? What would happen to Lyra if Pantalaimon, accidentally got swatted when he was moth-formed? Where did the night-ghasts come from, the ones that haunted Lyra after she switched the coins betokening their daemons? If they had been ghosts, they'd be trapped in the world of the dead, right? Do the mulefa have or need daemons? Are tualapi (those weird swan-things in the mulefa's world) animals (as their grazers clearly are)? Or are they some further order of conscious beings, like cliff-ghasts? Why do they obey Father Gomez? And Mrs. Coulter teaches the specters to fly. How can a specter learn something? Do they have individual memories, a social order, rules of behavior, communication skills that can be improved with effort?

This could go on forever, rather tediously, as we try to compile all the types of beings and all their interactions—

who can communicate with whom, who can hurt whom, and so on. We need a method of sorting it all out. Normally a good way to begin to put things in order in cosmology is to ask two questions: "When does it exist?" and "Where does it exist?" Where and when would a person expect to find whatever it is we're looking for? If you know the space and the time, you can begin to tell a story about how it all fits together, by hypothesizing what caused what. Here we always assume that what comes later is caused by something earlier (time), and we expect to find things that cause one another in close proximity (space). Such is the structure of standard cosmologies.

But this method won't work for sorting out Pullman's cosmology. That's because he has taken a certain delight in messing around with our ordinary ideas about space, time, and causality. He explicitly holds constant a few features of space and time and cause, but not reliably. In his naughtiest moment, he actually has Will use the knife to cut through time, by just a few moments, when he and Lyra and the Gallivespians are looking for the world of the dead. Will had been using the knife as a tool to cut across spatial dimensions, or dimensions of possibility, but then Pullman just teases us by having it cut through a few minutes of time. How wicked.

In terms of space, it's good to remember that Pullman also has the worlds of dreaming and waking in close spatial relation, as when Serafina Pekkala projects into Mary Malone's dream so as to awaken her without frightening her, and Lee Scoresby accompanies John Parry on the mission to destroy Zeppelins in his dreaming state. Pullman also has Mary do something akin to astral projection from her platform high among the wheel-pod trees. These are not the sorts of space-time-cause relations that we can explain with modern physics, so our ordinary assumptions about the relative constancy of space and time and cause will not help us tell the story of Pullman's cosmology.

Mephistopheles Is Not My Name

This slippage of space, time and cause is to be expected, however. Pullman is no doctrinaire defender of modern science. If anything, he sees the scientific revolution as a moment when humankind, in many worlds, lost its way. He explicitly dates the time when things start to go "wrong" as being three hundred years ago, when Newton was framing his physics in our world, the Guild of the Philosophers was creating the subtle knife in Cittàgazze, the experimental theologians were devising the alethiometer in Lyra's world, and the wheel-pod trees began to fail in the world of the mulefa.

Pullman is toying with the idea that modern science, and its fetish for technology, is a sort of Faustian bargain human beings made with themselves (not the devil) by being overly curious and greedy for knowledge. Every world has suffered from their unwise quest for a kind of truth that destroys beauty. This is not even the fault of the Church, in Pullman's tale—it's one of the few things he does not blame on the Church. The point is that trying to use a cosmology of space, time, cause, and nature to grasp this cosmology will not work.

Another Day in Paradise

Instead, we need to remember that there is a certain "mythic" cast to the trilogy that reminds us of some basic features of mythic consciousness (and of dream consciousness), which need not obey the laws of space, time and cause we take for granted these days. If I had to name a single cosmology from history that is most akin to Pullman's it would be John Milton's, which has the same odd mix of modern science and mythic beings, and it offers the same judgment of humans when they get too curious about nature. Of course, unlike Pullman, Milton (as far as I can tell) actually believed in all these sorts of mythic beings. That's hard to do these days, but the stories still tug at our feelings. A lot of people still believe in angels.

In Pullman's universe you can't even pin down identity, let alone space and time. People do remain more or less who they are from one world to the next, but identity is plural in Pullman's cosmos. He has a favorite strategy for handling the issue of plural identity, which is to give a separate identity to every layer of the self he can imagine. Every time he catches himself imagining a basic layer of self-experience, he externalizes and personifies it. So, for example, our human souls become daemons, and a bear's armor is an external soul of a different sort, and our deaths are outside of us, but always nearby. The insects of the Gallivespians are external manifestations of their nurturing instincts and their clan idenities (Salmakkia feeds hers on her own blood at one point, yuck). This is Pullman's standard move: externalize, personify.

If we had eyes to see every level of conscious existence at once, and we saw Lyra coming down the High Street in Oxford, we would behold a veritable crowd: her regular body, the small amount of Dust she attracts, her death, her daemon, her ghost, and, I assume, the part of her that is spirit or mind (the part that can become an angel, if someone helps her like Balthamos helped Baruch). Maybe we would also see some witch oil. Who knows? And then, having externalized and personified all these aspects of the self, Pullman likes to pull the various identities apart—just like the golden monkey does with bats and Gallivespians, and whatever it can get hold of. Pullman uses his imagination to part children from their daemons, and Baruch from Balthamos, and in death, he cuts off ghosts from their physical bodies, and finally, he tears apart Lyra and Will, banishes them forever to different worlds. It seems like a cruel experiment, actually, to spend one's time wondering what a person would be without his spirit, or without his soul, and so on. But that is part of the clue to figuring out how Pullman's cosmology really works, what principle is really behind it. It's about cutting things.

Rock, Paper, Scissors

When you can't quite count on space, time and causality to give you the order of the universe, you have to start looking around for other ideas that help in grouping things in order. It's like a game of rock, paper, scissors, which is a complete triad of dependency relations. You know the game: rock smashes scissors, scissors cut paper, paper covers rock. There are three ways of being: smashing, cutting, covering. And we have three types of entities that do these things, each being limited by one of the others. It's a perfect cosmology.

If you go back before the time when we decided cosmology was about space, time and cause, you discover that philosophers have been playing rock, paper, scissors for the whole of Western history. Their three favorite entities are the Good (which is sort of a rock), the True (which is like a pair of scissors), and the Beautiful (like the paper), but people don't agree on the rules or the functions or the ways that each limits the other. Plato started the game, and he enjoyed playing all three. Ever since then, philosophers have tended to favor one and to try to get it to do the work of both of the others.

In the last hundred years or so, the philosophers who like the True have had all the power. The defenders of the Good, after a brief period of disorientation, have been climbing back into the conversation, but the believers in the Beautiful have been both cut and smashed. They had their heyday in the Renaissance, with a flurry of further prominence during the two generations dominated by Romanticism. The lovers of the Good owned the Victorian era. Now we have these boring philosophers who only care about Truth. If I had to guess, I would predict that we are in for another round of dominance by the lovers of Beauty in the near future, when everyone tires of the True (the dominance of science in this case).

I'm tired of Truth myself. I'd rather be lied to, which is why I like Pullman. And in fact, Pullman is definitely one of the friends of the Beautiful. I have some sympathy for the Good, but not very much, and that is how I read Pullman too. And that is why his cosmology is difficult to understand by means of either a moral order or a scientific (or logical or epistemological) ordering. And thus, we have our clue. The Pullman cosmology obeys aesthetic principles, the logic of imagination and feeling, not the order of good and evil or of truth and lies (for more about those types of order, see my other essay in this volume).

The Beauty in the Beast

Aesthetic cosmologies follow the order of images and possibilities, what images can suggest. Here we are not very interested in arguments and what they logically imply, or in moral principles and what they demand. Cosmologies of the True and the Good are built around necessary relations—not what can be, but what must be. Cosmologies of the True and the Good are stern and humorless companions. You wouldn't tolerate a novel, or a movie, or even a song that was just one long series of logical implications or moral commands. People who read the Bible as just one long series of moral requirements are missing a lot about the book—it's interesting literature. People who read the Bible as an explanation of the natural world, like a bit of science that is literally true, are very much to be pitied. Imagine being that unimaginative. I just can't.

One of the coolest things about aesthetic cosmologies is that they are built around possibility instead of necessity—what can we imagine, and what can we do in imagination? The cosmology of the Beautiful does not want to be told that "you can't really do that, it isn't physically possible," or "you ought not do that, it's morally wrong." And this is really the clue we need, to make sense of Pullman's cosmos. What's possible and what's impossible in his story? Doing useful philosophy really depends on finding the right question and asking it in the right way. Simply being aware that cosmologies can proceed in different ways is important background knowledge, but until you have the question firmly before you, you have no direction.

Scholars are roundabout, but they usually get where they're going. I knew what my question was at the outset, but I only now share it with you, dear reader. The question is: what will the subtle knife cut and what won't it cut? Having settled on the idea that Pullman's universe is governed by aesthetic rules, it's easy to see that he's worried about possibility, not necessity. That's why he doesn't care to give us consistent physics or to solve impossible moral dilemmas with some set of clear rules.

Searching through the universe of Pullman's imagination for a key to the kingdom is not difficult. Three powerfully suggestive images jump out immediately:

1. **The Golden Compass (the alethiometer);**

2. **The Subtle Knife;**

and

3. **The Amber Spyglass (that is, the idea of learning to see Dust).**

I wonder: where might a semiobservant person get the idea that just these three images are important? Duh. In any case, thinking about these three and asking what is possible for them provides us with our rock, paper and scissors: the aesthetic order of Pullman's universe. We need only ask what is possible for these things and what is impossible, what they'll do and what they won't do.

Dust

Obviously, Dust moves the alethiometer. That's one thing it can do. If Mary Malone had been kind enough to point her spyglass in the right direction, I'm sure she would have seen the Dust dance. But it's also clear that Dust has limits. It can't do just anything. Its main limit is that it can organize itself into something communicative only in the presence of an appropriate intention. How this works would be a long story. Basically, Mary Malone thinks that the human brain had just the right sort of sympathy and resonance to permit Dust to organize itself in ways that communicate. Without that, Dust cannot become conscious of itself. This is not science, it's an invention of the imagination.

So even though Dust can express itself through computers and the I Ching and the alethiometer, it is not a powerful force at all. We have to expect to see it before we can make use of its benefits.

The benefits are: truth, goodness, and most of all, beauty. So when we understand the word "moves" in "Dust moves the alethiometer," I think we mean "moves" in a physical, a moral, and an aesthetic sense. Something "moves" us when we experience our whole moral and physical and emotional existence at the same time. That is what Dust does, it "moves" things that are susceptible to being moved, and that want to be moved. That includes the alethiometer, but not the knife.

The Compass

The relationship between the alethiometer and the knife is a little harder to understand, but properly used, the alethiometer actually guides the knife. That's one thing it can do. In an important conversation, as Lyra and Will are wandering around in Will's Oxford, he is unsettled at the idea that Lyra can use the alethiometer to know what she shouldn't know, to invade privacy. Will says: "that's enough. You've got no right to look into my life like that. Don't ever do that again. That's just spying." But Lyra's all important answer is:

> I know when to stop asking. See, the alethiometer's like a person, almost. I sort of know when it's going to be cross or when there's things it doesn't want me to know. I kind of feel it. This en't like a private peep show. If I done nothing but spy on people, it'd stop working. I know that as well as I know my own Oxford. (*The Subtle Knife*, pp. 104–05)

What the alethiometer can't do is tell the future, but that isn't as important as what it won't do. In the very next moment the question is raised about whether Will's father is still alive, an absolutely crucial question—and Lyra doesn't ask the alethiometer because Will doesn't direct her to do so. Why Will doesn't ask her to consult the device is hard to understand, except that he is consistent in this attitude throughout the whole story. He is struggling with freedom and fate, and he resolutely chooses not to know all sorts of things he could know, because he wants to preserve his sense of freedom (not his freedom itself, just his sense of it). So he chooses to preserve an aesthetic feature of his life, the feeling of acting freely, instead of knowing morally or scientifically what he "must" do.

The alethiometer, however, works with and through its interpreter, and so long as Lyra accepts Will's guidance, the instrument works to the "best" (meaning the most beautiful) purposes. That purpose is saving Dust, not because it is good or true, but because it is the basis of all that it beautiful in the world. This tells us what is possible and impossible for the alethiometer, and what we mean by saying that the knife "guides" it. We mean that Will the bearer of the power, tells Lyra when to use it and when not to, for the most part. And Lyra wisely obeys. Thus, the alethiometer submits to the knife.

Cut to the Chase

But the all-important and pivotal cosmological function is that of the knife itself. If you can tolerate an analogy for a moment, I will clarify. If I had been writing this chapter on Tolkien's *Lord of the Rings*, I would have made almost the same argument about aesthetic cosmologies, because I think he and Pullman are kindred spirits (C.S. Lewis is different; his cosmology is clearly moral). But if this were about Tolkien, I would have analyzed all the rings—nine for the humans, seven for the dwarves, three for the elves, and then, the One Ring, the Ring of Power—to find them and in the darkness bind them. Clearly Tolkien's cosmology is symbolized in what becomes of these rings, and one is at the center.

The subtle knife is like that for Pullman. It plays the part of the one ring, which is the reason it has to be destroyed, in the end (and that is an old trope in imaginative literature, that the power that tempts us must be destroyed). I am quite certain that Pullman is giving a nod to Tolkien when he has Will destroy the knife, and when he has so many characters say that it "never should have been made," and when he places its origin in a Tower in a land that has fallen into ruin. I think Pullman makes it clear enough that the knife is the center of his cosmology. But an especially revealing passage is worth quoting, since it brings together Pullman's panpsychism and cosmology all at once. Iorek Byrnison is speaking:

> I don't like that knife. I fear what it can do. I have never known anything so dangerous. The harm it can do is unlimited. It would have been infinitely better if it had never been made. With it you can do strange things. What you don't know is what the knife does on its own. Your intentions may be good. The knife has intentions too. . . . The intentions of a tool are what it does. A hammer intends to strike, a vise intends to hold fast, a lever intends to lift. They are what it is made for. But sometimes a tool may have other uses that you don't know. Sometimes in doing what you intend, you also do what the knife intends, without knowing. (*The Amber Spyglass*, p. 161)

Even ordinary tools have intentions. Lyra tries to talk the bear into fixing the knife with a fairly lame argument, but the bear is moved only by whether the alethiometer recommends fixing it. Thus, there is a sense in which the alethiometer has a power over the knife's continued existence. This completes the circle of rock, paper, scissors, but there is more to be observed. The alethiometer's power is not ultimate because we don't know the knife's intentions, or how to handle them. But, like the alethiometer, the knife needs a human actor to carry out its intentions, and like the alethiometer, only the right sort of human can use it.

That actually makes our quest for the cosmic order of Pullman's universe a lot easier. All we have to do is look at our ontology of conscious beings, all fourteen of them, and ask "what's possible for the knife, and what's impossible?" You can have a hell of a lot of fun going back and doing this now. I won't do the whole thing. I just want to call your attention to some really interesting stuff that tumbles out of this. The impossibilities, what the knife cannot do, are far more revealing than what it can do. But let's look at what it can do first.

In the right hands, the knife will cut the bear's armor, it cuts through space and time (and that's a heck of a trick), one assumes that it will kill or damage pretty much anything on the list of beings, with a few interesting exceptions. It wards off specters and harpies but we don't know whether it can kill them. The knife kills cliff-ghasts, and certainly could kill ordinary animals, talking animals, humans, witches, and daemons.

There are a number of interesting open questions, like whether the knife can affect night-ghasts and ghosts. And I wanted to use that knife on the creepy Boatman on the lake of the dead, but Pullman has the old fellow claim he can't be hurt by it. I would like to find out for sure. I also don't know whether one could kill one's own death with it, but I suppose not. Death is already dead, right? Since it is called the "god-destroyer," one assumes that the knife can kill angels. And the knife can cut Dust. The energy in Dust is released not only by the knife, but by a blade less fine: the guillotine at Bolvanger can do it, so certainly the subtle knife can. But the ultimate power the knife has is to sever the delicate membrane that protects the many worlds from the Abyss.

A Matter of Love

Pullman is silent on the issue of whether there was a creator who first set the Abyss (Chaos) and the Cosmos in their separate domains. He allows that perhaps there was a creator, but the Authority was not the Creator. All we can know is that the most powerful thing the knife can do is to rejoin Cosmos to Chaos, such that Chaos comes in (as specters) and Dust (the basis of conscious order) flows out. And if Iorek Byrnison is right, then this is what the knife intends: to undo the work of the creator. But we also have a clue as to what is powerful enough to smash the knife: love. Thus, when we know what Pullman means by "love," we know what's stronger than the knife, stronger than the golden compass, and stronger than Dust.

Both times that the knife is broken, it is the power of Will's love that does it: for his mother in the first instance, and for Lyra in the second. But Pullman's ideas about love are not Romantic, they are cosmic, aesthetic ideas, summed up in his statement that "Matter loved Dust. It didn't want to see it go" (AS, p. 404). A number of philosophers in history have spoken of "love" in this way, notably St. Augustine and St. Thomas Aquinas. One finds John Milton speaking this way also. The traditional cosmologies of love are usually Christian. But we all know that Pullman has little sympathy for that. The philosopher whose ideas about love most closely correspond to Pullman's are those of the American philosopher Charles Sanders Peirce (1839–1914). The reason Peirce's view is closer to Pullman's than the traditional Christian cosmologies is basically because Peirce, like Pullman, is an evolutionist. I will not weigh you down with a long description of Peirce's cosmology, called Agapasticism (after the Greek word agape, love). Suffice it to say that this is an aesthetic cosmology, in which everything that exists is built on mutual feeling. Here is a little sample:

> Three modes of evolution have been brought before us: evolution by fortuitous variation, evolution by mechanical necessity, and evolution by creative love. . . . the mere propositions that absolute chance, mechanical necessity, and the law of love, are severally operative inthe cosmos, may receive the names of tychism, anancism, and apgapism. (*Philosophical Writings of Peirce*, p. 364)

Peirce believes the universe allows all three types of evolution to exist, but he doesn't think all three modes are equally operative in what exists. Agapism is the more comprehensive proposition. It accounts for "the bestowal of spontaneous energy by the parent upon the offspring, and . . . the disposition of the latter to catch the general idea of those about it and thus to subserve the general purpose. . . In the very nature of things, the line of demarcation between the three modes of evolution is not perfectly sharp. That does not prevent its being quite real."

Peirce carries on about all this, brilliantly, for quite a few pages. If you now look back to where we began with this chapter, you'll see that Pullman handles evolution by chance and by mechanical necessity as being modes that work at a lower level of explanation than his idea of "love." So he is consistent, he just isn't interested in logical consistency. He plies the trade of the story-teller, which requires aesthetic and imaginative rules, not logical, scientific or moral ones.

But Peirce is a little further down that same path. He actually reconciles, with logic and science, these different modes of evolution using viable philosophical arguments— although it isn't as much fun to read as Pullman is. Now, you may never have heard of Peirce, and I have no reason at all to think that Pullman has ever read him. And you might think, "Well, other philosophers and scientists and even theologians must think Peirce is daft, to defend such ideas as 'evolutionary love'." But that would be very far from the case. Peirce's influence has been steadily growing for many years, and even his critics stand in almost perfect awe of his intellect and his learning, which are only recently beginning to come into common understanding. You might want to read a little ways into Peirce's philosophy, since I know you like Pullman's ideas.

My point is that if you follow Pullman's knife right into the world of contemporary cosmology, you might be surprised to find out how viable his most central ideas are. You don't need to travel to other worlds or believe in them. All you need is an open mind and a fair command of the game of rock, paper, scissors. If you don't believe me, check your own alethiometer.

As Lyra once said, "I'm the best liar there ever was. But I en't lying to you, and I never will" (*The Subtle Knife*, p. 103).

3
Why the Dead Choose Death

RICHARD GREENE

Lots of people die in Philip Pullman's *His Dark Materials*. In fact, lots of creatures both natural and supernatural, including God (a.k.a. The Authority) die throughout the work.

Lee Scoresby is shot to death (his corpse is eaten by his panserbjørne friend Iorek Byrnison), the powerful angel Metatron, along with Lord Asriel and Mrs. Coulter fall to their deaths into an abyss, and Iofur Raknison is killed in hand-to-hand (or, rather, paw to paw) combat with Iorek Byrnison, just to name a few. Much like our real—non-fictional— world, a lot is made of death. It's to be avoided, it's considered to be tragic, it's something to be mourned, the death of one individual can greatly affect the lives of billions of others (in ways both positive and negative), and dying can be quite unpleasant, though it need not be.

What is it to be dead? What constitutes death? Is death permanent? Can you survive your own death? What makes death bad? *His Dark Materials* addresses some of these questions and turns others on their ears.

The Puzzling Nature of Death

The Epicurean philosophers of ancient times held, oddly enough, that death couldn't be a bad thing. They thought that as long as you existed, then death wasn't present (at least not your death). Once someone died, then they didn't exist anymore, so there was never any death-related badness for that person.

This view was based on a couple of assumptions: 1. that upon death you cease to exist, so death doesn't involve something like an afterlife, and 2. in order for something to be bad for an individual, that person would have to somehow "experience" the badness. The Epicurean view, therefore, raises a puzzle about death. How can death be bad, if you aren't around to experience the badness?

Subsequent philosophers have raised a second puzzle about the badness of death, which is sometimes called "the asymmetry puzzle." The idea behind this puzzle is that the time before a person is born is not regarded as a bad thing, but the time after you die is regarded negatively, even though, metaphysically speaking, both times are identical—at each time you don't exist. Why should one period of non-existence be regarded negatively while another is regarded neutrally or with indifference?

Each of these puzzles could easily be resolved by taking the position that death is not bad. This, however, doesn't quite jibe with most people's feelings about death, and it certainly doesn't jibe with people's behaviors. People typically will go to great lengths to avoid death, including very religious people, who believe that upon death their lot will be greatly improved. Referring to the Pope driving around in his bullet-proof pope-mobile, Drew Carey quipped, "If that guy is afraid to die, then I'm really in trouble."

The various characters in *His Dark Materials* adopt pretty much the same attitudes with respect to death as do folks in the real world. In the very first pages of the trilogy our heroine, Lyra Belacqua, acts to prevent the murder of her "uncle," Lord Asriel. Will Parry's journey begins as he acts to save his feeble mother from sinister men looking for letters from her long-lost husband, John Parry, whom he believes pose a danger to his mother's life. Later Will grieves the death of his father at the hands of Juta Kamainen, a witch whose advances John Parry once spurned. The Gallivespians, two thumb-sized spies who travel on the backs of dragon flies, frequently leverage their position by wielding deadly poisonous spurs.

As regards death, even the moral attitudes of the characters in *His Dark Materials* parallel our own. For example, Father Gomez, a priest in service of The Authority feels the need to seek a pre-emptive absolution, which is a sort of pre-forgiveness, before setting out to murder Lyra (it was prophesied that Lyra's heroic journey would result in the end of The Authority's reign).

The similarities between Pullman's world and our own signal that the aforementioned simple response to our puzzles about death is likely not going to be applicable to the characters in *His Dark Materials*, either. Their attitudes and actions simply don't bear out that for them death is not a bad thing.

The Badness of Death

So just what is so bad about death? This question, as we've seen can't be answered by appealing to what death seems or feels like, because death isn't experienced. Many theorists endorse some version of what has come to be known as the "Deprivation View," which is the view that the badness of death lies in its depriving persons of the good things that life has to offer (if one is dead, one can't enjoy things such as Zeppelin rides or racing across rooftops).

The Deprivation View doesn't account for the badness of death by making reference to things experienced; rather, it cashes out the badness of death in terms of things not experienced. To illustrate, suppose that Father Gomez had been successful in his attempt to assassinate Lyra. Lyra would have missed out on almost the entirety of what promises to be a full and wonderful life. Lyra's future has her studying with the scholars at the Oxford of her world. She will learn to master reading the Alethiometer. She will enjoy deep personal relationships, she will travel, and so forth. As long as Lyra's future has more good in it than bad, the Deprivation View renders the judgment that Lyra's death is a bad thing. This will be true for anyone whose future is worth living: their death will be a bad thing in virtue of the future goodness of which they are deprived by death.

Another plausible view of the badness of death that doesn't account for the badness of death by making reference to things experienced is the Desire Frustration View. Advocates of this view hold that death is bad because it signals the frustration of desires; desire frustration is generally taken to be a bad thing, although it is certainly true that having certain desires frustrated is probably good (for example, it would appear to be a very good thing were my desire to inject heroin to be frustrated). Suppose that Iofur Raknison had been victorious in his battle to the death with Iorek Byrnison. Since Iorek had a number of significant desires, such as regaining his position among the panserbjørne, serving as the ruler of the panserbjørne, and helping Lyra on her quest, to the extent that his desires would have been frustrated by his death, his death it appears would have been a bad thing.

I'm not going to attempt to adjudicate the debate over which of these views (if either) is the correct view of the badness of death. Both look promising, each provides a response to our two puzzles about the badness of death, and each *seemingly* applies equally well to Pullman's worlds as they do to our world.

Death in the Worlds of *His Dark Materials*

So, what exactly happens when a person dies in the worlds of *His Dark Materials*? At first glance it appears pretty similar to death in our world—bodies go limp or explode or burn (depending on the circumstances of the death), and all signs of life vanish. There is one important difference: in those of Pullman's worlds, such as Lyra's world, in which persons have dæmons, the daemon can be seen to vanish at the precise moment of death. (There's a healthy debate going on in both philosophical and medical communities as to whether a whole-brain or a higher-brain criterion should be employed when determinations of death are made. The occurrence of a vanishing dæmon would go a long way toward resolving a number of the issues surrounding determination of death.)

There are a couple of things worth noting about this difference. First, it points to a sort of dualism, at least for human beings, in Pullman's worlds (the panserbjørne, for example, don't have dæmons): humans have a physical body and a soul of sorts, which roughly manifests itself as a dæmon. This is a non-standard dualism, as the dæmon is also physical, in nature, but this is not of great concern for our purposes. Second, there's nothing about this difference (the addition of a vanishing dæmon upon death) to raise a problem for either the Deprivation View or the Desire Frustration view of the badness of death as being applicable to Pullman's worlds. In fact, it lends some support to the claim that these views get things right in those worlds in which persons have dæmons.

The assumption that proponents of the various accounts of the badness of death make is that death is an "experiential blank." Recall the Epicurean puzzle: when you're dead you have no experiences. A common reaction to the literature on the badness of death involves raising the possibility of an afterlife. What if death is really good? What if you go to Heaven when you die? Stories involving an afterlife typically involve explaining how a part of us survives death—the body dies, but the spirit or soul or mind lives on. Well, if the physical body dies and the soul dies (that is, the dæmon dies), then there's nothing left to survive our death, and stories of an afterlife don't factor in to the discussion of death's badness.

The World of the Dead

The accounts of the badness of death we've been considering have fared well thus far. Unfortunately, matters are not quite as simple as they first appear. In *The Amber Spyglass*, the third installment in *His Dark Materials*, Lyra and Will decide to venture into the world of the dead in order to make contact with Lyra's friend Roger and Will's father.

Upon entering the "suburb of the dead"—a dreary "shanty town" just across the river from the world of the dead, Lyra and Will discover that each person has a ghost that survives his or her death and has what is called a "death." Your death is a shadowy figure that comes into existence when you're born, sticks around unnoticed throughout your life, and at the moment of death taps you on the shoulder and escorts you across the river and into the world of the dead.

So, there is at least one thing that survives your dying: your ghost (your death also survives, but it is not clear whether your death is a part of you or just something assigned to you at birth). This means that the situation regarding the badness of death in Pullman's worlds is a bit more complicated that it initially seemed. In addition to your physical body and your dæmon, you have a ghost. Perhaps your dæmon is not your soul after all, but rather, the place where the soul is housed during your life. Perhaps, alternatively, the soul is itself not a simple thing—one which partially inhabits your ghost and partially inhabits your dæmon (Plato held that the soul actually had three parts: the reasoning part, the spirited part, and the appetitive part). Pullman's writing is not entirely clear on this matter. At any rate, it's not obvious that either the Deprivation View or the Desire Frustration View will be able to account for the badness of death, or for that matter, it's not, at this point in the discussion, clear whether death is even a bad thing in Pullman's worlds. It all depends, of course, on what lies across the river.

Upon attempting to cross the river into the world of the dead, Lyra is informed by the boatman—a character strongly reminiscent of Charon the boatman from ancient Greek mythology who would ferry the dead across the river Styx and into the underworld—that her dæmon will not be allowed to accompany her on the voyage. Lyra reports a sensation of her dæmon, Pan, being ripped from her heart. Will and the Gallivespians report experiencing a similar sensation, even though they don't themselves have dæmons (presumably it's their souls that are being left behind, but again, it's not entirely clear). Upon reaching the world of the dead Lyra and her party are attacked by harpies. Ghosts inform the group that the world of the dead is a miserable place where nothing ever happens except torment by harpies. The harpies cause hopelessness and despair in the ghosts by constantly reminding them of bad things about themselves and their lives.

So, this seems sufficient to account for the badness of death in Pullman's worlds. The afterlife is full of bleakness and periods of boredom, which are only broken up by despair inducing torment at the hands of the harpies. Moreover, the pain that Lyra felt upon becoming separated from Pan is perpetual and not limited to those persons that have a dæmon. Recall that Will and the Gallivespians felt the same sensation as Lyra. It turns out that any creature with a soul will, upon entering the land of the dead, become separated from their soul and experience the same misery.

Thus, death *is* a horrible experience after all in the worlds of *His Dark Materials*. The Deprivation View and the Desire

Frustration View are unnecessary, in that they were employed to explain how death can be bad given that death is an experiential blank. Moreover, to the extent that the dead are still deprived of the good things in life and their desires are still frustrated, those facts appear to be far outweighed by the sheer misery of spending eternity in the world of the dead, being tortured by harpies, and experiencing a painful separation from one's soul (or dæmon, as the case may be).

Why the Dead Choose Death

While it appears that we've accounted for the badness of death in Pullman's worlds, we've not yet answered the central question of this chapter: why do the dead choose death? That's because our story still contains a twist or two.

As it turns out, the afterlife is not exactly death. People's bodies have died, and their dæmons have vanished into thin air (in the movie version of *The Golden Compass* dæmons appear to explode upon death), and all that remains is a sort of ghostly existence, but there's one final step that the dead might possibly take.

Will and Lyra desire to help the dead. They negotiate with the harpies to stop tormenting the ghosts in exchange for the ghosts regaling the harpies with interesting stories from their lives, but this is not enough—Will and Lyra want to release the dead from the world of the dead (even without the harpies' torment, there is still the pain of being separated from their dæmon and the day to day boredom of being in the world of the dead). They accomplish this by using Will's knife (the titular "subtle knife") to cut a hole into another world. The dead (well, most of them anyway) flee the world of the dead without hesitation. As they enter the new world, they vanish in a fashion similar to dæmons upon "death." At this point their atoms link up with their dæmons' atoms and they join the universe. The resulting state is nirvana-esque.

So now we have the answer to our question. The dead choose death because it is better than the afterlife. Again, the afterlife is mind numbingly dull and full of despair. Death is, at minimum, neutral, with some possibility of being a positive experience, since the dead ultimately become Dust, which is the basis for conscious experience. Again, the text is a little sketchy on the details. At any rate, on any utilitarian calculus, death is a preferable state of affairs to the afterlife. At the point in which death is an option, the afterlife is the only other option.

Does this mean that since the afterlife is distinct from death in Pullman's worlds, the Deprivation View and the Desire Frustration views are back on the table? Recall that they only failed to account for the badness of death when the afterlife was actually considered to be death, since it is not, perhaps they should be reconsidered.

Here's one reason for considering that death (not the afterlife, but actual death) is bad (even though it is nirvanaesque). Suppose that you were given the option of living the rest of your life or being dead in a join-the-universe-and-become-Dust sort of way. Would you choose to die if death were neutral (that is if death were an experiential blank)? Presumably nobody with a life that had positive value would trade it for something neutral. To do so would be irrational. But what about the second possibility—that becoming Dust was positive in nature? Here, I suppose that some would opt for that, but it is far from certain that most people would give up their positive experiences (along with their negative ones) for such a constant and unvarying existence.

Admittedly I'm basing this claim on purely anecdotal evidence, but for years I've been getting people's reactions to Nozick's "experience machine." Nozick imagined that we could have the option of being plugged in to an experience machine, which would give us all the sensations and subjective experience of living a wonderful life and doing important things, though these experiences would be entirely delusory and we wouldn't be doing anything in reality. It turns out that people are seldom willing to trade their real lives for the completely convincing illusion of a different and more wonderful life.

While we can conclude that life may be preferable to death (for most or all depending on the details of what death is like), we haven't been given reason to think that death is bad. In our world death is bad because of what it deprives us of or because of the desires it frustrates, but what we are deprived of or what desires are actually frustrated depends greatly on our circumstances.

Suppose that I have been offered a teaching position at Jordan College, which I must accept prior to December 1st of this year or the offer will expire. Suppose further that I do nothing with respect to the offer (it simply expires) and on January 15th of the following year I am devoured by an armored bear. While it may be plausible to suppose that my death deprived me of certain things, it is not plausible to suppose that my death deprived me of the job at Jordan College. That offer was already off the table. Similarly, the good things in life are already off the table at the point in which the residents of the world of the dead choose death. The only things that death deprives them of are boredom and pain. The good things that life has to offer are well in the past. So, the Deprivation View cannot account for the badness of death, since death doesn't actually deprive anyone of anything good (nor will it, as the afterlife is, by hypothesis, unchanging in its essential features).

The Desire Frustration View doesn't fare much better. Suppose that I desire to be a professional baseball player someday. This desire may be strong, but given that it's never going to be satisfied (I can't hit a curve ball, my vision is beginning to falter, and I am rapidly approaching "advanced" age), it's not plausible to suppose that death is bad because it frustrates this desire. Death will only be bad to the extent that it frustrates desires that have a reasonable chance of being fulfilled.

Again, once we find ourselves in the world of the dead, there are very few desires (if any) beyond the desire for death that may ever come to fruition. So, the badness of death cannot be accounted for by the Desire Frustration View, either. So, where does this leave us?

In the worlds of *His Dark Materials*, death simply isn't a bad thing. Perhaps it's not as good as living, but it sure beats the afterlife. That's why the dead choose it!

4
Characters in Our Own Stories

Rachel Megan Barker

Daemons are more than a good fiction device: they answer a need in us.

—Karen Traviss

In Lyra's world, every human being has a daemon; a physical manifestation of their soul, which has a name, its own personality, and which takes an animal form. A daemon's form will change whilst the human is a child, but when the child hits puberty the daemon will settle into a fixed form, a form that in some way is supposed to represent who the human is.

What does it mean for our sense of identity to be represented in a way that is fixed, unchanging, and visible to ourselves and everyone around us? Is there a way to understand the idea of these settled forms that translates to our own understanding of identity in our world?

The idea that we even *have* fixed identities is hotly debated. After all, we change throughout our lives. Most people would probably argue that it *feels* as if we have a sustained personal identity. In my case, the I that is writing this essay feels like the same person that I was when I was eleven years old. But I am also a fundamentally different person from that person. My physical body has changed almost entirely, and my personality is radically different in many important ways. So am I still the same person I was then? And this is not just a phenomenon that manifests between childhood and adulthood—while most adults have more stable personalities than most children do, a person will still undergo huge changes in terms of who they are and how they act throughout adult life.

When we meet Lee Scorseby in *Once Upon a Time in the North*, he is a man who can fly a hot air balloon and who is attempting to make enough money to settle down and live an easy life. It is his meeting with Lyra in *The Northern Lights* that initiates a Han Solo–like transformation into a character who is ultimately willing to lay down his life for a cause greater than himself. But, throughout this whole process, his daemon Hester is an arctic hare.

How, then, can Hester's form represent Lee throughout this period of great change for him? And how can we say that Lee is the same person throughout the series, when he changes so dramatically?

Similarly, in the original trilogy, Lyra's daemon Pan settled as a pine marten. But in *The Secret Commonwealth*, Pan himself comments to Lyra on how much she has changed since the events of *The Amber Spyglass*. And yet, his form remains the same.

So what gives either the characters in the story, or us, any kind of consistent identity? Perhaps it is the story itself. The ongoing role we play in the narratives that are our own lives position us as singular actors moving through a narrative, in contrast to the other actors moving around us. Therefore, a daemon's form does not represent a person's personality, but rather the role that a person takes in their own story.

A Narrative Center of Gravity

In his 1992 article titled "The Self as a Center of Narrative Gravity," Daniel Dennett drew the comparison between our understanding of ourselves as a singular entities, and our understanding of characters in stories as singular entities. He argues that we do not exist as a singular fixed identity in any "real" way, but rather "it does seem that we are virtuoso novelists, who find ourselves engaged in all sorts of behavior, more or less unified, but sometimes disunified, and we always put the best 'faces' on it we can. We try to make all of our material cohere into a single good story."

For centuries, philosophers have argued over what gives a human being a consistent identity, or whether we have one at all. There are many schools of thought that would maintain that we simply do not, that there is nothing that makes who a person was a year ago the same person as who they are now. Therefore everything about our existence is merely a series of transitory present moments.

Identity is both a psychological and social necessity. We need some sense of consistent self that exists throughout our lives; society needs to be able to treat each individual like a single self. The idea of self as a narrative centre of gravity fits neatly with the idea of the settled daemon form, and gives us a solution to the question of identity by looking for a coherent identity not inside of ourselves but instead at that point where we meet the world. I exist as a singular identity because my life, regardless of what happens to me throughout it, is one singular narrative, with everything that has happened in my past leading directly to everything that is happening in my present, which in turn will lead onto everything that will happen in my future.

Whilst daemons are often, somewhat inaccurately, compared to the ideas of spirit guides or witch's familiars, a better mythological parallel would be the fylgja of Norse mythology. This is a spirit, which like a daemon takes an animal form, and like a daemon is born alongside a person. The fylgja is tied to a person's fate. While many of us, myself included, do not believe in the idea of fate as inevitable destiny, the idea that the fylgja represents or is tied to the story that a person must live out provides a wonderful parallel to the significance that a daemon's form holds for the narrative role their human will play in the world.

What We Can Learn from a Seagull

Take old Belisaria. She's a seagull, and that means I'm a kind of seagull too. I'm not grand and splendid nor beautiful, but I'm a tough old thing and I can survive anywhere and always find a bit of food and company. That's worth knowing, that is. And when your daemon settles, you'll know the sort of person you are.

—*The Northern Lights*

In *Northern Lights*, Lyra meets a seaman called Jerry, who's daemon Belisaria is settled as a seagull. The way that Jerry talks about his daemon's form illuminates how Jerry perceives himself, which resembles a common perception of seagulls.

We don't ever find out more about Jerry's story than what we learn through his short conversation with Lyra, but what he tells us about the form of his daemon is as much about the way he participates in his own life as it is his personality.

He is someone who is tough, yes, but this means he is someone who will survive in harsh situations, and who is always going to be able to find the things he needs to sustain that survival. He gives the impression of a rugged, seafaring, and nomadic life; this is the narrative that he lives, and what Belsaria's form therefore represents.

Tell Them Stories

Tell them stories. They need the truth. You must tell them true stories, and everything will be well, just tell them stories.

— *The Amber Spyglass*

In *The Amber Spyglass*, we journey with Lyra and Will into the world of the dead. There, the children make a deal with the harpies who inhabit that world that they will allow people safe passage through the world, and out into the world of the living again, in exchange for stories from those people about their lives. This is a rallying call from Philip Pullman about how he believes we should live our lives; to make them stories that are worth telling.

While Daniel Dennett asserts that the narrative nature of our identities makes them somehow less real, I contend that it is the narrative nature of our identities that gives us our reality. In the same way I can understand Marisa Coulter as a singular person through the narrative arc that unfolds around her, through seeing her both as an actor and a character acted upon in a way that unfolds into one long storyline, so I can understand my own identity. I understand my actions as my own; and the ways in which I have changed and evolved are not a change to my core identity but part of it. As any character in a story has character development, my personal development is part of my singular narrative.

Lyra's own story is still unfolding. In the latest addition to the *Book of Dust* trilogy, *The Secret Commonwealth*, we meet a twenty-year-old Lyra who is going through a difficult time in her life. She no longer has the vigor and optimism that she did as the young teenager who's daemon settled as a pine marten. Her relationship with Pan is falling apart, and the once silvertongued liar has fallen into a hyper-rational way of viewing the world that is destroying her imagination.

The proposal that daemon forms represent a person's personal narrative works in very broad brushstrokes. Most animals have a variety of sometimes contradictory symbolism surrounding them in different cultures and through different times in history. But in various mythologies about pine martens, we see the running themes of brave heroes, lucky spirits, and often of a creature that may prove unexpectedly dangerous.

Despite the huge changes that she has gone through since the events of *The Amber Spyglass*, Lyra remains very much a heroic figure. And she remains someone who, despite so much adversity, always seems to run into what she needs to continue on her path; there is a real element of luck in her journey. Furthermore, she is still deeply dangerous to the Magisterium and the establishment in her society. We can see these narrative tropes that are so central to her life reflected in Pan's settled form.

The entirety of what Lyra's story contains, of course, is vast, and Pan's form does not tell us anywhere near everything there is to know about Lyra's journey. It is, rather, a reflection of the broad themes of that journey. The pine marten form represents Lyra's particular narrative, in which Lyra herself is her own centre of narrative gravity.

An Arctic Hare, a Snow Leopard, and a Marmoset

"Finding out that you're an arctic hare. That's surprising. Damn, I was surprised."

"Surprised? Why the hell were you surprised? I ain't surprised." said Hester. "Iorek's right. I always knew I had more class than a rabbit."

—*Once Upon a Time in the North*

Lee Scoresby's daemon, Hester, takes the form of an arctic hare. Lee's character arc is a huge journey, involving a great deal of change on his part. There are a wide variety of myths and legends surrounding hares, across various cultures. They are often seen as unreliable and as self-interested tricksters, which mirrors who Lee is when we first meet him in *Once Upon a Time in the North*. But the way that hares move—hopping—is thought to symbolize a huge change in someone's life, representing Lee's journey from aeronaut for hire to a person who's willing to sacrifice himself to save Lyra. Hares are also associated in many cultures with involvement in the creation story, mirroring Lee's involvement in Will and Lyra's story. Their story itself mirrors the story of Adam and Eve.

Stelmaria, Lord Asriel's daemon, meanwhile, takes the form of a snow leopard. There are some obvious parallels to Asriel's story in this form; his journeys to the North, his role killing Roger (mirroring the snow leopard's nature as a predator), as well as some less obvious parallels—indigenous beliefs suggest that snow leopards remove people's sins from past lives, which reflects Asriel's mission to end the rule of the Church over humans' lives and behavior. This highlights his desire to do away with the idea of sin.

A character we see in the original trilogy, but get to know properly in *The Book of Dust* books is Hannah Raif. Her daemon takes the form of a marmoset. The pygmy marmoset is thought to be magical by the Matsigenka, as well as dangerous; it is said to lead hunters astray. This magical nature reflects Hannah's ability to read the alethiometer, and that they are seen as dangerous reflects how she becomes a growing danger to the Magisterium, through both her alethiometry and her involvement in the rebel organization Oakley Street.

A Story We Cannot Yet Know

By its mimetic intention, the world of fiction leads us to the heart of the real world of action.

—Paul Ricoeur, *Hermeneutics and the Human Sciences*

Wrapping your head around the idea that a human exists in a concrete way via our own narrative is entirely instinctively logical to some people, and an entirely alien concept to others. Some of us instinctively think more "narratively" than others. But for all of us, the thing that most clearly holds "us" together as singular individuals is that every present moment of ours is immediately preceded by our most immediate past moment, which is then immediately followed by our next future moment. This then threads itself together into one continuous narrative, which functions in the same way as a story, albeit a much more complex and longer story than you would normally find in a book, movie, or TV show.

Philip Pullman's choices of daemon forms for his characters do not, and arguably cannot truly encompass everything about the character's story; they are shadows of the much bigger and more complex picture that they represent. But they represent the fact that that story is there; that every character is a narrative centre of gravity, moving through their own story.

Will, a boy from our world, discovers his own daemon, Kirjava, who takes the form of a cat, when returning from the world of the dead. Mary Malone, meanwhile, learns how to see her daemon—an Alpine Chough—through a technique she learns from Serafina, despite her daemon not having a physical form. But there is no such magic in our world. We're not able to see a daemon form to represent the story that we are living. There is no ability to step outside ourselves and see our story from beginning to end. But the idea of that full story exists, and the idea of a settled daemon form provides this wondrously unique metaphor for the reality of that overarching narrative we are all individually living.

And if we see ourselves as central characters in our own personal narratives, then we can see the truth in one of the core messages of the series—*tell them stories*. The series pushes us to see ourselves as our stories, and to make those stories ones that we can be proud and excited to say that we have lived.

Part II

---

*"Without stories,
we wouldn't be human
at all."*

5
Mrs. Coulter:
The Overwoman?

RANDALL E. AUXIER

She's Cleopatra and Mata Hari and Madame Bovary and Joan of Arc all rolled into to one, isn't she? Maybe you should add in your favorite Bond Girl to complete the list.

Back when they tried to make the first novel into a movie (2007), they cast Nicole Kidman as Mrs. Coulter. I guess they needed star power. Hell, they had Daniel Craig and Sam Elliott. I don't know about you, but I don't really picture Nicole Kidman when I try to imagine her.

Don't get me wrong, I'm a huge fan of Nicole Kidman, but she just doesn't quite have the right *femme fatale* sort of energy (plenty *femme*, not enough *fatale*). She's also not crazy enough. And in a two-hour movie she had to get evil too quickly. Mrs. Coulter is far beyond *Noir*, anyway, don't you think? Ruth Wilson has a longer arc to develop the character. But there's still a big diff between a three-season series and three substantial novels.

Philip Pullman created this character before Claire Underwood (*House of Cards*) appeared on the scene, and yet, I wonder whether Robin Wright read the novels and thought "hmmm, I'll play Claire like *that*." So I guess I want Robin Wright to get the part. She's a little bit too old, but she could pull it off. I spent years trying to imagine Mrs. Coulter, and then, like magic, there was Claire Underwood.

I'm going to have to confess something. I don't really dislike Mrs. Coulter as much as I'm supposed to. Well, maybe I'm actually supposed to *not* dislike her, but for me it goes beyond that. In fact, I have a silly crush on her more wicked side, not her (oh so transient) vulnerable side. Part of it is that I can't quite get her character to "hang together" in my mind, which is intriguing all by itself. I'll bet I'm not the only person out there who gets her (or fails to get her) this way. She's a deliciously mysterious babe, and quite a dangerous one to have around (ask Lord Boreal). And part of the attraction is that she's a fictional character, which is the safest sort of dangerous woman to be infatuated with.

So, there you have it: she's dangerous *and* she's safely non-existent, and I think about her all the time (well, a lot of the time). It could be a problem. Fortunately, that's my job. Good work if you can get it (and keep it).

My Theory

]So I came up with a theory. Philosophers like theories quite a lot. Not so much as we like chocolatl, but chocolatl doesn't pay our bills and theories do (oddly enough). I started off just wondering whether Mrs. Coulter is really religious at all (it would spoil the attraction if she were; don't ask me why). Her ambiguous religiosity seemed to be at the heart of the puzzle, or so I hypothesized, and since it was *my* puzzle, no one prevented me from thinking so.

It is not easy to tell the difference, by the bye, between good philosophy and people just thinking stuff up. If you are beginning to get the sense that philosophers sit around making stuff up, I would say you're getting the message here. I'm going to do what I can in these pages to show you a few things about how to make stuff up and call it philosophy (and get away with it). Sociologists and psychologists also make things up, but (from what I can tell) their theories need not have anything to do with reality, so philosophy is more constrained.

Back to my theory. I decided that there are two main ways we might understand Mrs. Coulter's obsessions and motives (this is how philosophical theories usually start: on the one hand . . . on the other hand . . .). First, Philip Pullman offers, on several occasions, the suggestion that Mrs. Coulter is *afraid* of Dust and genuinely wants to use the power of "experimental theology" to spare people from sin in the future.

You gotta love the idea that what we call "physics" could have been "experimental theology" had a few things been different in our world (like the hilariously creative notion that John Calvin becomes Pope). And frankly, if Einstein's General Relativity isn't theology, nothing is. (I am far from the first to assert this.) Anyway, we might call this anti-Dust crusader the "religious" version of the Coulter character.

But on many other occasions, Pullman suggests that Mrs. Coulter is really only interested in power, and she uses all the means available to a woman in her world to gain it. Echoes of *The Handmaid's Tale*, and Serena Waterford, no? Now there's a thought. Give this part to Yvonne Strahovsky. In Mrs. Coulter's quest for power, she doesn't seem to be afraid of *anything*, least of all sin. On the face of it, these seem like two different people. I will get to the bottom of this with my theory, and I hope to get it done before Mrs. Coulter gets to the bottom of the Abyss.

I think that there is a sort of genius in the way Pullman finishes off Mrs. Coulter: locked in an eternal struggle with Metatron, who symbolizes the *religious* craving for power, in all its perversity, and Lord Asriel, who symbolizes its contrary, the *worldly* will to power, all falling forever together, kicking, biting, pulling hair. Their plunge is, I think, intended to allude to the fall of the angels banished from heaven in Milton's *Paradise Lost* (I, 44–75; VI, 860–877). Shades of Golem and his Precious at the Cracks of Doom, right?

But what would you bet that Mrs. Coulter switches sides whenever either Metatron or Asriel gets the upper hand in that endless struggle? And they all fall into a pit so deep that a physical body would starve before it hits the bottom (to use Pullman's image), and then their ghosts continue falling and fighting forevermore. I think that Pullman was telling us not to expect a final resolution between these contending forces, but Mrs. Coulter seems to hold them in balance by never quite committing herself wholly to one or the other.

There was a good deal to think about here. I had so many questions and so few answers. So I did what anyone with too much free time would have done: I started poking around in likely books to see where Pullman got all this stuff, and to try to figure out his angle on Mrs. Coulter. I really think that the TV writers who created Claire Underwood and adapted

Serena Waterford must surely have read Pullman. The characters are just too close to be accidental. But that was AP (After Pullman). I went looking BP specifically for a model for her character in all this ancient sacred literature and also in John Milton, who were sources for this story. I think I found Mrs. Coulter, but I will save that for near the end (don't peek).

Paradise Re-lost

Lots of people have commented that Pullman sort of rewrote Milton's big ol' poem about the war in Heaven and turned the story on its head. In terms of the *content* of the trilogy, I think there is a pretty good case for seeing it this way. But what's going on *philosophically* with Pullman is really a different story. Let's cover Milton first. You may recall that in the days before the world was created, a third of the angels took up battle with the Almighty. It didn't turn out well for anybody, really. Maybe Pullman didn't buy the way Milton depicted Adam's attitude toward the tragedy of world history near the end of the big ol' poem, when our common progenitor pretended to be grateful for all the blood, sweat, and tears shed by his many sons and daughters, just so that his heirs could be "saved" later on. Well, did Pullman rewrite Milton? Was that what he set out to do?

Someone had to "take one for the team," so I did it. I went and reread *Paradise Lost* to see what all came from there that later shows up in Pullman's trilogy. The writers of the HBO series surely did the same. I found some stuff that others haven't noticed, mainly because no one really wanted to reread the whole thing. Do they still teach Milton in high school? God, when I was a youngster, everyone had to read this blasted thing, which I always wanted to rename "Boredom Gained." But I now know that it's a better read when you get older.

Okay, I'm not quite being truthful. I bought the audio book version and listened to it on a car trip to Kansas City. But I did dig out my old high-school textbook version, snickered at my comments in the margins from when I was seventeen, and marked it up anew as I came to things I recognized from Pullman. And I am coming clean about this because I need you to be aware that there is a fantastic audio version of this book, read by Anton Lesser, whose vocal interpretation of the poem is so good that the whole thing became comprehensible to me for the first time. It's published by Naxos audio books and it is worth every cent of the $40 it costs

Anyway, here is some stuff I found.

Many Worlds

We don't need recent physicists like Hugh Everett (1930–1982) to find the "many worlds" hypothesis, although Pullman does have Mary Malone mention Everett's hypothesis by name in Book III (*The Amber Spyglass*, p. 77). Milton already had a similar idea: "Space may produce new worlds; whereof so rife / There went a fame in heav'n that He ere long intended to create" (I, 650–51). So, there are many worlds. No big deal. Further, the same idea occurs in the very line that gave our trilogy, and our HBO series, its name, where Milton says that all the several causes of the world would struggle in endless chaos, "Unless th' Almighty Maker them ordain / His dark materials to create more worlds" (II, 915–916).

In fact, it is mildly un-Biblical (as Milton knew) to pretend that God made only one world. Certain passages, especially in Genesis, but also elsewhere, whenever angels are being discussed (such as Psalm 82, or Revelation), only make sense by supposing a vast cosmos of many worlds, and many levels of existence beyond our familiar realm of the senses.

The idea that these many worlds might exist right on top of each other *in dimensions of possibility* is not in Milton, however. So the business in Lyra's world about the "heretical" Barnard-Stokes Hypothesis (which is supposed to correspond to the Everett hypothesis) is only intended to remind us of how the church has been suspicious, historically, of new ideas and science. This "many worlds" idea is not heretical in *our* world, so making it a part of a heresy in Lyra's world is a difference between hers and ours. I can't see that Milton would have had a problem with the plurality of worlds in dimensions of possibility. And the idea is probably not heretical.

Milton was very, very smart, and he was more than just a poet. He wrote some philosophical prose that philosophers still read and teach, especially his defense of the free press.

In the big ol' poem, he articulated a fairly subtle theory of knowledge, suggesting a dynamic physical intercourse (Milton loved the word "intercourse") between the worlds of spirit and sense. For example, the inhabitants of these two worlds might eat the same food (V, 475–505), which is probably why the angel Balthamos eats a mint cake when Will offers him one in Book III. But most importantly, the inhabitants of heavenly domains can have sex and reproduce with humans. Yes, that's in the Bible.

We will get to this point in a while, but I want to make it clear that Milton vehemently denied that it was sex between Adam and Eve that made them "fall." Milton explicitly has Adam and Eve doing the deed in paradise (it isn't dirty yet), and he says they would have had children, eventually, even without falling. The difference is that there was no lust in the pre-fall intercourse of Adam and Eve. There was pleasure, but no lust, which I find a bit difficult to imagine, fallen sinner that I am. In any case, those who want to attack Pullman for promoting sex as a perfectly sinless thing should examine and compare his presentation of sex between Will and Lyra (sorry to those who aren't reading, only watching, but yes, there is sex in store for Lyra—you haven't met Will yet, but you'll like him) with Milton's description of sex between Adam and Eve *before* the Fall. My point for now is that angels are *physical* beings. The relevance of sex will become clearer in a few moments.

Dust to Dust

The idea of "Dust" is also in Milton, just before the line about "his dark materials." He is speaking of the elements and forces that make up the physical world, and he says that Hot, Cold, Moist, and Dry each have an army of particles contending with one another "unnumbered as the sands" and these atoms are "levied to side with warring winds," and "To whom these [particles] most adhere, / He rules a moment" (see II, 898–908). That explains a few things, like the dust winds discovered by Mary Malone on her platform high in the crown of the seed-pod trees. It also explains the relationship between Dust and the *will to power*. Milton has it right there: those who rule a moment. Such individuals as Mrs.

Coulter and Lord Asriel are probably very "dusty," but maybe not in quite the same *way*—for example, I think Asriel is probably Hot and Mrs. Coulter is probably Cold (that's my suggestion about why Pullman names her "Coulter" and insists on calling her that throughout the trilogy—she's a cold customer, colder than Asriel in any case).

The idea of dust occurs in much the same way that Pullman speaks of it near the end of Book I (*The Golden Compass*, pp. 370–74, 376–77), when Lord Asriel is explaining to Lyra, in his comfy prison near Svalbard, where Dust comes from. Asriel quotes the famous Biblical passage from Genesis "for dust thou art and unto to dust shalt thou return" (p. 373). Milton has Adam pondering this same admonition and his own "death," and Milton comments about whether our human inability to be satisfied might continue beyond death, but "That were to extend / His sentence beyond dust and Nature's law" (X, 805–06). Milton is saying that desire and dissatisfaction die with physical death and do not extend beyond our dissolution to dust. Dust is an ultimate destiny for us, which is a point Pullman uses freely. It is not heresy unless Milton is a heretic (although plenty of people, such as William Blake, have said he was).

So, an aside about Milton and heresy. The more I studied him, the more I realized both that Milton is a heretic and that a bunch of people in his time and his court knew that perfectly well. But he was just too well-positioned with the Lord Protector for anyone to do anything about it. He was "Secretary for Foreign Tongues to the Council of State" for ten years (1649–1659), meaning that he was basically in charge of making sure that all business and political dealings of the government under Cromwell which were to be expressed in two or more languages (especially with those tricky French folk, the clever Dutch, and the still pesky Spaniards) said exactly the same thing, legally speaking, in the other languages as they said in English. It's hard to openly accuse a man who is *that* useful.

Returning to dust, as we always do, it is good to be aware that the tradition of orthodox Christian theology makes a place for this sort of idea, this dissolution to dust. For example, when Macrina (324–379 C.E.) explained her theology to her brother, whom we now know as St. Gregory of Nyssa, he asked her how the final resurrection of the body is possible, given that the bodies of the disciples have (by the fourth century) dissolved into atoms. Macrina said that the atoms have "known" each other in life and will recognize one another when God ordains their rejoining. This is not heresy, it's integral to the Christian tradition, and it also turns out to be the truth about the physical universe. We now call it "quantum entanglement" (see *The Amber Spyglass*, p. 156). Many of us don't expect God ever to ordain or command a final resurrection, but both Milton and Pullman are well aware that Christianity requires an interpretation of the simplest particles that compose the physical world. Pullman is not making this up and it isn't even an inversion of Christian doctrine, or of Milton. It's orthodoxy.

Touched by an Angel

Pullman's description of the huge battle between the forces of Lord Asriel and Metatron in Book III owes a good deal to Milton's description of the first war in Heaven, a war replayed on the Plain of Armageddon in the Christian book of Revelation.

Regarding this battle, Pullman suffers from the same sort of problem as Milton and the writer of Revelation: how do we describe, in *physical* terms, a conflict among angels, none of whom can quite be killed or even go to war in the ordinary sense? (see Milton, VI, 345–354). The writer of Revelation gets all symbolic and cryptic and indecipherable. Milton just has Raphael (the archangel who brings all the messages from God to Adam) lament that this is a "Sad task and hard, for how shall I relate / To human sense th' invisible exploits / Of warring spirits?" (V, 564–66) It just sounds silly when we bring it down to a level of description we can grasp. So the Archangel decides to describe it *as if* it were a war among human-like beings, and warns us that this is only an analogy. Something similar is going on at the end, with the fall of Mrs. Coulter, in an endless . . . well, it's a threesome. There. I said it. And not for the last time. It's the threesome to end all threesomes. The Mother of all Threesomes. A trinity, if you will. Sort of the condemned counterpart of that other threesome, the Holy Spirit, God the Father, and the Holy Virgin. (Am I getting too imaginative?) Jesus. I'll quit.

Mrs. Coulter: The Overwoman?

This narrative strategy of Raphael is reminiscent of the disclaimer made by the first angels we meet in Pullman's Book II, when Queen Ruta Skadi encounters angels who look like human forms to her only because she is unaware "that she saw them as human-formed only because she expected to" and that, really, they were more "like architecture than organism, huge structures composed of intelligence and feeling" (*The Subtle Knife*, p. 141). This corresponds to Milton's description of angelic nature as "All heart they live, all head, all eye, all ear / All intellect, all sense; and as they please / They limb themselves, and color, shape, or size / Assume, as likes them best, condense or rare" (VI, 350–54).

This explains why Balthamos can play the part of Will's daemon if he so chooses, and why it is humiliating for him to condense himself in a mere bird. Much of Pullman's angelology follows Milton, but both also follow certain older texts. The Jewish angelology of the time of Jesus is very similar, and descends from an older Hebrew counterpart, of course, which itself traces back to ancient Persia and Mesopotamia. St. Augustine's views are explicitly mentioned, but also there are the shared sources of the Bible and the *Pseudepigrapha*. I'll get to that in a minute, since I know you're just dying to find out all this stuff. The point is that Milton is hardly the original source.

But the idea that humans of flesh and blood can sometimes *become* angels is also in Milton, in much the way Pullman describes it. Remember that Balthamos was *always* an angel, but he helped Baruch, who had been a man, the brother of Enoch, *become* an angel; meanwhile, the Authority also made Enoch an angel, renamed "Metatron." Milton says that men and angels differ in degree but are of the same kind (V, 490), and has Raphael say to Adam: "Wonder not then, what God for you saw good / If I refuse not, but convert, as you, / To proper substance. Time may come when men / With angels may participate, and find / No inconvenient diet, nor too light fare; / Your bodies may at last turn all to spirit, / Improved by tract of time, and winged ascend / Ethereal as we, or may, at choice / Here or in heav'nly paradises dwell" (V, 491–501). So, it looks to me like Pullman intends to stick with Milton on this relationship between angels and humans, and if you found Pullman's description of angels a bit unfamiliar, it's because you forgot how it works in *Paradise Lost* (or because you never read that far).

That Knife

The subtle knife, the star of the second book and presumably of Season Two, itself also comes from Milton, at least partly, I think. It is modeled on the sword of Michael, the Archangel who leads God's troops into battle, and who clashes with Satan himself. Milton says: ". . . the sword / Of Michael from the armory of God / Was giv'n him tempered so, that neither keen / Nor solid might resist that edge" (VI, 320–23). Michael slices Satan's sword easily with it, and then cuts right into the Fiend himself, yet "The girding sword, with discontinuous wound / Passed through him; but th' ethereal substance closed / Not long divisible," (VI, 328-331) which may have given Pullman some ideas about how to describe cutting into other worlds. Also, when we consider how Will's fingers are cut off and simply won't stop bleeding, the explanation might be that the knife has cut not only his body but also his spirit and his ghost, each of which might have some role to play in the processes of physical healing.

That Compass

Everyone knows that the phrase "His Dark Materials" came from Milton, but not as many know that the American title of Book I, *The Golden Compass* is also from Milton. The Son is creating the world we inhabit, at God's behest, and in carrying out the task, "He took the golden compasses, prepared / In God's eternal store, to circumscribe / This universe, and all created things" (VII, 225–27). This is not the alethiometer as a device, it is just the phrase that was used for the title, but it's hardly an accident that it is in Milton. Still, my point is that it's there.

The Sons of God

Enough already? Not quite. The juiciest bit of Pullman's story is drawn from a very strange passage in the Bible, from Genesis 6:1–4:

> When men began to multiply on the face of the land and daughters were born to them, the sons of God saw that the daughters of man were so fair. And they took as their wives any they chose. Then the Lord said, "My Spirit shall not abide in man forever, for he is flesh: his days shall be 120 years." The Nephilim were on the earth in those days, and also afterward, when the sons of God came in to the daughters of man and they bore children to them. These were the mighty men who were of old, the men of renown.

Weird, huh? I never heard a sermon on this passage. One wonders what a preacher would convey as the moral message here. The Bible proper doesn't say much more about this little episode, but what happens next (in the Bible) is that the people turn away from God and become wicked, and then God slays them all in a flood—I think you've heard about that part.

But more than a few people have scratched their heads at this passage. What's up with the "sons of God" doing the dirty deed with the "daughters of men." If you're curious, there is a great deal more about this obscure part of world history in the Deutero-cannonical writings (I'll say more shortly on that topic), but for now what's important is that Milton takes up and explains all this stuff. In Book XI, lines 556–715 (I know, you never made it that far in high school), Michael has been sent to kick Adam out of the Garden of Eden, but he consoles Adam by showing him all of the future, including the salvation of humanity by the Son of God (Michael does not mention Pullman's novel to Adam, for some reason, but then, I guess it's just a sketch of the future, not the details).

Milton explains this odd passage from Genesis by expanding it. The world was pastoral and good, Michael says, but somewhere another angel was up to something naughty, deep in a cave, pounding on an iron forge, "Laboring, two massy clods of iron and brass / Had melted . . . the liquid ore he drained / Into fit molds prepared; from which he formed / First his own tools; then, what else might be wrought" (XI, 565–573). In Greek mythology, this naughty fellow is called Hephaestus, while the Romans called him Vulcan. He has a Hebrew name too. Wait for it. This naughty angel heads down to the world of human beings with a troop of followers and teaches the humans metal craft, including how to make weapons and to adorn themselves with jewelry made of fine metals.

It's pretty much all downhill from there. The human race in intercourse with these lusty angels make war, and build their cities, and they forget about God as they fall into what Michael calls "effeminate slackness." Basically, when all is said and done, the "sons of God" and the "daughters of men" have created a whole race of giants who are violent and very difficult to feed. These are "the mighty men of old" from Genesis, and Michael describes them as "Destroyers rightlier called and plagues of men" (XI, 697).

Pullman knows this story from Milton, but he also has studied the writings on this strange episode from the *Pseudepigrapha*, which is a name given to various ancient writings in the Biblical style (often held in esteem and given some degree of authority, the Deutero-cannon, or secondary authorities). Important among these writings are three apocalyptic writings called First, Second, and Third Enoch, and also Second and Third Baruch. Pullman draws heavily from these writings for his content. For example, the idea that Enoch, the seventh generation from Adam, became an angel renamed Metatron comes from chapters 3–4 of Third Enoch. There's a great deal more from these apocryphal writings that Pullman uses for his story, but for the moment, the important event comes when an angel with the interesting name of Azazel (which is Hebrew for "scapegoat") takes a notion to pay the Earth a visit:

> In those days, when the children of man had multiplied, it happened that there were born unto them handsome and beautiful daughters. And the angels, the children of heaven, saw them and desired them; and they said to one another, "Come, let us choose wives for ourselves from among the daughters of man and beget us children . . . And they took wives unto themselves, and everyone respectively chose one woman for himself, and they began to go unto them. And they taught them magical medicine, incantations, the cutting of roots, and taught them about plants. (First Enoch 6: 1–2, 7: 1–2)

Here we find the origin of the witches of Lyra's world, and the reason they live so long (they are the daughters of angels), and what sort of magic they can perform. But there's more. "And Azazel taught the people the art of making swords and knives, and shields, and breastplates, and . . . decorations" (8:1). For disclosing the arts of metallurgy to the humans, Azazel is punished by God, who tells Raphael: "Bind Azazel hand and foot and throw him into the darkness!" (10:4). Enoch says to Azazel: "There will not be peace unto you; a grave judgment has come upon you. They will put you in bonds, and you will not have an opportunity for rest and supplication, because you have taught injustice, and because you have shown the people deeds of shame, injustice, and sin" (13:1–2). Milton also mentions Azazel by name, and designates him as the standard bearer for Lucifer's army.

So, putting two and two together, here's what you get: the model for Asriel is Azazel. Lord Asriel is not a man, he's an angel who has chosen a wife from among the daughters of men, namely Mrs. Coulter. The enmity between Enoch (Metatron) and Asriel goes back to the time when Asriel was cast down and bound. The angel of light in Pullman is not Lucifer but is Xaphania, and she and Asriel have planned this new challenge to the old order, and have done so by repeating the "sin" of Genesis 6:1–4. Holy cod. You wanna talk about a spoiler alert? This isn't a piece of imaginative fiction Pullman wrote, it's a freakin' adaptation.

The witches have a prophecy about Lyra because they are the surviving female offspring of the fallen angels who retain the wisdom they learned back in the days before the first war in Heaven. They know that the sign of the new challenge will come when one of the defeated angels has a daughter by one of the daughters of men. This hypothesis about Asriel is confirmed when the witch queen Ruta Skadi describes her visit to Lord Asriel's Adamant Tower ("Adamant" comes from the name "Adam" which is a Hebrew word that means primal material, or . . . dust). The Tower (Of Babel? Of Cirith Ungol?), which was raised to make war with heaven:

> How has he done this? I think he must have been preparing this for a long time, for eons. He was preparing this before we were born, sisters, even though he is so much younger . . . But how can that be? I don't know I can't understand. I think he commands time, he makes it run fast or slow according to his will. (*The Amber Spyglass*, p. 270)

The queen's erotic desire is inflamed and she does with Lord Asriel what the witches did back in Genesis. The suggestion that witches are the daughters of the angels is, as far as I can tell, Pullman's invention, but it nicely draws the story together. There is a great deal of crypto-matriarchy being suggested here, which may be the reason that instead of Lucifer, the principal among the fallen angels is female. And perhaps the angel Xaphania is really in charge of all this rebellion. Her name is probably taken from the *Pseudepigrapha* also, from the Apocalypse of Zephania, which is (among other things) a study in angelology and their orders and places in the heavenly city.

The discussion of Pullman's use of sources beyond Milton could go on forever, so I bring in the *Pseudepigrapha* here more to suggest where you might look for more information. I mention it only to the degree that this information solves some riddles that remain from the trilogy.

Pullman never really explains that Asriel is an angel who has succeeded in breaking his ancient bonds and condensing into a substantial form so that the re-enactment of the sin of Genesis 6 is now possible again. Pullman never tells us why Lyra is so special, or what gives her the standing to play the part of Eve again, but the key is Genesis 6. Pullman gives us enough clues to work out who Asriel is, if we're willing to follow the trail. And obviously, this tells us a bit about Mrs. Coulter too. She is irresistible to the angels, whether Asriel or Metatron. But why? She is not Eve, after all.

A hint is to be found when Milton, describing Eve as she serves supper to Adam and Raphael in paradise, says, tantalizingly: "Meanwhile at table Eve / Ministered naked, and their flowing cups / with pleasant liquors crowned. O innocence / Deserving Paradise! If ever, then, / Then had the Sons of God excuse to have been / Enamored at that sight; but in those hearts / Love unlibidinous reigned . . ."

To paraphrase a bit, here is Eve without so much as a fig leaf, pouring a righteous single malt for Adam and Raphael, and they don't even lust after her, *but Milton does.* He is sitting there thinking to himself "those idiots, there is *womanhood itself* right in front of you, and you're just drinking and chatting!" Granting, Mrs. Coulter isn't Eve, but she's the freaking Mother of Eve, which might be, well, matriarchally speaking, more of a challenge. Hmmm. Lilith. Yes, that was the name I was looking for . . .

Beyond Good and Evil

As interesting as it is, none of this source material is "philosophy," *per se*. It is important to look at some of it so that we understand what sort of dark materials Pullman is working with, but until the materials are placed in some sort of order (whether human or divine—or daemonic), there is really nothing more here than a lot of images and ideas. But these are not your run of the mill images. They are archetypes. A dance of the archetypes, in the dust.

The more I have read his sources, the more I have become convinced that our man Pullman has intentionally modeled a number of his characters on types that are "beyond good and evil." It is not the fact that they are angels or children, or men and women, that is crucial; it is how these characters understand morality as a set of conventions that they might or might not choose to believe (and stay within). This is the famous idea (and book title) belonging to Friedrich Nietzsche (1844–1900). This little guy was withdrawn, very quiet, and a profoundly tortured soul. He wrote as if it was his personal calling to cast thunderbolts from the clouds at every conventional value or traditional practice.

Nietzsche has been dead for well over a hundred years, but he still makes religious people (and a lot of non-religious ones) very nervous. He was most notorious for having proclaimed that "God is dead." In Book III of the trilogy, Mrs. Coulter, confronts Father MacPhail (President of the Consistorial Court of Discipline) with the same idea, in words quite similar to a famous passage by Nietzsche. Father MacPhail says: "There are some people who claim that God is dead already. Presumably Asriel is not one of those, if he retains the ambition to kill him."

To this, Mrs. Coulter replies; "Well, where is God, if he's alive? And why doesn't he speak anymore? . . .Where is he now? Is he still alive, at some inconceivable age, decrepit and demented, unable to think or act or speak and unable to die, a rotten hulk? And if that is his condition, wouldn't it be the most merciful thing, the truest proof of our love of God, to seek him out and give him the gift of death?" (*The Amber Spyglass,* pp. 293–94).

This passage clinches the deal. It is pure Nietzsche, and Pullman intends us to know this. He built into Mrs. Coulter's discourse not only words and dialectical twists exactly in the style of Nietzsche, but also included a description of how Nietzsche spent the last twelve years of his own short life—"decrepit and demented, unable to think, act, speak, and unable to die." I do believe I discern Pullman's desire to go back in time and free Nietzsche from this suffering. And Nietzsche famously spoke of "Free Death," the heroic choice to die at the time of one's own choosing, just a few pages away from his most infamous passage about the death of God in his book *The Gay Science.* There is no question in my mind that Pullman intends us to understand Mrs. Coulter in association with Nietzsche. He even adds, after Mrs. Coulter has challenged Father MacPhail, that "Mrs. Coulter felt a calm exhilaration as she spoke. She wondered if she'd ever get out alive; but it was intoxicating, to speak like this to this man" (p. 294).

Once it's clear that Pullman intends his readers to see an engagement with Nietzsche's philosophy in his writing, other things about the story fall into place. He also intends us to see the characters of Lyra and Will, along with those of Asriel, Mrs. Coulter, John Perry, and Metatron, as carrying out a cosmic battle that is "beyond good and evil," which is to say, they employ a kind of judgment that is incomprehensible from within conventional moral standards and ideas. None of these characters feels the least bit bound either by conventional morals or by any kind of ordinary human emotion. They are "overmen," or in German, *Übermenschen.*

This doctrine of Nietzsche's has caused a lot of problems historically—the idea that a race of men will appear that supersedes and replaces humankind as we now know it. To such beings as these, we seem like insects, almost brainless slaves to everything that is weak and contemptible. Overmen don't live by our standards, and they ought not to, since our morality is devised by the weakest, most envious and vile among us—in Nietzsche's word, "Christians." Pullman stays away from any serious critique of Jesus or Christ, but this only reinforces Nietzsche's distinction between The Church, which was the invention of St. Paul, whom Nietzsche detests, and Jesus, whom Nietzsche admires as one who was too good for this world. Pullman steers clear of anything praiseworthy in the history of conventional religion and concentrates on the aspects of religious history that Nietzsche roundly condemned.

Asriel and Metatron are neither villains nor heroes; they are contending forces more powerful than we humans can understand. Their concerns are beyond our ken, and our moral judgments regarding them are of no interest to them. If you don't especially like Lord Asriel, who mercilessly murders Roger the kitchen boy so that he can re-establish his forges and smithies in an empty world, well, you aren't *supposed* to like him, and what's that to him? If Metatron seems to be a lecherous old angel, he isn't even slightly ashamed of it. Shades of Trump? Well, time is a funny eternal return, ain't it? You and your silly little moral qualms can go to blazes for all they care.

What about our favorite children, Will and Lyra? How does a child exist beyond conventional morality, and become stronger than all others, in spite of having conventional morality constantly thrust upon him/her? First, Pullman is careful to give the children extra-ordinary genes (and we have already noted Lyra's genealogy), but then he also devises childhood settings that deprive them of ordinary experiences. He suggests, by way of his plot choices, that the paths that lead to a girl version and a boy version of the "overman" are quite different.

On the "boy" side, Will is driven by *will*—not the will to power in the conventional since, but the will to fulfill his fate (*amor fati*, as Nietzsche says), to take up his father's mantel of warrior and shaman, and to exist beyond the limitations of ordinary men by the strength of his will. The Freudian implications of his bearing a "subtle knife" are obvious enough, I suppose, as are those of fighting with one's own father in the dark. There is nothing subtle about the positioning of Will's mother between him and his father. Apparently, the boy doesn't automatically evade the oedipal struggle just by being beyond good and evil. As with Nietzsche's overman, Will simultaneously detests violence and uses it without a moment's hesitation. The boy rises to overman by means of his will, it seems.

The girl rises to overwoman by more subtle and complex pathways. Pullman names her "Lyra" to emphasize the stark contrast between truth and lies. There's a difference, Nietzsche says, between "truth-and-falsehood," which is a conventional, intellectual idea (driven by a simple-minded logic and infected with conventional judgments about good and bad), and between "truth-and-lies," which is a contest of imaginations.

> In all cases we try to survive by inventing simulations, but this is the means by which the weaker, less robust individuals preserve themselves . . . In man [not overman], this art of simulation reaches its peak: here deception, flattery, lying and cheating, talking behind the back, living in borrowed splendor, being masked, the disguise of convention, acting a role before others and before oneself—in short, the constant fluttering around the single flame of vanity is so much the rule and the law that *almost* nothing is more incomprehensible than how an honest and pure urge for truth could make its appearance among men. (*The Portable Nietzsche*, p. 43).

But Lyra will overcome this dilemma. Here, in a nutshell, is the tension Mrs. Coulter has to face as she tries to ascend from the fetters of convention and the church to her genuine nature, which is beyond all that, Lilithly (say that five times fast, but not to a mirror in the dark). It's difficult, isn't it, Marisa, to be a substitute for Mary? Lyra, on the other hand, is given, by her nature, a perfect command of both truth and lies. She doesn't read that damned device, *it* reads *her*.

Both overcomings require practice, but both arts come easily to Lyra: the lies come not by way of imagination (Pullman makes a point of saying she is unimaginative), but simply because Lyra feels no constraint; and truth comes to her by way of a technology of symbols, *active* symbols. As Nietzsche puts it: "What, then, is truth? A mobile army of metaphors, metonyms, and anthropomorphisms" (p. 46). In short, truth is an alethiometer. Vivid imagination is not to blame for Lyra's lies. Xaphania's later teaching about the value of imagination, and the difficulty of learning to travel by its means, is at stake here. I sure hope they include that in the HBO series.

Thus, Lyra tells the truth just as she lies: from beyond conventional morality. By analogy, Will is the true despiser of violence but finds himself continually obliged to engage in it to preserve his own unalterable purpose. His violence is not the violence of blind followers or of those who oppress others and call the situation "peace" or "order" or "law." Thus, one of the more peculiar passages in the trilogy is explained. When Lyra first encounters Will in Cittàgazze. Lyra asks the alethiometer "*What is he* [Will]*? A friend or an enemy?* The alethiometer answered: *He is a murderer*" (*The Subtle Knife*, p. 28).

Now, I don't know about you, but if I was in Lyra's spot, I wouldn't be inclined to think of that as good news. But Pullman says, "When she saw the answer, she relaxed at once. He could find food, and show her how to reach Oxford, and those were powers that were useful, but he might still have been untrustworthy or cowardly. A murderer was a worthy companion. She felt as safe with him as she'd felt with Iorek Byrnison, the armored bear."

That's it. That's pretty much the whole explanation we ever get from Pullman. There is a tiny bit of elaboration on it later in the story, but the bottom line is that Lyra trusts Will *because* Will is, like herself, operating outside of conventional, cowardly morality, where no one can be trusted. And as Nietzsche puts it, "Is it not better to fall into the hands of a murderer than into the dreams of a lustful woman?" (*Thus Spoke Zarathustra*, "Of Chastity," p. 81). There we pretty much have Nietzsche's version of the story of Will rescuing Lyra from the sleep into which Mrs. Coulter has delivered her.

But notice that Lyra's path to overwoman is not a fight, it is a decision about which boy to follow. When she does anything apart from following Will, she gets into terrible trouble and messes everything up. Will on the other hand always knows what to do, because he does what he *has* to do and nothing else. Eventually, Will even begins to tell Lyra when to use the alethiometer, and she pretty much does whatever he says. We will discover more about the overwoman later, but for now, I just want to register with you, dear reader, that this arrangement between overman and overwoman follows Nietzsche's very controversial views about women. He rather famously characterizes them as being clever liars, but the hardest pills to swallow these days are these three remarks:

1. Everything about woman is a riddle, and everything about woman has one solution: pregnancy.

2. The man's happiness is: I will. The woman's happiness is: He will.

3. Are you visiting women? Don't forget your whip!

These are all from the same section of *Thus Spoke Zarathustra* ("Of Old and Young Women") which would be worth your while to read in full, thinking all the while of Lyra and Mrs. Coulter. Uncomfortable as it may be, Pullman is following this line of thinking in Nietzsche as well. He retains the ideas of active masculine virtues and passive feminine virtues. If anything, Mrs. Coulter rather than Lyra poses a challenge to this scheme of things, which is part of the reason Mrs. Coulter is more interesting than her daughter.

Pullman has written his epic trilogy on a latticework of Nietzsche's philosophical ideas about the death of God, about the ideas of good and evil, truth and lies, the will to power, and overmen and overwomen. It is not quite right to think of him as having rewritten John Milton or the Bible or *The Chronicles of Narnia* or Tolkien's trilogy with an inverted theology. Those elements contribute to the content of Pullman's trilogy, but the *ideas* under consideration are pretty much Nietzsche's. Pullman has narrated what Nietzsche called the "transvaluation of all values" in the form of a fable—which is exactly what Nietzsche himself did in *Thus Spoke Zarathustra*. But Pullman's story is for children, the children of the future, after the long-awaited death of God.

Pullman names Nietzsche in interviews about this subject, and the evangelical Christians have been very quick to exploit Nietzsche's "bad reputation" as a weapon against Pullman. I might add here that it is less comfortable for me to contemplate the other author who attempted this, Ayn Rand. Her lead characters were beyond good and evil, and Lord Asriel bears a striking resemblance to John Galt in *Atlas Shrugged*. But in my judgment, if one has any affinity for Nietzsche at all, one does well to skip Rand and just read Nietzsche. Rand's writing and ideas are caricatures of Nietzschean ideas and lead only to narrow-minded selfishness, not to anything morally interesting. Pullman, by contrast, has far greater subtlety. And I don't see Pullman endorsing Nietzsche's views or advocating them. I think he is probably offering a critique of Nietzsche.

Now maybe this little journey through Nietzsche hasn't been all that much fun (as far as I can tell, Nietzsche never had fun in his life), but hold your horses for a second –Nietzsche's last act before they institutionalized him for insanity was to collapse at the sight of a horse being beaten, but I won't beat your horses, I just want them held. Pullman is not a raving Nietzschean, I promise.

In Mrs. Coulter's Cave

In Book III, Pullman has Mrs. Coulter and Lyra re-enact the mythic drama of Demeter and Persephone, in which Will, acting the part of Hades, steals Lyra (Persephone) from Mrs. Coulter (Demeter) and takes her to the underworld to be queen there. Afterwards, Mrs. Coulter is altered. She is now (and only now) at the mercy of the power of motherhood, and she provides several drippy (and to my mind over-written and overwrought) apologies for motherhood. It is all pretty unconvincing. This is *not* Mrs. Coulter, or at least, it isn't the Mrs. Coulter I have a crush on. Even Asriel expresses something like contempt for this new, simpering, shadow-of-the-woman-she-was. Yes, she still plays each side off against the other, but there is a change. Now Mrs. Coulter is bereft of all religiousness, which is the power of fear, and this had been a source of her mystery and strength.

I want to make two points about where Pullman goes with his wicked woman: 1. Pullman created a character so powerful he didn't know what to do with her. Demeter was a cop-out. Mrs. Coulter, he says, is what happens to woman in a world dominated by the two overmen, Metatron and Asriel. There is no way for a woman to prevail in such a world, and that leads to my second point.

2. Sending Marisa (Lilith) Coulter into the abyss with Asriel and Metatron suggests to me a no-win situation for the Nietzschean overwoman. Pullman is not endorsing the world of Nietzsche and is suggesting that in such a world, the superior woman has no real place.

The most interesting path would have been to let Mrs. Coulter's character go where she naturally would have—which is to say, in a fearless novel, Mrs. Coulter *prevails* (like Claire Underwood). Why should Lyra (and motherhood) be such a weakness for a woman who is corruption incarnate? And with a choice between a woman who is beyond good and evil and a rival man, my money is on the woman. This is the woman who can break the subtle knife, see witches when they're invisible, tortures a witch without a moment's hesitation, and has the entire Church trembling in fear. This is the woman who can even command the specters, which is to say that she even commands the abyss. And she isn't equal to the task of being Lyra's mother? Seriously?

Mrs. Coulter, if you must know, is the woman Milton was lusting after when he imagined Eve, the babe so righteous looking that she could seduce an angel or a man as upright as Adam. But having created her, Pullman pulls back from the edge. Having created the *perfect* character, the one that might have won him literary infamy, he chose to cripple her with motherhood. It is interesting that, as far as we know, he spares Lyra that burden. So I'm not happy about Pullman's effort to weasel out of his dilemma by using the *Demeter-ex-machina* strategy. But this is not about me.

Thus Spake Philip Pullman

So what is Pullman's "teaching?" I think many people have misunderstood his point. There are so many characters with so many variant points of view that it might be difficult to extract the genuine moral theme from the trilogy. But with a little reflection, his point comes clear. Pullman puts his teaching into the words of Mary Malone, Serafina Pekkala, and the angel Xaphania.

Mary is the wisdom of clear-headed scientific understanding that is not the servant of dogma and also not closed to spiritual realities. She is the "sister" of the witch, whose understanding of nature is intuitive rather than scientific, and the relevant witch has also reformed the traditional ways of witches with a willingness to consider innovation and to overcome dogma as it has settled in to the society of witches. Xaphania speaks for the spiritual wisdom of the ages, and for the proper use of human imagination. All of this is offered in the final chapters of Book III. It isn't very exciting.

Pullman also provides Will's and Lyra's responses to their womanly teaching. Will, the masculine principle, takes Mary as his friend and guide. Lyra takes Serafina as hers. In so doing, Lyra overcomes the lies, but also loses access to truth when she can no longer read the Alethiometer—unless she is willing to commit a lifetime of study to the task. Pullman is saying truth isn't easy. But in the underworld she learns that truth is really *narrative* in form—the way to stay within the truth involves faithfulness to one's *own* narrative, not to a piece of technology.

Will's peculiar challenge is that of freedom and determinism. He has struggled throughout the story with whether he is determined to be a warrior by "his nature." He declares war on his fate early in Book III when he says that even if he can't choose his nature, he can choose what he does. Nietzsche has counseled that the overman is able to love his fate, but Will (and Pullman) takes a different view. Xaphania suggests the same.

But in the crucial moment, when Will has asked Xaphania what his "task" in life is, he stops her from telling him, because knowing her wisdom only perpetuates the struggle between freedom and fate. Thus, Pullman isn't saying he has a solution to the issue of freedom and fate, or of truth and lies. He is saying that even for Will and Lyra, after the crash and collapse of the world of powers beyond good and evil, still the philosophical problems remain. Pullman's advice is: truth is hard to know and knowing it takes work, and we are free to choose what we do, so long as we don't trouble ourselves overmuch about questions that are beyond our ken.

It is important that Pullman places all three teachings in the viewpoints of female characters. It's very clear that Pullman regards not only wisdom, but intuition and empirical knowledge as feminine virtues. That's why the "yearly meeting" is Lyra's idea, not Will's. They live in different worlds, but for an hour, in the noonday sun, on midsummer's day, they might quietly seek to occupy the same time in complementary spaces.

Xaphania's teaching is of the goodness of dust, and it sounds like the Boy Scout pledge: we are supposed to be cheerful, kind, patient, and curious, and that's how we renew the life force. But in particular, Xaphania wants to redeem imagination, and traveling by its means:

> We [angels] have other ways of traveling . . . It uses the faculty of what you call imagination. But that does not mean *making things up*. It is a form of seeing. . . . Pretending is easy. This way is hard, but much truer. . . . It takes long practice, yes. You have to work. Did you think you could snap your fingers, and have it as a gift? What is worth having is worth working for. (*The Amber Spyglass*, p. 443)

This is Pullman's theme, and it is equally critical of church and of state, and of any and every dogma. What he praises and advocates is not an overthrow of dogma, narrow-mindedness, and fear. He teaches that it always destroys itself, falls into the abyss under its own weight. And Nietzsche's world, which is our world, allows no place for feminine wisdom. Thus, Mrs. Coulter has no choice but to re-enact all that the collective unconscious determines her to do wherever the will to power is dominant. Pullman's interest in not in what happens to the will to power, but in what alternatives there might be. That is why he doesn't need to invert Milton, doesn't need to endorse Nietzsche, doesn't need to attack scriptural or mythic traditions, or anything of the sort. His positive suggestions may not be so startlingly new or profound, but they do have the tinge of common sense.

Incidentally, Xaphania's teaching also fulfills what I promised at the outset. Philosophy, like the travel of angels, isn't just making things up, at least not really. It requires imagination, but also a lifetime of work. But it's worth working for, and by taking the time to read thought-provoking literature, like Pullman's books, you are well on your way to learning that way of traveling.

6
The Terrifying Power of a Young Girl to Change Worlds

NINA SEALE

> The one thing he didn't want to do was hurt the boy. He had a horror of harming an innocent person.
>
> — *The Amber Spyglass*

So thinks the religious assassin, Father Gomez, as he watches a young boy and girl walk in the open savannah of a strange world. He observes how "it was clearer than ever that the boy and the girl were walking into mortal sin," and yet, the boy remains innocent in his eyes and he carefully focuses his rifle sights on the dark-blonde head of Lyra Silvertongue.

This hunt through the world of mulefa and tualapi is the last remaining attempt on Lyra's life in *His Dark Materials*. Only a few chapters before, the Regent Angel Metatron is lured to his death by Lyra's mother Mrs. Coulter, who says she can bring him to Lyra's father Lord Asriel and her dæmon so both can be destroyed. And before that, a stolen lock of golden hair is used to detonate a bomb which tears a huge abyss between the worlds in the land of the dead, only just missing its target.

Lyra is twelve years old and her dæmon Pantalaimon has not yet settled. She has undergone a great many adventures across worlds, but she did not chose her fearful destiny, and is not aware of the greatness of her actions, as Dr. Lanselius says "she must fulfil this destiny in ignorance of what she is doing, because only in her ignorance can we be saved."

Unlike Will, she has not killed. She is innocent, and yet, the massive authoritarian force of the Church pursues this twelve-year-old with a mission to destroy her.

Like everything else in this fantasy series, the persecution of Lyra is larger than life. However, the persecution of young women who have never incited violence, terror, or other forms of harm, is not fictional. Philip Pullman chose a female protagonist to lead these books which, in his own words, "are about killing God" (*Sydney Morning Herald*, 2003). Father Gomez looks beyond Will, is even horrified at the thought of harming a young innocent (though, of course, Will is a killer), to set his rifle's sights on Lyra.

The persecution of women is one of the many recurring themes of the dark and bloody history of humanity, and it is still pervasive today. Though many of the themes and characters of *His Dark Materials* draw on past institutions, ideologies and literature, there are many parallels we can draw between the fear of Lyra Silvertongue and the way innocent young women are treated today. What is it about young women that strikes fear into people and institutions with so much more power?

Fear of the Feminine

Then a bath, with thick scented foam . . . Pantalaimon watched with powerful curiosity until Mrs Coulter looked at him, and he knew what she meant and turned away, averting his eyes modestly from these feminine mysteries as the golden monkey was doing. He had never had to look away from Lyra before.

— Northern Lights

How nonsensical. Generations of readers must have frowned at this. Half of your soul, look away from you because you are female and it is male?

This moment shows a difference between children and adults, a learned behavior we see reflected in society that does not exist innately in our natures. Feminine mystery. Look away. The separation of male and female, even though each person exists with both masculine and feminine traits, illustrated by the sex of most dæmons being different from their humans'. In the world of dæmons, masculinity and femininity exist within one person just as they exist in society. One of our many ancient patriarchal philosophers, Plato, said "Humans have a twofold nature," but human society has not been built on the foundation that these two sexes exist together in equal strength, as the rest of Plato's sentence agrees "the superior kind should be such as would from then on be called 'man'."

Plato believed that men's superiority was defined by the divine—their souls are superior, and if a man leads a bad life, he will be reincarnated with an inferior soul: that of a woman. Plato's colleague Aristotle disagreed (for being so sure of their superior souls, they had to spend their time picking apart how and why women were so inferior to them) and thought that female inferiority came from biology; they were weaker both physically and mentally across the animal kingdom. Aristotle describes the female as "softer" (*History of Animals*, IX) in disposition than the male, describing the female as "more mischievous, less simple, more impulsive, and more attentive to the nurture of the young: the male, on the other hand, is more spirited than the female, more savage, more simple and less cunning."

So these two bearded Greek philosophers with their "superior souls" agreed that women are inferior, with a stronger tendency to immorality: "A woman's natural potential for virtue is inferior to a man's, so she's proportionately a greater danger, perhaps even twice as great." This belief is described most famously in the Bible itself, as it is Eve who is tempted and drives the downfall of man, which is the role the Magisterium believes that Lyra plays in the universe.

Fortunately, the essence of woman is no longer only discussed publicly by bearded men in their patriarchal echo chambers. A bourgeois Parisian by the name of Simone de Beauvoir shook the boat in 1949 with her book *The Second Sex*, which ripped at the fabric of patriarchal philosophy woven by Aristotle, Plato and many, many others.

Recall Lyra's "feminine mysteries" from which Pan has to look away. De Beauvoir accuses men of a similar offense. Men separated women by cloaking them in a false aura of mystery. They used stereotyping (women are prone to flightiness, to quick tempers, to immoral behaviour) as an excuse not to understand women's problems or try to help them. De Beauvoir also applied this pattern to other separations in society by more powerful classes: race, class and religion. These stereotypes are bolstered by the people in the empowered class with the loudest voices, and used to organise society into a hierarchal system that undermines those who are "different."

So, naturally, anyone who threatens these stereotypes threatens to topple the whole system. A young woman seeking the truth about Dust, perhaps . . .

Fear of Awakening

"Because if they all think Dust is bad, it must be good . . .

"We've heard them all talk about Dust, and they're so afraid of it, and you know what? We believed them, even though we could see what they were doing was wicked and evil and wrong . . . We thought Dust must be bad too, because they were grown-up and they said so. But what if it isn't? What if it's—"

She said breathlessly, "Yeah! What if it's really good . . . ?"

—*Northern Lights*

Out of all the changes we see Lyra undertake as she embarks on her adventures and grows into her adolescence, this moment is one of the most significant. It's the first time it dawns on her that she and Pan can make better decisions than the adults she has known, and at various points idolised and trusted. It's a moment most young people have, when they realise their parents are not perfect, when they disagree with them about something important for the first time (though admittedly most of us aren't standing on an ice bridge into another world).

This first moment carves Lyra's path, as it gives her and Pan strength in their convictions and the belief that they can choose the right path, the good path, without the need of another authority. Without this conviction, they would never have believed that they could defy Asriel by refusing the Gallivespians and travelling to the world of the dead. This way of thinking even forces the bond between Lyra and her dæmon, because she chooses to abandon Pan on the shore of the mist-covered lake because she knows rescuing Roger is the right thing to do.

This kind of awakening is one of the biggest threats to an authoritarian regime. I believe it is Lyra's scariest trait, and that of real-life Lyras. One real Lyra who has been threatened and discredited in her birth country is Yeon-mi Park, a young woman who escaped North Korea with her mother when she was thirteen. She attracted the attention of the world on the stage of the One Young World Summit in Dublin, 2013, when she was twenty-one years old and has since expanded on the horrible reality of life inside the secretive communist regime in interviews, speeches, and her book *In Order to Live: A North Korean Girl's Journey to Freedom*.

Yeon-mi has since described the reaction from North Korean leadership, saying it "continues to threaten me through YouTube videos and has threatened my family members who still live in the North. The Kim regime does everything to silence me, even now. I don't think anyone should have power over me, or have the right to tell me what to say or how to think. That's not right. I want to be free" (*Deutsche Welle*, 2016).

This treatment is not unique to Yeon-mi. Many of her fellow defectors have been threatened in the same way and, more horrifying, is the way that people who appear think past the tight bars of thought built by the regime around its citizens. In her book, Yeon-mi describes how foreign media is banned and enforced to prevent Western ideas from infiltrating society. She says that the day she secretly watched a pirated copy of *Titanic* on her uncle's VCR (with the windows covered): "I couldn't believe how someone could make a movie out of such a shameful love story. In North Korea, the filmmakers would have been executed . . . In North Korea, public executions were used to teach us lessons in loyalty to the regime and the consequences of disobedience."

Freedom of thought is the biggest threat to an authoritarian regime. And what is the source of freedom of thought? Knowledge.

Fear of Knowledge

Why then was this forbid? Why but to awe,
Why but to keep ye low and ignorant,
His worshippers; he knows that in the day
Ye Eate thereof, your Eyes that seem so cleere,

Yet are but dim, shall perfectly be then
Op'nd and cleerd, and ye shall be as Gods,
Knowing both Good and Evil as they know.

  —*Paradise Lost*

Philip Pullman drew great inspiration from *Paradise Lost* when he penned *His Dark Materials*. Although it mimics the events in the biblical Fall of Man, the serpent Tempter in *Paradise Lost* is eloquent, intelligent, and sympathetic, and his argument to persuade Eve to disobey God, who seeks to oppress humanity in low ignorance, is a strong, righteous one.

From the moment Lyra and Pan leave their world, they seek truth and knowledge. They visit Dr. Mary Malone in her college in our Oxford to ask her about Dust (or dark matter, as we know it), and even in our world we see the forces of the Church from Lyra's world, who terminate Mary's research. Even after all the incredible adventures of the trilogy, it ends with Lyra taking a place at St. Sophia's College in her Oxford to begin a formal education for the first time in her life.

Another real-life Lyra who was attacked for pursuing freedom of thought is Malala Yousafzai, who survived an attempted assassination by the Taliban to eliminate the threat she posed as an advocate for women's education in Pakistan. After the attempt on a sixteen-year-old child's life, a spokesperson for the Pakistani Taliban labelled Malala as "the symbol of the infidels and obscenity" and added that she would be targeted again if she survived. The Taliban claimed that "even a child can be killed if he is propagating against Islam."

Malala's advocacy for education, particularly for young women, has become an international movement. She is the embodiment of the power that a young woman can have to overthrow suppressive regimes if she wields knowledge, and so the terror she incited in terrorists is understandable. She has said "With guns you can kill terrorists, with education you can kill terrorism."

The fear these Lyras instil in these real-life embodiments of the Church is a fear of loss of power, a fear of change. The powerful potential of a young girl armed with truth and knowledge can cause a tidal change in thinking. And yes, to those who oppose free thought, these young women are terrifying.

Fear of Change

"My daughter!" cried Lord Asriel, exulting. "Isn't it something to bring a child like that into the world? . . . Did we know what we were taking on when we started this rebellion? No. But did they know—did they know what they were taking on when my daughter got involved?"

— *The Amber Spyglass*

From ignoring and dismissing Lyra, Lord Asriel expresses great admiration for his daughter and eventually sacrifices his life for her safety with Mrs. Coulter. All the things he attempted, with all his strength of character, ambition and determination, were achieved by his young daughter: seeking the source of Dust and saving it, crippling the Authority by undermining their power in releasing the Dead, and building the Republic of Heaven (well, the latter is the endeavour she takes up at the close of the trilogy).

In *The Amber Spyglass* we learn that the strength of the Authority that Lord Asriel seeks to destroy does not lie in the great mystical figure "God, the Creator, the Lord." When the reader finally meets this figure, he is merely an aged being who "could only weep and mumble in fear and pain and misery." The strength of the Authority lies in its followers—the masses which make up the Church—people who believe steadfastly in the righteousness of their beliefs even in the face of the cold, stark truth.

In the bleak world of the dead, where the Authority imprisons souls to an eternity of nothing, when Lyra and Will offer the chance to leave, one person speaks up: "This is not a child. This is an agent of the Evil One himself! The world we lived in was a vale of corruption and tears. Nothing there could satisfy us. But the Almighty has granted us this blessed place for all of eternity, this paradise, which to the fallen soul seems bleak and barren, but which the eyes of faith see it as it is, overflowing with milk and honey and resounding with the sweet hymns of the angels. *This* is heaven, truly!"

This eloquent speech by a damned soul seems inspired by the (admittedly not so eloquent) tirades you can read online which condemn Greta Thunberg, the young climate activist. The willful ignorance of the masses and their reluctance to see that change is needed is one of the strongest weapons within an oppressive authority's armoury. Climate change deniers like President Donald Trump feed off this disgust towards change and appetite for falsehoods that support their way of thinking. Taking action against climate change would mean huge sacrifices for the most privileged and powerful, but finally voices such as Greta's have forced a global call to action that can no longer be dismissed.

Yet, wilful ignorance and decrying of Greta as a puppet of her parents and the environmentalist movement can still be found by people whose arguments are shallow and transparent. Australian political commentator Andrew Bolt justified his criticism of Greta by using her autism diagnosis to undermine her, writing "I have never seen a girl so young and with so many mental disorders treated by so many adults as a guru . . . Her intense fear of the climate is not surprising from someone with disorders which intensify fears." In the face of the change she has already created in the political climate, these attempts to discredit her are pathetic, and call to mind the blinded bleating of the damned soul who decries Lyra to "remain here in our blessed paradise."

The Power of Lyra Silvertongue

"We know what we're doing is important, after all."

"We don't know it," Pantalaimon pointed out. "We think it is, but we don't know. We just decided to look for Dust because Roger died."

"We know it's important!" Lyra said hotly, and she even stamped. "And so do the witches."

— *The Subtle Knife*

As the power of an authoritarian regime does not lie in its leader, but the conviction and strength of its followers, each of the real-life Lyras described above are strengthened by their allies. Lyra picks up many allies on her journey: the Gyptians, Lee Scoresby, Iorek Byrnison, the witches of Lake Enara, to name a few.

The bonds created with these allies come from a common thinking and belief in Lyra's goodness. This was described by the writer behind the BBC's joint adaptation of the trilogy with HBO, Jack Thorne, who described Lyra as an anti-superhero: "The thing I love about Lyra is that she's constantly following the path of the good. I really believe we should be following our goodness now."

That goodness is the strongest defence that real-life Lyras have. Just as Lyra herself has faults in her dishonesty, her selfishness and temper, real-life Lyras are not perfect either, and clever opponents who fear them will use their weaknesses to denounce them. But so long as Lyras choose the path of the good, righteous people will be drawn in to help them and their power is inconceivable. The Authority is right to fear them.

7
From Pantalaimon to Panpsychism

PETER WEST

If you're reading this then I take it you're a fan of *His Dark Materials,* or maybe you've just discovered Lyra's story via Philip Pullman's new trilogy (*The Book of Dust*) or the new television series.

I'm a fan too: I grew up reading and re-reading the *His Dark Materials* trilogy, gripped by the fantastic images conjured up by the descriptions of the worlds that make up Philip Pullman's fictional universe. From Lyra's Oxford with its zeppelins, colleges, and Gyptians from the Fens (which is where I grew up!), via the world of the mulefa with its giant birds and elephant-like motorcycle gangs, and finally to the battlefield where the forces of the new Republic of Heaven face-off against Metatron and those fighting on behalf of the Authority. In hindsight, the concepts introduced in Pullman's books have continued to shape the way I think long after I first read them. Not that I ever really *stopped* reading them: I finished the latest addition to the series, *The Secret Commonwealth*, almost before the first reviews came out.

As a fan of *His Dark Materials,* I think it is worth knowing where the roots of these stories and the ideas contained within them might lie. Pullman himself is upfront in acknowledging that his work is indebted to several books from the history of English storytelling. Most fans will know that *His Dark Materials* draws on books like John Milton's *Paradise Lost* and the prose of William Blake, as well as faerie stories dating back to the Middle Ages. But I want to draw the attention of fans to a connection between *His Dark Materials* and another important figure in the history of English storytelling: a seventeenth-century philosophy and fiction writer called Margaret Cavendish. Knowing about the philosophy and fiction of Margaret Cavendish enhances our appreciation of *His Dark Materials*.

I think there are two reasons why *His Dark Materials* fans should be interested in Cavendish. Firstly, she wrote a short story called *The Blazing World* which tells a very similar story to Lyra's journey in *Northern Lights*. *The Blazing World* is a story about a woman who travels through the North Pole into another world where she meets talking bears. This should sound familiar to anyone who has read *Northern Lights*. Several literary scholars and historians of philosophy think *The Blazing World* is the first example of science-fiction writing in the English language: it was written almost two-hundred years before Mary Shelley's *Frankenstein*. The second reason fans should be interested in Margaret Cavendish is that she defended a philosophical view called panpsychism.

Panpsychism is a philosophical theory that tells us that everything in the world around us, from grains of sand to human beings, is *conscious*. It literally means all or everything ("pan") is soul or mind ("psychic"). (Pantalaimon, the name of Lyra's daemon, means "all-forgiving" or "all-compassionate." Of course, we see Pan's forgiving side stretched to its limit in *The Amber Spyglass* when Lyra leaves him behind to enter the world of the Dead).

As surprising at it may seem, panpsychism is becoming quite a popular view amongst philosophers today who are interested in consciousness and the mind. However, Cavendish held this view over three-hundred years ago when most philosophers were defending a *mechanistic* account of the universe: one which likens the world around us to clockwork or mechanical instruments. On the mechanistic account of the universe, we are alone in being conscious. One prominent mechanist, René Descartes, believed that even animals were simply complicated machines or "automata."

Why should this be of interest to fans of *His Dark Materials*? Because Philip Pullman is himself a panpsychist and has said so in several interviews. I think we can better understand

Pullman's world if we understand panpsychism. In particular, understanding panpsychism helps us understand why Dust is so important in Pullman's fictional universe. Over the course of both trilogies—*His Dark Materials* and *The Book of Dust*—we learn that Dust, a mysterious substance that attaches itself to human beings, is at the bottom of everything. And, Dust, we learn, is closely connected to consciousness.

I'm not saying that Philip Pullman must have read Margaret Cavendish or *The Blazing World*. In fact, he told me (on Twitter) that he had not. But he also told me, when I asked him about Margaret Cavendish, that "books can influence you even if you don't read them." I think fans of *His Dark Materials* should know about Margaret Cavendish because *The Blazing World* tells a remarkably similar story three-hundred years before *Northern Lights* was ever written and because Cavendish defended panpsychism long before it was a popular philosophical view. In my view, the connection between Cavendish's writing and Pullman's stories provides an added dimension to the connection between *His Dark Materials* and the history of English storytelling.

New Worlds

Both Philip Pullman and Margaret Cavendish explore the fascinating idea that our world is connected to other worlds at its poles. This idea is perhaps inspired by the fact that, for a long time, maps seemed to depict one world connected at the hip to another (when really they were depicting the two "sides" of the Earth). In 1666, over three hundred years before *Northern Lights* was released, Margaret Cavendish published the weird and wonderful story of a woman's journey to *The Blazing World* (the protagonist is never named, but later in the story is referred to as the Empress). A year earlier, in 1665, a scientist named Robert Hooke published a book called *Micrographia,* in which he argued that microscopes—a new and exciting scientific instrument at the time—could show us, as he put it, "new worlds." This idea, of catching glimpses into new worlds, captured people's imaginations and Cavendish's story, which takes us on a journey into her own invented new world, was heavily influenced by such scientific claims.

In the story, an unnamed woman is abducted and taken onboard a ship that sails towards the North Pole. The crew die on the journey north but the woman is spared and when the ship reaches the North Pole it sails right through it and into a completely new world. We are told that our own world and this new world are joined at their poles:

> . . . for it is impossible to round this World's Globe from Pole to Pole, so as we do from East to West; because the Poles of the other World, joining to the Poles of this, do not allow any further passage to surround the World that way; but if any one arrives to either of these Poles, he is either forced to return, or to enter into another World. (*The Blazing World*, Project Gutenberg edition)

Like *His Dark Materials*, *The Blazing World* takes place in a multiverse: a universe that consists in multiple worlds—not just different planets, but worlds that exist in their own dimensions (although there are only three worlds in Cavendish's story, while the number of worlds in *His Dark Materials* seems to be limitless). The woman now finds herself in a new world, the Blazing World, so-called because its sky is full of blazing stars regardless of whether it is day or night. To anyone who has read *Northern Lights*, the similarities between the first act of *The Blazing World* and the plot of the first book in the *Dark Materials* trilogy are striking. *Northern Lights* follows Lyra's journey north where she discovers that the General Oblation Board have been separating children from their daemons at a research station in Bolvangar. When she finally escapes from Mrs. Coulter, thanks to the help of Iorek Byrnison, Lee Scoresby, and the witches, Lyra finds a bridge to the stars. Following this bridge, Lyra looks up at a "blazing sky" before crossing (*Northern Lights*, p. 396). The book concludes on a cliff-hanger as "Lyra and her daemon turned away from the world they were born in, and looked towards the sun, and walked into the sky" (p. 397).

Polar Bears

Bears are also an important bridge across the three-hundred-year gap between *The Blazing World* and *His Dark Materials*. Iorek Byrnison (surely the best character in *His Dark*

Materials: he's a talking polar bear who wears impenetrable armour, drinks heavily, and comes out on top in pretty much every scrap he's involved in), the fallen bear-king, accompanies Lyra on her journey towards the northern lights and saves her life on more than one occasion (and fixes Will's Subtle Knife later on in the story).

She pays him back by helping him take back his throne in Svalbard, where the armoured bears live. But Lyra is not the only world-hopping protagonist who is rescued by talking bears. In the *Blazing World,* the heroine of the story, having crossed over to a new world via the North Pole, comes across a group of strange creatures. She looks across the icy landscape and sees: "walking upon the Ice, strange Creatures, in shape like Bears, only they went upright as men." She is afraid at first but soon realizes that the Bear-men mean her no harm. In fact, she quickly realizes that the

> Bear-like Creatures, how terrible soever they appear'd to her sight, yet were they so far from exercising any cruelty upon her, that rather they shewed her all civility and kindness imaginable; for she being not able to go upon the Ice, by reason of its slipperiness, they took her up in their rough arms, and carried her into their City.

Like Lyra, *The Blazing World's* protagonist is accompanied through the icy terrain to safety by human-like bears who, though they are strange and fearful in appearance, are ultimately kind and protective. Both protagonists eventually find themselves in a city inhabited by talking bears.

Mad Madge

These are some obvious similarities between Margaret Cavendish's *Blazing World* and Lyra's journey in *Northern Lights.* That's one reason fans of *His Dark Materials* should know about Cavendish. But what's all this got to do with philosophy? Well, it's because Cavendish was best known during her lifetime as a philosopher—and quite a remarkable one at that.

Seventeenth-century England was a very different society from the one in which we now live. It was an especially different place for women. It was very unusual for women to be educated, and even rarer for them to attend university, let alone write philosophy. At the time, a public intellectual named Samuel Johnson said that seeing a woman engage in intellectual pursuits was like seeing a dog walk on its hind legs: "It is not done well, but you are surprised to find it done at all." A woman writing philosophy in the seventeenth-century would find herself in a similar position to an atheist in Lyra's world where the Magisterium determine what is and isn't socially acceptable: derided, criticised, and, for the most part, marginalised. This is the intellectual climate in which Margaret Cavendish found herself. Yet, she defied social conventions to become both a prolific writer and the first woman to attend a meeting of the Royal Society of London, a prestigious group of scientists and philosophers in England.

Cavendish was nicknamed "Mad Madge" because of her eccentric personality and dress sense, and because of the eclectic mixture of poetry, fantasy fiction, and philosophy she wrote over the course of her life. This unflattering nickname also reveals the extent to which women writers were dismissed by their male counterparts. Just as Lyra, the scruffy girl who enjoys mud-fights with the local boys in Oxford, is seen as an oddity by the stuffy scholars of Jordan College, Margaret Cavendish was viewed as a spectacle by most of her philosophical contemporaries. Samuel Pepys, the famous diarist, followed her around London for a week just to catch a glimpse of her! But like Lyra, despite social norms that placed limits on her intellectual freedom, Cavendish made a lasting impact on the way we think about the world around us.

Is Everything Conscious?

Panpsychism is the philosophical view that everything in the world around us, from people like you or me, through to animals and plants, and all the way down the "chain of being" as far as mountains, rocks, grains of sand, and bars of chocolatl, is conscious. Panpsychism sits somewhere between materialism, the view that everything is purely material or physical, and idealism, the view that everything is mental (idealists think that everything either *is* a mind or exists *in* a mind). Panpsychism, materialism, and idealism are three different philosophical systems or "pictures of reality." Idealism had its hey-day largely in nineteenth-century Germany, and materialism was very popular for much of the twentieth-century (especially in the UK and US). Right now, however, panpsychism is an increasingly popular view.

Margaret Cavendish endorsed panpsychism long before it was anything like a mainstream philosophical position. Cavendish's argument is designed to make sense of the fact that we live in a well-ordered universe. She argues *backwards* from the fact that we live in a comprehensible and predictable world full of laws of nature (apples fall from trees, the sun rises in the morning, and where there is smoke there is fire) to the conclusion that everything in the world around us must be conscious. There's only one explanation for such order and regularity in her eyes: things in the world *must* be conscious. As she sees it, if every different part of nature were *not* conscious of what the other things in the world around it were doing, the world would be chaotic. But it isn't. So everything in nature *must* be conscious. (Cavendish makes this argument in *Observations Upon Experimental Philosophy*.)

An example might help make her point clearer. Imagine walking down a busy street in Oxford whilst trying to read your alethiometer (or while texting on your phone). You would probably end up walking into a naptha lamp, another person, or (God forbid) someone else's daemon. This wouldn't happen if you pay attention to—if you were *conscious* of—what was going on around you. All of this means that if you walk down a busy street, and people *aren't* bumping into each other or their daemons, then you can reasonably infer that they *are* conscious of one another. Likewise, if you see someone stray into another person's path, you might reasonably assume they weren't paying attention.

Cavendish thinks that the same is true of the universe in general. Things *aren't* chaotic, in fact, the workings of nature seem to make a great deal of sense. The more we learn about nature by engaging in biology, chemistry, and physics—the natural sciences (what Cavendish would call "natural philosophy" and the scholars in Jordan College would call "natural *theology*")—the more we can accurately predict what's going to happen in the world around us. We should understand the universe in general, Cavendish thinks, in just the same way we understand the various parts of the universe we interact with every day—just on a much greater scale. In this way, Cavendish gives us a philosophical reason to believe in panpsychism.

Dust and Consciousness

In *Northern Lights*, we learn that the scientists in Bolvangar, who cruelly conduct experiments separating children from their daemons, are interested in Dust. By the end of *The Amber Spyglass*, it has become very clear that Dust is at the root of conscious life as we know it. Philip Pullman himself said he was so interested in Dust, and what it might be, that he had to write a new trilogy (*The Book of Dust*) so he, and we, could learn more about it.

The Magisterium in Lyra's world and the scientists in Bolvangar are interested in Dust because they think it is connected to Original Sin. The Magisterium believe that by learning more about Dust they will be able to better understand what happened after the Fall of Adam and Eve. However, in *The Amber Spyglass*, thanks to the research of Mary Malone and the time she spends among the mulefa, we learn that Dust is closely connected—and perhaps even the source of—consciousness. After she constructs the Amber Spyglass, Mary can see that humans like her or Will, as well as humans who have daemons (like Lyra or Lee Scoresby), are surrounded by Dust. She also realises that the mulefa are surrounded by Dust, whereas the other animals in their world which don't seem to be intelligent or capable of speaking, are not:

> Everywhere she looked she could see gold, just as Atal had described it: sparkles of light, floating and drifting and sometimes moving in a current of purpose . . . where she saw a conscious being, one of the mulefa, the light was thicker and more full of movement. (*The Amber Spyglass*, p. 243)

Mary learns, by using the Amber Spyglass, that *more Dust equals more consciousness*. All the worlds in *His Dark Materials* are full of Dust. The connection between Dust and consciousness makes the Magisterium begin to look even scarier. For, not only are they looking to impose an authoritarian regime on multiple worlds, but their fear of Dust indicates that they feel threatened by the very existence of consciousness itself.

Dangerous Philosophers in *The Secret Commonwealth*

The *Dark Materials* trilogy contains many subtle allusions to panpsychism and philosophical theories about consciousness, especially as we learn more about Dust. However, in *The Secret Commonwealth* (Volume Two of *The Book of Dust*), the connection is much more explicit.

The book begins with Lyra as a university student in Oxford. We learn that she has read two books written by two popular philosophers: Simon Talbot and Gottfried Brande. Both are fictional philosophers but represent real philosophers (in our world), throughout history, who have painted pictures of reality that subtract from it life, knowledge, and consciousness (for another fictional philosopher, who has similar views to Simon Talbot, see Flann O'Brien's novel *The Third Policeman* which contains references to a fictional philosopher called de Selby who tells us that all of human experience is an illusion). We learn that Pan is not happy with what is suggested by Talbot and Brande's philosophical views because they imply that daemons are just an illusion too. In the end, this pushes Pan to leave Lyra and search for her lost imagination.

Pan is quite rightly frustrated by Lyra's obsession with these two philosophers. Simon Talbot, we learn, is "a radical sceptic, to whom truth and even reality were rainbow-like epiphenomena with no ultimate meaning" (*The Secret Commonwealth*, p. 79). Talbot's philosophy removes all meaning from the world, reducing human experiences to temporary, fleeting illusions, like a rainbow in the sky on a rainy day. Pan is even more alarmed by Gottfried Brande's philosophy which is presented in the form of a story set in a world where human beings have no daemons. The take-away message of Brande's philosophy is that daemons are an illusion too. As Pan puts it, "daemons are merely—what is it?—psychological projections with no independent reality" (p. 78). All of this is extremely worrying for Pan, who watches as Lyra is swept up by these two philosophers endorsing views which take all meaning, imagination, and even life out of the world they know (and we came to know in the original trilogy). Eventually, Pan tells Lyra that if this is what philosophy is like then philosophy itself is contemptible:

> If philosophy says I don't exist, then yes, philosophy is contemptible. I *do* exist. All of us, we daemons, and other things too — other *entities* your philosophers would say — we *exist*. Trying to believe nonsense will kill us. (*The Secret Commonwealth*, p. 81)

Over the course of *The Secret Commonwealth,* Lyra's narrative arc takes her away from the views of these sceptical "illusionist" philosophers and back to the belief that there really is life and knowledge in the world around us.

The message from Pullman could not be clearer: don't be fooled by those who tell you that life, knowledge, and consciousness are the privilege of people like us alone—or that it doesn't really exist at all. Like Margaret Cavendish, whose panpsychism offered a stark contrast to the mechanistic world-view defended by most of her contemporaries in the seventeenth-century, Pullman's aim is to show that there is no great divide between ourselves and the rest of the world around us: there is no line between conscious and unconscious (for *everything* is conscious). Although they have quite different reasons for doing so, both Pullman and Cavendish defend the view that we live in a living, knowing universe.

A passage from *The Amber Spyglass* makes it clear that, in Pullman's fictional universe, there's no divide between consciousness and unconsciousness—that, in fact, everything in the world around us contains life and knowledge. This is the moment that Roger's ghost steps out of the word of the Dead through the window cut by Will:

> The first ghost to leave the world of the dead was Roger. He took a step forward and turned to look back at Lyra, and laughed in surprise as he found himself turning into the night, the starlight, the air . . . and then he was gone, leaving behind such a vivid little burst of happiness that Will was reminded of the bubbles in a glass of champagne. (*The Amber Spyglass*, p. 382)

8
Is Pullman Corrupting the Young?

ABROL FAIRWEATHER

In 399 B.C., Socrates was put to death for corrupting the young and for not believing in the gods revered by his fellow Athenians. The latter charge, impiety, was the cornerstone of securing the former charge of corrupting the young.

Surprisingly, 2,400 years later, Philip Pullman finds himself responding to similar charges, although in the court of public opinion rather than a court of law. Amidst astonishing world-wide success, Pullman's *His Dark Materials* has managed to stir quite a controversy over the purportedly anti-religious message and 'sinister agenda' conveyed to a young following. Fortunately, unlike Socrates, Pullman is not fighting for his very life in court. *His Dark Materials* was, however, one of the top five most challenged books in the United States in 2007 as reported by the American Library Association, all for "Religious Viewpoint."

The religious controversy sparked by Pullman's trilogy is a mixed bag. On one hand, the fact that Pullman is not facing a trial like Socrates is a testament to our progress in the protection of fundamental freedoms and human rights. On the other hand, it shows that vestiges of Socrates's problem are still with us.

One tyrannical aspect of the Authority, the primary antagonist in Pullman's trilogy, is the suppression of ideas that question the absolute authority of the Authority. In his public response, Pullman delights in the fortuitous irony of endeavors to suppress his writing by the Catholic Church and other religious groups, when that is one of the primary evils of which his writing warns. While it's difficult not to appreciate the irony, Pullman's strong response to his religious critics has furthered their fury. Pullman's ongoing public response is nuanced, passionate, harsh, and often insightful, but neither conciliatory nor polite to the offended parties. On the other side of the coin, religious groups continue to raise deep concerns about the author of *His Dark Materials*, the spiritual bankruptcy of his trilogy, and the danger of exposing our children to either. Socrates may be smiling right about now.

The richness and complexity of *His Dark Materials* opens a number of directions for Pullman's defenders. There is his inveterate dislike of C.S Lewis's *Chronicles of Narnia*, which Pullman has called "a peevish blend of racist, misogynistic, and reactionary prejudice" (BBC interview, 16th October 2005). There is the clear influence of Milton, many references to Blake, and even to quantum physics. There is also the powerful presence of existentialism and Friedrich Nietzsche.

The legal challenge to *His Dark Materials* has not succeeded and is unlikely to succeed. However, once we grant that Pullman's trilogy counts as legally protected speech, there might still be moral objections to it. There are plenty of human activities that are lawful, but morally problematic: adultery, hate speech, and many cases of lying. These actions will often pass legal muster, but will also often be deemed morally deficient. Legality and morality are two different things. In light of this distinction, the concerned parties in the United States will note that simple appeals to the First Amendment are not sufficient to put the moral basis of the religious concern to rest. *His Dark Materials* may raise a host of moral concerns, even if its author is protected by rights to freedom of expression.

Supporters of *His Dark Materials* may request a clarification from his religious detractors: What, exactly, is the moral objection? It can be seen as a combination of special features of Pullman's readership, and special features of the content of his message. The trilogy is written for and marketed to children. In John Stuart Mill's classic defense of individual freedoms in *On Liberty*, children are not granted the full range of freedoms enjoyed by adults. Unlike adults, children are yet to achieve "the maturity of their faculties . . . to guide their own improvement by conviction or persuasion." Because children cannot yet conduct "experiments in living" and "pursue their own good in their own way," others may rightfully decide for them until they reach the maturity of their faculties.

The very reason for which Mill restricts full political liberties for children speaks to their increased vulnerability to psychologically forceful content. Adults with a fully formed (though hopefully evolving) sense of identity have more effective resources to defend themselves against affronts to their dignity as persons. They can offer reasons and arguments and maintain confidence in their self-worth in the face of even the most disparaging criticism.

Children, still in the midst of forming their sense of identity, lack these essential defenses, leaving their nascent identities easier victims to personally threatening messages.

Moving from features of Pullman's readership to features of his message, we must appreciate the influence of the provocative German philosopher Friedrich Nietzsche. Nietzsche is the author of the infamous line "God is dead." This line is often attributed to the Prologue of *Thus Spoke Zarathustra*, where the death of God is indeed pronounced. However, the first occurrence is in *The Gay Science*, section 108, and most famously from the mouth of the madman in section 125.

Nietzsche says not only that "God is dead", but that "we have killed him." Much of the religious concern has its origin in the Nietzscheanism lurking between the lines of *His Dark Materials*, perhaps at the forefront of its author's mind, and which reaches the vulnerable ears of eager childhood readers. The clear link between Authority and the God of the Abrahamic monotheisms, and the central plot theme of Will, Lyra, and Lord Asriel to kill the Authority suggest "killing god" as the central message of the trilogy. This is certainly the message his religious readers have seized upon as the ground of their grave concerns.

A provocative statement of Pullman's in the *Sydney Morning Herald* (13th December, 2003) sparked an Internet frenzy that quickly led to claims about the sinister agenda lurking between the lines of *His Dark Materials*. Pullman is here on record saying, "My books are about killing God," amplifying an earlier statement in the *Washington Post* that "I'm trying to undermine the basis of Christian belief." These public comments lead to a highly effective and widely disseminated chain-email attributing to Pullman the more alarming claim that "The purpose of my books is to kill God in the minds of children." This particular wording has never been confirmed as really being from Pullman, but has gained considerable traction in religious circles, and has ultimately led to Pullman's branding, by Peter Hitchens, as "the most dangerous author in Britain."

At the core of Pullman's religious disenchantment is not that theism is false on matters of fact, as an adherent of evolution might complain to an adherent of creationism, but that it "makes doing evil feel so good." Theism is not just false; it is harmful. Nietzsche would certainly be a Pullman supporter on this point.

Putting these points together, the message of *His Dark Materials* is perceived as more than a "God is dead" ideology, but rather an exhortation to be the killer. It is precisely the killers of God that his young readers identify with in the trilogy, who may in turn feel a sense of complicity in the act itself. The combination of Pullman's violent expression of his religious disbelief (killing God), the complicity of minors in killing the Authority, and a psychologically vulnerable readership constitute the hub of the moral objection.

A Special Form of Violence?

There is no established rating system for books comparable to what we have for movies, and the idea has been consistently rejected when broached. However, the way movies are rated for different age groups may help to clarify the issues. The main variables used to determine a rating from G to R for a movie include sex, nudity, drugs, and violence. While the romance between Will and Lyra may make a young reader blush, there is of course no explicit sex. But there is some violence. If Pullman's religious critics can show that objections to *His Dark Materials* rest on the widely accepted goal of protecting children from violent content, the burden of proof may fall to Pullman's defenders.

However, since we see plenty of graphic fantasy violence in *Harry Potter*, *Lord of The Rings*, *The Chronicles of Narnia*, and countless classics for young readers, there would appear nothing exceptional about the many violent acts described in *His Dark Materials*. To ground a concern based on violent content, there must be something special about the violence in the trilogy which sets it apart from the violent content which, perhaps regrettably, children are exposed to on a regular basis.

Perhaps there is something different about killing the Authority. *His Dark Materials* is not only about killing a character of fiction, but, as Pullman himself suggests, killing the God worshipped and loved by well over a billion human beings, and undermining the basis of their spiritual life in the process. The American Psychological Association recognizes a form of violence that damages the human soul, but which does not require an overt act of violence to do so. This subtle, but deep injury to a person is called "spiritual violence," and it is particularly damaging to children. In a narrow sense, spiritual violence diminishes its victim's self-worth because of his or her religion, or for failure to meet the standards of some religion. Religious condemnations of homosexuality are often cited as a paradigm case.

In a broader sense, spiritual violence targets a person's identity, their essence as an individual, and the structures that give meaning to their life, whether these are found inside or outside of religion. All too familiar examples include hate crimes and hate speech. An interesting recent argument has been made that hate speech, while in itself nothing more than sounds in the air or marks on a page, should qualify as a "tort," the legal term for an actionable injury against a person. This movement has, thus far, met the same fate as the legal challenges to *His Dark Materials*, but this failure may simply reinforce the yawning gap between legality and morality in a liberal society.

Seeing the trilogy in conjunction with Pullman's public remarks, religious readers may experience *His Dark Materials* as violence done to their identity, aggression against their essence as a person, condemnation of who they are because of their religion. Recalling Mill's point, the identity of a Christian child will be particularly susceptible to such an attack. Perhaps *His Dark Materials* should come with a warning for spiritual violence.

In *The Golden Compass*, we're introduced to a dangerous brain child of Mrs. Coulter: Intercision. This is an ingenious literary device, and a perfectly fitting example of spiritual violence. To sever the connection between a person and their dæmon denies them the formation of a complete, matured identity. Intercision is violent, leaves its victims less than fully human, and can be fatal. The moral complaint against Pullman can be expressed using his own image of what makes us fully human. *His Dark Materials* may sever a reader's connection to God by either severing an already established connection, or preventing a connection from forming in the first place. In either case, the victim is denied a complete spiritual life. If this form of spiritual deprivation is the purpose of his trilogy, Pullman's writing should be seen as alarming by his own lights. While it is a testament to his ingenuity and genius as a writer, intercision may provide religious critics with their best expression of the moral concern raised by *His Dark Materials*.

While this would be an interesting irony, Pullman's defenders would no doubt respond by arguing that religious institutions in countless cases throughout history, and no less in the present day, are the true perpetrators of spiritual violence, with atheists amongst their primary targets. Atheists have long been the victim of an intercision at the hands of religion, and the cultural institutions trapped within its yolk. Seen in this light, whatever spiritual violence there may be in the trilogy and the mind of its author, it is a form of spiritual self-defense.

While this may give Pullman's supporters some ammunition against his detractors, it sounds like returning an injury with an injury. The self-defense rebuttal to the spiritual violence charge could provide some justification against the moral concern, but this comes at the cost of granting that the trilogy is injurious. This is not an ideal approach to assuaging the moral objection. A better line of defense will show that there is a constructive purpose to killing God.

It cannot be denied that *His Dark Materials* is a work of considerable spiritual depth. However, the depth of Pullman's message may work against him unless he can assuage concerns that he is pulling off an intercision against the faithful amongst his readers. The heart of the matter for our purposes is why Pullman wants to kill god. What comes next? What is ultimately accomplished? How, and if, the moral basis of the religious objection is answered rests largely on how we answer these questions. We now consider the positive, constructive purposes of atheism, rather than seeing it merely as the destruction of theism and the spiritual life it supports.

A Public Atheist?

Philip Pullman is not the only outspoken and unapologetic atheist in town. The religious outcry against *His Dark Materials* has catapulted Pullman into a small, but growing group of 'public atheists'. The renowned biologist Richard Dawkins (*The God Delusion*), cable talk show host and director Bill Maher (Religulous), and Christopher Hitchens (*God Is Not Great*) are high-visibility figures, each of whom has made a point of stoutly affirming his atheism.

These figures are fighting to gain public acceptability for a creed which has long been denied a storefront in the marketplace of ideas. The atheist movement is particularly strong in the United Kingdom, the British Humanist Organization purchased ads on public buses saying "There's probably no God. Now stop worrying and enjoy your life." If an ideology is denied public visibility and acceptance, its adherents are denied the right to "living truths," to use Mill's felicitous phrase. For an individual to enjoy their own good in their own way, the creed by which they live by must be allowed expression and discussion in the larger conversation that animates community life. While it ruffles some feathers, Public Atheists are claiming this fundamental right for themselves and other atheists.

The controversy over *His Dark Materials* has catapulted Pullman into the role of an important Public Atheist, but it does not address our main question, for two reasons. First, the legal right to espouse atheism is not at issue here. Our question is about the moral status of Pullman's particular brand of atheism, not his legal right to preach it nor the legitimacy of the atheist movement as a whole. Furthermore, we still want to know why Pullman is so intent on killing God. While the protests over *His Dark Materials* have had the unintended consequence of placing Pullman in the rarefied company of other elite public atheists, not to mention a big bump in sales for the trilogy, our concern is about one atheist in particular, specifically about his "sinister agenda."

The False God

In their 2007 book, *Killing the Imposter God*, Donna Freitas and Jason King deny that Pullman is an atheist, public or otherwise. They claim that he is rejecting a traditional monotheistic understanding of God, and the oppressive social institutions erected in God's name. They argue that Pullman is rejecting the "tyrant God," not God per se. This reading of Pullman would radically reconfigure the moral controversy over *His Dark Materials*, as well as much of the media coverage of the trilogy.

Freitas and King read Pullman not as an atheist, but rather a "panentheist." Panentheism means "all in God"; a subtle variation of "pantheism," which means "all is God." Panentheism doesn't define God as a creator separate from creation. Traditional monotheism radically separates God from the created universe, and from mankind itself, and sees God as a rational, rule-giving authority standing over the mind of man. The traditional concept of God has Creator and creation as radically distinct entities, the latter subservient to the former. We may have something of God's nature, but we do not live where God lives, and we are virtuous when we are subservient to divine commands. Panentheism, on the other hand, places man and God in the same world.

Freitas and King read Dust as Pullman's theological successor to the transcendent, tyrannical, oppressive creator of the world, and the institutions which enforce its ideology. Dust is "the ultimate, unifying, and animating principle in the universe, . . . the 'spirit' of human beings and all matter but also the 'form' of angels." Dust is wisdom, the spiritual force immanent in the worlds of the trilogy, and is the God of *His Dark Materials* according to Freitas and King.

While this keeps Pullman at odds with the Catholic Church and other mainstream religions, the panentheist interpretation has Pullman engaging in intra-religious debate over the true nature of God, rather than thrusting a dagger into the heart of all gods. Perhaps Pullman is redefining rather than killing God. Perhaps *His Dark Materials* is just a rallying cry against oppressive religious institutions, rather than an attack on religion, per se.

As well as being an interesting and in some ways persuasive interpretation of Pullman's religious views, *Killing the Imposter God* is also of interest because Nietzsche is discussed as a significant influence on Pullman's unusual theology. While the authors are right to note the influence of Nietzsche on Pullman, their reading of both appears to miss the mark in some ways.

Nietzsche is not really an atheist, according to Freitas and King, but is simply rejecting an outmoded Christian God. However, Nietzsche clearly rejects not just a Christian God, but all "otherworldly" ideologies. Nietzsche's concern is that placing the locus of ultimate value in a non-human deity and a world beyond our own abdicates a deep personal responsibility that comes with human freedom. If God is the creator of values, the deepest act of human freedom is rendered obsolete, pointless, already achieved. For Nietzsche, the highest purpose in human life is to create and live in light of values of one's own making. This is to be truly an individual. The heart of Nietzsche's concerns is that God stymies true individuality. Anything that does this, whether religious or not, will earn Nietzsche's contempt. Nietzsche's concerns go further than authoritarian religious institutions.

Freitas and King tell us that Pullman, like Nietzsche, only rejects authoritarian religious institutions, "tyrant Gods." Killing the Authority is killing this God, not every God. If their reading is correct, then it's incorrect to categorize Pullman as an all-out atheist. Admittedly, their panentheist, non-atheist, interpretation provides an interesting perspective on *His Dark Materials* that would seem to undercut the religious controversy in which Pullman is embroiled. However, like their reading of Nietzsche, I think more is going on in killing the Authority than objecting to oppressive religious institutions, and for similar reasons.

The interpretation of Pullman in *Killing the Imposter God* essentially makes a god out of Dust. But, one thing we don't want Dust to do is simply replace the overreaching moral authority of the Authority. This would be like reading Nietszsche's Overman, the creator of values, as replacing one "otherworldly" religion with another, when Nietzsche's problem is with "other worldly" ideologies as such. Likewise, Authority is not only an oppressive social institution; it deprives individuals of the essential purpose of human freedom. The Authority denies the most important creative act in human life by relegating the meaning of individual lives to a logic of discovery, rather than a logic of creation. It's not clear that panentheism does any better on this score, if the values we ought to live by still lie fully formed in God, whether a God of this world or of another world.

It would be rash to conclude that the panentheist interpretation is wrong, although it does appear that Pullman wants to be an atheist. Perhaps we should just let him be one. In either case, what does seem clear is that, whether Pullman is an atheist or a panentheist, Dust should not play the same role in defining the values individuals should live by as does the Authority. Dust would then be no friend of freedom.

What Is Freedom For?

Freedom is central to the purpose of killing God for both Nietzsche and Pullman, but how exactly are the two connected? In different ways, both Will and Lyra exercise freedom at critical junctures in the story. A fairly obvious connection between the Authority and freedom in *His Dark Materials* is that the former impedes the latter, to the point of threatening its extinction. Nietzsche recognizes a similar threatening connection between God and freedom, but he also describes the birth of a new freedom that is achieved by killing God. Here, Nietzsche tells us what freedom is for, and hence presents killing God as a constructive act. Perhaps Pullman's full message about the connection between freedom and the Authority has the mark of Nietzsche on this critical point. The moral concern now comes down to the connection between killing God and freedom.

What exactly is freedom? One of many strands in the history of theorizing about the nature of freedom is the distinction between Negative Freedom and Positive Freedom. To possess negative freedom is to be "free from"—free from obstacles, barriers, and strong constraints on the exercise of autonomy. We lack negative freedom when some significant, contrary force impedes the natural operation of the human will; we are unable to act as we choose to because something outside of us resists the power of our will.

To possess positive freedom is to be self-directed, to act in such a way as to take control of your life, and realize your fundamental purposes. Positive freedom is what we are free for, or what we are able to actually do. Freedom here moves us toward its positive aim, end, or goal. Negative liberty is typically lost by the interference of something external to the agent of action, whereas positive freedom is often abdicated by the agent himself. Complete freedom is to possess negative freedom and to exercise positive freedom.

The Authority clearly constitutes a barrier and constraint on agency and autonomy, and thus undermines negative freedom. By implication, the Authority also undermines positive freedom because the former is necessary for the latter. However, restoring negative liberty by killing the Authority achieves only a necessary, but not sufficient, condition for exercising positive freedom. Killing the Authority is thus not itself the realization of full freedom. We should not diminish the importance of this aspect of Pullman's message, for many have suffered, and continue to suffer diminished negative freedom at the hands of God. However, the full message of freedom will include some conception of positive freedom. This tells us what freedom is for and it gives us the key to answering the religious concern—or seeing that it cannot be answered.

Assuming we are at no significant loss of in terms of negative freedom, there are two ways in which positive freedom can be lost. We can abdicate positive freedom by falling into what Sartre calls "bad faith." This includes (but is not limited to) believing that one's fate is determined, that we are subject to, rather than being the creator of, the force that drives our life. Positive freedom may also simply remain unactualized, dormant, a mere possibility. If you are deeply indecisive or non-committal, or suffer from some kindred anemic condition of the will, your life will not be robustly self- directed. Kierkegaard discusses this way of losing yourself in

Either/Or, when Judge William warns us not to lose sight of "the headway" that time itself is making when we linger too long in the moment of decision.

In both cases, we fail to choose in a robust way, and are not meaningfully directing our own lives. To achieve positive freedom, we need a robust commitment to a motivating value, principle or aim. But, to avoid bad faith, we must resist a commitment which denies our responsibility for freely making the commitment in the first place. Our life aim is what it is because we have willed it to be so. To have no principle of action, to choose nothing, is to be stuck in nihilism. Achieving full freedom requires avoiding nihilism without falling into bad faith.

Killing the Authority could undermine positive freedom in the latter sense, if we're left without a successor system of values. This is often a concern raised about atheism; it leaves us with nothing to care about, and thus deprives us of full freedom. The loss of freedom to nihilism is a concern Pullman must address if he wants to kill God while preserving positive freedom. However, if a successor system of values is determined by the pantheistic reading of Pullman's would-be God, the deification of Dust, as the Pullman of Killing the Imposter God would have it, the threat of bad faith looms.

If the answer to what values should direct our life is lying, fully formed, in the universe itself, we have really abdicated, rather than fulfilled the responsibility that comes with full freedom. This is also at the heart of Nietzsche's interest in killing God. Religion threatens to stamp out deep positive freedom.

Nietzsche's Child and Answering the Moral Objection

One of the most compelling and concise pieces written by Nietzsche is the story of "The Three Metamorphoses," the first section of *Thus Spoke Zarathustra* directly following the famous pronouncement of God's death. Nietzsche here tells us how the camel of the spirit became a lion, and the lion finally became a child. It is fitting that, given our concern about impact of the trilogy on young readers that the child represents the achievement of full freedom for Nietzsche. Nietzsche's child tells us why God must killed.

Nietzsche's spiritual allegory begins with the "Camel of the Spirit," the beast of burden which kneels down to bear any load placed upon it. The camel's burden is not of its own making, but yet defines the camel's purpose and highest achievement. The camel is reverent to the intriguing and powerful figure, the "Great Dragon," also called the great "thou shalt." The Great Dragon claims to encompass all possible values. No values, points, or purposes for life can be thought which do not already glisten on its scales. The Great Dragon demands obedience as the ultimate authority, it stands above man as its law giver, until the Lion of the spirit kills it. The Lion makes freedom possible when it slays the great "thou shalt"; the great symbol of all external authority is the Lion's prey.

This killing is extremely important; it is man's escape from the spiritual tyranny of religion. However, it is not itself freedom, but merely its possibility. The Lion, like the Camel, is wholly dependent for its life purpose on the Great Dragon. The Lion is not creating its own way, but merely destroying the obstacle that stands in its path. Without the great the Great Dragon, neither the Camel nor the Lion would have anything to do, and thus they do not give their own purpose to life.

The Child is the final stage of the spirit. Its will is its own, not simply a response to something outside of it; the spirit of the child is sui generis. Nietzsche tells us that the Child may be the world's outsider because it lives outside of all existing values, but it thereby wins itself. The Child of the spirit is the epitome of positive freedom, and is only possible given the death of the Great Dragon. With the realization of this freedom, Nietzsche tells us that we achieve true individuality. For Nietzsche, the point and purpose of killing God is the deep positive freedom and individuality achieved by the Child.

Is this Pullman's message? The figure of the Great Dragon is an amazing fit with the Authority and Mrs. Coulter. Lord Asriel, Will, and Lyra would fittingly be cast as the Lion of the spirit, and the Camel is the diminished spirit of those living under the Authority.

But what of Nietzsche's child? The Child is not an attack against anyone's identity or self-worth, and thus is not a symbol of spiritual violence. The development of the spirit toward full freedom occurs within one person, not in aggression between many. It would be a simplification of Pullman's nuanced and diverse intellect and creativity to see his ultimate message as nothing but Nietzsche's Child. However, if it were, it does not seem to fit the bill for spiritual violence, nor would the moral objection be borne out.

Another answer to the moral objection comes as we see the connection with Nietzsche fade. Pullman gives us a different way to think about positive freedom in the Republic of Heaven. This not only replaces the religious ideal of the Kingdom of Heaven, but it has a clear social and political message and applies to individuals connected to communities, not isolated individuals. Nietzsche's message is far more individualistic, and may raise real concerns if large groups of people were to live out the Nietzschean ideal. Pullman may be radical, but he does not appear radically Nietzschean at this point.

Pullman invites his critics to recall the virtues that triumph in the trilogy: courage, compassion, love, kindness, intellectual curiosity. These values do not stand outside of all existing values like Nietzsche's Child, nor do they represent a corrupting, concerning ideology for young people. The moral basis of the religious challenge to *His Dark Materials* is severely deflated at this point. The message of the trilogy is, at bottom, neither sinister, harmful to children, nor at odds with the moral core of many religions. At this point, Pullman's religious critics are left grasping for straws in the attempt to locate what we should find so objectionable.

There will, no doubt, be some who continue to criticize Pullman for using provocative images and ruffling religious feathers. Fortunately, we have laws on the books protecting our right to do that, and our freedom to describe our own good in our own way. Pullman is thus unlikely to suffer the same injustice as did Socrates. In Pullman's own words, he does have an agenda: he wants his readers to turn the pages of his books, enjoy life and exercise their intellectual curiosity. Pullman himself sums it up best:

Is Pullman Corrupting the Young?

And I think it's time we thought about a republic of heaven instead of the kingdom of heaven. The king is dead. That's to say I believe that the king is dead. I'm an atheist. But we need heaven nonetheless, we need all the things that heaven meant, we need joy, we need a sense of meaning and purpose in our lives, we need a connection with the universe, we need all the things that the kingdom of heaven used to promise us but failed to deliver. And, furthermore, we need it in this world where we do exist—not elsewhere, because there ain't no elsewhere. (The Republic of Heaven Speech)

Part III

*"This is a different
kind of knowing . . .
It's like understanding,
I suppose . . ."*

9
How Not to Die of Despair

JIMMY LEONARD

What would I ask an alethiometer? Something profoundly philosophical about which course of action would do the most good for humanity, I hope, right after I used it to find the remote.

Really, though, why doesn't Lyra use the alethiometer more? She holds a device that can answer *any* question, and she can read it with a speed and comprehension unmatched by scholars who've studied the instrument for years. With that kind of power, she should be poring over life's deepest moral quandaries and unlocking the vast secrets of the universe. Her omniscience should have her a thousand steps ahead of the Magisterium, and yet half the time she keeps the thing buried in a rucksack. What gives?

It's the Master of Jordan College who first tells us that Lyra must play her part in some cosmic conflict "without realizing what she's doing" (*The Golden Compass,* p. 28). Serafina later confirms that Lyra is "destined to bring about the end of destiny," but "if she's told what she must do, it will all fail" (p. 271). Oh, and just in case that's not dramatic enough, the witch clarifies that *failing* means death will rule every universe and obliterate all free thought and emotion, now and forever. So, no pressure.

Yet it's a strange juxtaposition. Lyra, who could know *anything* from the alethiometer, must know *nothing* about her fate, lest we all die. It's especially odd considering the overall bent of Pullman's trilogy against oppressive authority. We might expect our young heroine to dismantle the Magisterium with bold proclamations of truth. Instead, she's surrounded by characters who keep secrets, mislead her, or otherwise rob her of the ability to make an informed decision. As for Lyra herself, she's rash and impassioned, not exactly one to spend her time deconstructing moral precepts. Neither does she outwit her opponents, for although she's clever with Iofur Raknison, her deceptions ultimately fail with No-Name the harpy.

No, it's not what Lyra knows that saves the world. On the contrary, Lyra's highest moral capabilities and most forcible influence are founded in her *ignorance*.

So what do we make of this paradox, that a girl with an all-knowing symbol reader can only achieve her purpose if she doesn't know it all? It's not so far-fetched to imagine a real-world alethiometer. Machine learning solves problems in healthcare and banking and shipping logistics. Algorithms select advertisements most relevant to users, and predictive text finishes our search queries before we even know what we're asking. Consult a golden compass or ask Siri—the goal is essentially the same. We're approaching godlike omniscience in our everyday lives, and yet the more we move to solve problems, the more we inevitably face Lyra's dilemma. Scientists might wonder if we *could* know everything. Philosophers ask if we *should*.

The Truth Nobody Wants

Utilitarians argue that something is morally acceptable when it maximizes benefit to society and limits harm. There are other philosophical views of ethics that say something can be virtuous for a given person or situation, even if it doesn't maximize the benefit to others. But given the Master and Serafina's talk about Lyra's destiny to affect every living creature, the utilitarian view is the one worth considering here.

According to utilitarians, something seemingly immoral might become a righteous course of action when viewed with a wide-angle lens. Clearly, the Master of Jordan College subscribes to this theory, seeing as his botched attempt to poison Lord Asriel is done because the consequence of *not* killing him might be far worse. (Although a repeated theme in Pullman's trilogy is that murderers are trustworthy companions, so perhaps the Master's just trying to fit in.)

In Lyra's case, it seems that everyone knows the prophecy regarding her destiny, but nobody bothers to share it with her. Dr. Lanselius tells Farder Coram, Serafina tells Lee Scoresby, Lena Feldt tells Mrs. Coulter, and by *The Amber Spyglass,* the Magisterium and Asriel's forces in the Adamant Tower all know the prophecy. In fact, they all talk pretty freely about this thing that Lyra's definitely not supposed to know. Beyond that, Lord Asriel and Mrs. Coulter conceal the fact they're Lyra's parents, Lord Boreal and John Parry operate under aliases, and of course Lyra herself lies to just about everyone she comes in contact with—endearingly, though, nothing like the ruthless deceit of her mother. The alethiometer's truthful, but hardly anyone else is.

When it comes to deception, we don't have to think hard to find morally excusable examples. Heck, as an educator, I've lost count of how many times I've said *you can do it* or *I believe in you* when a student probably can't or I most certainly don't. But we tell these lies with good intention, and I'm happily proved wrong when that same student goes on to surprise me.

See, nobody really disputes the ethics of sharing good news. It's only in the case that something might go wrong—or already has—that we weigh the relational and emotional costs of burdening someone with the truth. With the alethiometer, Lyra could easily discover Lord Asriel's intentions when she and Roger arrive at his house on Svalbard. Yet Roger sagely remarks, "There's been terrible things we seen, en't there? And more a coming, more'n likely. So I think I'd rather not know what's in the future" (p. 322).

Bad call, Roger.

Then again, maybe it's best that she doesn't look. From Lyra's perspective, Roger's murder is devastating. From a utilitarian perspective, it's necessary. We're supposed to believe that Roger's death is preferable to his survival because only through his sacrifice can Lyra find her way to the land of the dead and free the souls of every world. So, then, the loss of one is worth the salvation of many—limit the harm, maximize the benefit. Critically, Lyra's ignorance about Asriel's plot preserves the most ethical outcome for the multiverse. Roger has to die.

To be fair, this kind of conclusion marks a significant inadequacy of utilitarian reasoning. Justifying child sacrifice for the greater good presents a slippery slope that might make us no better than the Oblation Board, and it's a dangerous start to call Asriel's actions ethical. Then again, maybe some equivalent witch-prophecy existed for Roger and this was his purpose all along. As much as we sympathize, perhaps it was his destiny to be the first soul set free in the land of the mulefa.

Indeed, it's a stroke of great luck that she never inquires about the future. Yet even if Lyra would have pressed the alethiometer for details, she might not have received an answer.

Lyra never asks about her destiny, but, conversely, the alethiometer never tells.

When Fates Have Wings

It certainly could have. Of course it could have! This is the same alethiometer that, unprompted, urges Lyra to find Tony Makarios, slyly informs her that Master Lanselius already knew about the intentions of the Tartars, and gets all prickly with her for asking the same question twice while she's trapped in Iofur's palace.

When Mary Malone wonders who's behind the Cave—her own version of the alethiometer—she receives the answer, "angels" (*The Subtle Knife*, p. 220). Well, then. That's worth considering.

We ought to be skeptical of whatever conscious presence drives the needle on the alethiometer. These beings, whoever they are, very well could be manipulating Lyra or misrepresenting the facts. For what's it worth, when John Faa asks if the symbol reader is "playing the fool" with Lyra, she says, "It never does, Lord Faa, and I don't think it could" (*The Golden Compass*, p. 182). She might be right, but she's also naive. If the alethiometer can't blatantly deceive her, it certainly can lie through omission.

Yet if these angels are wise and ancient beings that make even a witch queen like Ruta Skadi feel young when she flies among them for a night, we can reasonably assume that they are rational enough to make informed, ethical decisions, at least when compared with humans. Any misleading of Lyra would be done with good reason. If the angels had wanted Lyra to save Roger's life, they could have been more explicit than telling her that she's bringing Lord Asriel "something" that he needs (*The Golden Compass*, p. 315). They could have told her to turn around and forget Svalbard, or at least been upfront about it: "So, Lyra, full disclosure, in just a few hours, your dad is going to murder your best friend in a seemingly heartless action that ultimately leads to the redemption of the universe. Let us know if you have any questions."

In fact, Lyra later tells Will, "The alethiometer's like a person, almost. I sort of know when it's going to be cross or when there's things it doesn't want me to know" (*The Subtle Knife*, p. 92).

Catch that—there are things that these rational, truth-telling angels *don't* want her to know. Philosophers love debating fate and free will like Lee Scoresby loves a game of hazard, but we should wonder, what moral obligations belong to the fates themselves? If we accept that Lyra *could* have refused her destiny, that she *could* have saved Roger and never ventured to the land of the dead, then we must admire the cunning of the fates. They trick Lyra into walking the exact path required to save the world, safely eliminating her choice in the matter.

Or is it the other way around? Lyra avoids any dread or obligation, and perhaps she takes the right path precisely because she has the freedom to do so.

It's a curious aspect of destiny—especially in literature, when we have the privilege of viewing a closed system in its entirety—that "free will" often makes more sense looking forward while "fate" makes more sense looking back. Certainly, it's Lyra's decision to escape Mrs. Coulter's flat or to tell Iorek how to find his armor or even to leave Pantalaimon on the shore as her boat pushes off into the water. Indeed, the core drama of the trilogy hinges on the possibility that Lyra could choose a different outcome—

supporting free will—and yet, in retrospect, her every action seems preordained.

Like Schrödinger's cat, the fate-free will question is an entanglement of two possibilities. Lyra both keeps her daemon and betrays him on the dock; she both loves Will and selflessly lets him go. At every crossroads in the trilogy, either decision is *permissible*, and yet for the good of every soul in the land of the dead, only one decision is ever truly *possible*. When Lyra realizes she can only leave one window open, it has to be the one for the souls. It's heartbreaking, of course, but no other option is ethically defensible.

Serafina tells Lee Scoresby, "We are all subject to the fates. But we must all act as if we are not or die of despair" (*The Golden Compass*, p. 271). In other words, life's one big cup of chocolatl as long as we're free to follow our hearts. But, according to Serafina, inherent in our beings is some predetermined purpose about which we have as little choice as we do about what forms our daemons will take. (Incidentally, mine would be a bear, and I often stress about how that'd play out in social situations. I guess if Asriel can manage with a snow leopard, I'd figure it out too.)

She's not wrong, though. Deep down, all of us sense our limitations, but it's unhelpful to think only of the heights we can't reach. It's a disquieting exercise to dwell too long on our futures. If we peek behind that curtain between the worlds, if we stumble upon that tree and taste the knowledge of our destiny, then we shall surely die.

Lyra in the Garden

Milton tells it like this:

> So near grows Death to Life, whate'er Death is,
> Some dreadful thing no doubt; for well thou know'st
> God hath pronounc't it death to taste that Tree. (*Paradise Lost* IV, 425–27)

Except, Eve does doubt that Death's a dreadful thing, just as Lyra doubts that Dust is as harmful as the Magisterium fears. Lyra's tempter, Mary Malone, isn't some evil serpent but someone we actually like, and Lyra's quest doesn't bring about death but rather creates an escape from it. Instead of God banishing her from Eden, Lyra literally returns to the garden—the botanic garden at Oxford—in the final pages of the trilogy.

In short, she wins. The original Fall narrative is inverted. Tasting knowledge saves the world instead of ruining it, and instead of bringing about death, Lyra fulfills Lord Asriel's bold declaration that "death is going to die" (*The Golden Compass*, p. 331).

So, then, we have two competing premises. One, Lyra can only achieve her destiny when she knows nothing about it, and, two, Lyra's full knowledge of good and evil is what ultimately allows her to restore order to the world.

It's a beautiful paradox. Lyra can't know what's required of her until the precise moment that she's ready to make the right choice. The Master of Jordan College predicts Lyra will make a great betrayal, and most first-time readers believe this is Roger, a betrayal borne from tragic *ignorance*. But the true betrayal comes when she leaves Pantalaimon crying on the shore (*The Amber Spyglass*, p. 254). This time, it's Lyra's *knowledge* that makes the sacrifice. She understands exactly what she's doing. In the Garden, Eve is tempted and indulges her curiosity; she chooses herself and shatters her paradise. Yet Lyra's choice is self-denying. Instead of gratifying her own desires, she pays a great price and rebuilds the paradise lost.

Lyra's ignorance, then, is not an ultimate goal but rather a means to a purpose. In Trollesund, Lyra thinks she'd rather die than be parted from Pantalaimon, meaning she would have never agreed to leave him from the outset of her journey (*The Golden Compass*, p. 171). Therefore it's sensible for the alethiometer to conceal the needed sacrifice until Lyra's mature enough to make it. In the words of John Faa, "To strike a day too soon is as bad as striking a hundred miles off" (p. 122). In our youth, there are some truths we're not ready for, and the mental capacity for knowledge precedes the maturity to use it wisely.

Yet supposing we're all adults here and can handle whatever truth is thrown at us, there's still the matter of interpretation—how do we know we've read the facts correctly? I don't mean this in a "How do I know a chair is a chair" sort of way; it's a matter of considering our preconceptions.

Some philosophers might say it all starts with defining truth itself. How do we know anything is true? The danger with an alethiometer, however, is not necessarily proposing that the answers given to any question are true; the problem is asserting that any one person's *interpretation* of those answers is true. The layers of nuance and understanding to even the simplest of questions might extend as far down as the ladders of meaning for any symbol on the alethiometer itself. When Lyra first inquires about the spy Benjamin de Ruyter, Farder Coram says, "It's working all right, Lyra. What we don't know is whether we're reading it right. That's a subtle art" (p. 127). Humans reading the messages of angels are bound to lose something in translation. We're responsible not for a flawless reading of the instrument but for acknowledging our uncertainty.

Better Left Unasked

Before we sail too high into the philosophical ether, let's step outside the fantasy. I may not be a witch, but I can say with certainty that some future tragedies are "fated." Another natural disaster will strike; another violent crime will occur. I've no idea what I'll have for dinner this time next week, but I am wholly confident that bad things will happen in the world.

In ethics, philosophers talk about something called the veil of ignorance. It's the idea that decision makers should pretend to not know their social position in order to design a just society. If I wanted to make a law regulating Gyptian trading in the Fens, for example, I'd have to "forget" whether I myself am a Gyptian or a landloper, thereby removing my bias. Only from this position of ignorance could I fairly view both sides and decide the most equitable course of action. While the principle typically applies to lawmaking, it also fits for destiny.

I can read all I'd like about achievement gaps based on race, gender, or socioeconomic status, but even a compelling national trend has little merit when it comes to an individual. Of course a single person can outrun a stereotype—or at least, that's what we ought to believe and instill. "Write your own destiny," says every motivational poster and meme. Any rational person knows that opportunities aren't equal and probably never will be, but lying to someone about their potential is a cornerstone of inspiration. Like Lyra and her presumed *inability* to read the alethiometer, our self-actualization thrives in ignorance of the things we're not supposed to do.

It happens like this. We often approach problems looking for an optimized solution. I have my navigation app look up driving directions because I want to avoid traffic and find the fastest route home. Flight math is more convoluted as I'm weighing not only travel time but also financial and opportunity costs (what do I miss by flying out on one day instead of another?), and accordingly I involve more data and comparisons prior to making the decision.

Now, if I could write a program that limited my expenditure of stress, money, and time in order to maximize my peace of mind, the result would certainly be *Don't travel at all*.

It's an unhelpful answer because of my inputs. My common concerns about travel are decidedly myopic. What the tech world calls *garbage in, garbage out*—a program is limited by the inputs it receives. If I ask a poorly worded question to my alethiometer, I'll get a useless answer in return.

Perhaps I should ask, *What journey would provide the greatest inspiration*, or *which scenario would position me best to help others*, or *how will these trials prepare me for some future challenge in my life*? We might, in theory, extrapolate some principle from previous experiences that would actually lead to an answer, but the more likely scenario is a never-ending string of *what ifs* that creates a complete decision paralysis. In essence, it's a competing value system. I can logically conclude that leaving my house isn't worth the risk. This values the data-informed perspective that I cannot prevent terrible things from happening. Yet I can also intuit that any joy or fullness in my life will require the very risk I logically should avoid. Productively engaging with the world necessitates an *ignorance* of whatever hardships may occur.

The same is true on a global level. As an example, in the wake of numerous mass shootings in the United States, many have wondered if we're missing the warning signs. I've no intention to hop on a political soapbox, but it's a relevant ethical question. We *could* predict future criminals, but should we? No matter what concrete data we look at, one of the most problematic concerns is determining who chooses the criteria for a "likely threat."

Whoever turns the dials on the alethiometer will frame their question with assumptions in mind, and even the most spurious correlations between demographic factors and violent crime could easily parlay into inequitable public policy. For example, if we're thinking about 'red flag laws', seeking a correlation between gun violence and previous mental health treatment is loaded with assumptions. It's also true (and a favorite example of statistics classes) that ice cream sales are positively correlated to homicide rates. Should we arrest anyone who eats ice cream? As Farder Coram says, reading the symbols correctly is a subtle art.

To apply the veil of ignorance, we must "forget" if we are the accusers or the accused. It's a golden naiveté that believes all people are born equally into the world and are capable of good behavior, and yet this is exactly the childlike ignorance that preserves rights and due process. *Innocent until proven guilty* is logically absurd but ethically sound. Of course we can see patterns and predictors of criminal behavior, and yet, justice is always blind.

I remember taking aptitude tests and career assessments in elementary school, compiling the data on what would be the best path for my life. This might be informative, but never prescriptive. Suppose I could ask an alethiometer, *what career should I pursue?* Or, as I wanted to earlier, *which course of action would do the most good for humanity?* Surely we could find some statistically defensible answer, ever evolving as we refine the inputs and analyze increasingly large data sets. Yet Will puts it best: "If I end up doing that, I'll be resentful because it'll feel as if I didn't have a choice, and if I don't do it, I'll feel guilty because I should. Whatever I do, I will choose it, no one else" (*The Amber Spyglass*, p. 444). Such is the paradox of human progress: Our greatest potential lies in the ignorance of what our potential ought to be.

As Serafina says, we are all subject to the fates. As long as people are free to make choices, we are bound to self-destruct. We'll face rejection, disappointment, and betrayal. Yet perhaps limiting this harm is *not* what maximizes the benefit. Maybe humanity's strongest future exists when we don't ask those questions about our destiny. Only in ignorance of what should and shouldn't work can we create and discover, find new worlds and challenge whatever authority is meant to oppress us. Maybe every person on Earth has some part to play in our cosmic destiny, but we are better off not knowing what we're doing.

10
The Truth in Lyra's Lies

KIERA VACLAVIK

Swept along in the mounting drama which is the climax of *The Golden Compass*, it's easy to miss a classic case of narratorial hoodwinking. Asriel's plans are near completion; only one more ingredient is needed, and "it," we are told, is "drawing closer every minute" (*Northern Lights*, p. 363).

The missing link is, of course, Roger, and a "*he*" rather than an "*it*," as Pullman knows full well. But he covers his tracks and the suspense is maintained a little longer. Earlier in the novel, the connection between creativity and deceit is made explicit: both artists and liars, we read, must "be vague in some places and invent plausible details in others" (p. 283). It comes as no surprise, then, that Pullman has elsewhere described the storyteller as a "trickster" who "can persuade people of something that isn't true" (Parsons and Nicholson interview, p. 133).

The universe he has created is full to bursting with all manner of liars, tricksters, storytellers, and deceivers. From the Arctic foxes to the Almighty himself, almost every character—whether sympathetic or morally reprehensible—lies, deceives, or betrays at some point. The nurses at Bolvangar and Mrs. Coulter are of course at it, but so too are Lord Asriel, Will, his father, Mary Malone, and Iorek Byrnison—who, Lyra informs us, "never lies" (*Northern Lights*, p. 367).

Lyra's Lies

But can we believe Lyra when she asserts Iorek's truth-fulness here or indeed anywhere else, given that she herself is a liar to the core? As her name suggests, storytelling (Lyra, lyre, lyric), invention, deception, trickery, and bluff are at the very heart of Lyra's character. Time and time again, attention is drawn to this aspect of her persona, with 'liar' acquiring the status of epithet as the trilogy unfolds. Perhaps the highlight of her career as trickster comes in the final part of the first volume when she maneuvers the villainous Iofur Raknison into a fight to the death with Iorek Byrnison. Having adroitly identified her adversary's Achilles's heel, Lyra poses as the dæmon which is his heart's desire and persuades him with great guile to do her bidding. Lyra's lies here save the day.

It's on the strength of this performance that Iorek Byrnison christens her Lyra Silvertongue. Just as she welcomes this designation, so she (like Pullman) proudly assumes her trickster identity in a whole range of situations. But when it's held against her—an accusation rather than an accolade—Lyra angrily denies the charge ("I en't dishonest!") (*The Subtle Knife*, p. 170). Nine times out of ten such disavowals will themselves be falsehoods since the charges are usually well-grounded . . . But it's not because she's been found out that Lyra is enraged; it's because such accusations overlook her motives. Lyra's lies, deceptions, and inventions are invariably undertaken for very good reasons.

True, in the early stages of the trilogy her stories are a means of showing off, imposing herself, and impressing others by inspiring awe and fear. This—and nothing more honorable—is what's going on when she tells Roger the bravado-laden tall stories about her uncle's ability to strike his enemies dead with a single glance (*Northern Lights*, pp. 46–47). Yet Lyra's lies also serve to comfort and assist others, to preserve her independence and guarantee her existence. In the circumstances in which she finds herself, lying and pretense are simply unavoidable: her various alter-egos are no mere play-acting whims but strategies upon which her life depends. And when like Lyra you're involved in world travel—traveling *between* worlds—a lie often proves more credible, and therefore more efficient and efficacious, than the truth.

What Lies Beneath

Experience repeatedly impresses the value and efficacy of lying upon both Lyra and the reader following her journey. Until, that is, she ventures into the Land of the Dead in the final volume of the trilogy. It's here that Lyra the liar is most visible and, in all senses of the term, most exposed. For the umpteenth time, Lyra embarks upon an elaborate fiction in order to get around the obstacle she faces. This time, however, there's no triumph. Far from it. This time her efforts elicit physical attack and verbal abuse:

> . . . the harpy was flying at them again and screaming and screaming in rage and hatred: '*Liar! Liar! Liar!*'
>
> And it sounded as if her voice was coming from everywhere, and the word echoed back from the great wall in the fog, muffled and changed, so that she seemed to be screaming Lyra's name, so that *Lyra* and *liar* were one and the same thing. (*The Amber Spyglass*, p. 308)

This time there's no angry denial; Lyra merely wilts into the arms of Will who shelters her and removes her from the immediate danger. So in the Land of the Dead, Lyra is denounced and attacked for doing the very thing in which she excels and which has been so effective elsewhere: for telling tales.

Shortly afterwards the strategy shifts. Lyra manages to harrow hell by *telling the truth*. When she encounters the ghosts who populate this barren land, Lyra regales them with true stories of her past packed with sensory detail. Her words are a rich source of sustenance to the ghosts and harpies who crowd around her. In the subsequent negotiations and bargain which is struck, it soon emerges that such accounts—grounded in truth and in personal observation—will assure the salvation of every single individual. A clear contrast is set up between this new system and that of the Church whose assertions about the afterlife are shown to be manipulative and misleading lies, nothing but empty threats and hollow promises.

From now on, true stories rather than tricks and inventions seem to be the order of the day. The dead who have so benefited from truth-telling instruct Mary Malone to follow suit, and it's in this way, by recounting a series of lived experiences, that she accomplishes the temptation and therefore guarantees redemption. What's more, Lyra herself is a seemingly reformed character.

The journey through the underworld clearly marks an important stage in her development and maturation— emerging on the other side both she and Will are "no-longer-quite-children" (p. 410). It also seems to trigger a funda-mental shift in her character. "I promise to tell the truth, if you promise to believe it," she pledges in the trilogy's closing pages (p. 542). Pullman has elsewhere confirmed that in the Land of the Dead "She leaves fantasy behind, and becomes a realist" ("Writing Fantasy Realistically").

The Great Betrayal?

Could *this* (rather than Roger's death or Pan's abandonment) be the "great betrayal" prophesied for Lyra in the second chapter of the trilogy? The treacherous act which the Master of Jordan College knows she will commit unwittingly and at great emotional cost? In telling the truth, is Lyra true to herself? Her conversion seems to go against the very principles of realistic characterization upon which Pullman sets such store: where, we might ask, is the plausibility, the consistency?

Nor is this betrayal limited to the character of Lyra but extends to the trilogy overall and to its readers. It's as though we, like Roger, are deftly led to a great precipice where the footing abruptly fails. The apparent 180-degree turn to the truth effectively pulls the rug out from under the reader who, for over a thousand pages, has admired Lyra's ruses, enjoyed her fantastic tales, and—crucially— relished the work of fantasy in which she exists. Surely the implication is that we should all put away our childish things and take up memoirs, autobiographies, or confessions instead? The move towards truth seems to fly in the face of Pullman's own repeated valorization of stories and of storytellers, those tricksters who (let's not forget) succeed in persuading someone of "something that isn't true." Is Pullman's hard-sell of truth his ultimate act of treachery?

But should we believe him anyway when he—a storyteller—states that storytellers deal in lies? Can you ever trust a (self-avowed) trickster? How can we verify the truthfulness of his statements? We're faced here with a literary equivalent of a classic, age-old philosophical conundrum commonly known as "The Liar Paradox." Its earliest and most widely known formulation runs as follows: "'The Cretans are always liars,' said the Cretan." Is the Cretan lying? If he is, his statement is true . . . which means that he is lying.

Our mental footing starts to falter at this point. Lyra actually makes this kind of statement at one point in the trilogy: "You think I don't know about lying and that? I'm the best liar there ever was. But I en't lying to you, and I never will, I swear it" (*The Subtle Knife*, p. 107). Statements such as these appear irresolvable, impossible, and as disorientating as the trilogy's apparent move to truth. But just as philosophers have found ways around, and solutions to, the Liar Paradox so too is it possible to account for and understand the trilogy's own apparent paradoxes.

Solving the Paradox—I En't Dishonest

Firstly, Lyra's character is by no means as clear-cut as Pullman suggests in his comments concerning her evolution. Even before the pivotal moment of the journey to the Land of the Dead (or *katabasis* as it was known to the Ancient Greeks), Lyra is more than capable of telling the truth. She's even been described by one critic as the "handmaiden of truth," no less (Rachel Falconer, personal communication). In the trilogy's first chapter, she resists the temptation to run away or bury her head in the sand, and tells her "Uncle" the truth about the poisoned wine.

In the course of the novel, she opens herself entirely to the Gyptians and, later, her father, recounting what has happened to her up until that particular point in the narrative. Similarly, in the second volume, and despite the considerable risks of incomprehension and rebuff, she perseveres in her efforts to truthfully explain herself and her experiences to both Mary and to Will. So what happens in the Land of the Dead *is* prepared for, it doesn't just come out of the blue. Lyra *has* done this before. Finally, of course, and long before her katabatic travels, Lyra is able to read the alethiometer. So the truth is literally at her fingertips.

Lies (Cont'd)

And if the truth makes many an appearance prior to the *katabasis*, so too do lies and deceptions continue to occur afterwards. Indeed, at the end of the very chapter in which the salvationary dimension of truth is made clear, a lie is told—a white lie, a lie which seeks to assuage and comfort, but a lie nonetheless. Lyra asks Will whether the end is in sight: "He couldn't tell. But they were so weak and sick that he said, 'Yes, it's nearly over, we've nearly done it. We'll be out soon'" (*The Amber Spyglass*, p. 338).

Later on, Will and Mary will "decide on a story and stick to it" in order to negotiate the authorities and generally navigate their way, once back in their own world (p. 540). And long after the apparent shift to the truth, Mrs. Coulter stays absolutely true to form as the most inveterate of liars. The scene with Metatron is made up of a dizzying series of lies proclaiming themselves over and over as truths. Lyra's mother is perhaps the slipperiest of all the trilogy's characters, and even at this late stage in the proceedings, the reader is still not entirely sure what she's up to. Only because of the way the episode parallels Lyra's manipulation of the power-hungry bear is it possible to perceive Mrs. Coulter's (noble) treachery here.

Lies and Truth/Truth and Lies

But perhaps what really matters in all this is Lyra. Even the newly honest Lyra is not wholly exempt from breaking her word in the later stages of the trilogy. Lyra promises Mary that she and Will "won't go in among the trees" but, just six pages later, where else do we see them venturing but "into a little wood of silver-barked trees"?! (pp. 481, 489).

It's towards the end of the trilogy that Lyra loses the ability to instinctively read the alethiometer. This means that there is a very clear overall balance within the overall work. Pre-*katabasis* she deliberately lies a great deal (although she can tell the truth at times) and she can read the alethiomenter. Post-*katabasis* she endeavors to tell the truth (though does not manage it all the time) and—precisely because of that endeavor, that effort, and self-consciousness— is unable to read the truth-telling device. Truth and lies are distributed in a way which contributes to, rather than detracting from, the trilogy's internal coherence.

The cause of Lyra's loss will also be its cure: she will eventually regain her ability to reread the alethiometer by hard work and endeavor. Indeed, she will achieve something greater than her initial gift, as the angel Xaphania informs her: "But your reading will be even better then, after a lifetime of thought and effort, because it will come from conscious understanding. Grace attained like that is deeper and fuller than grace that comes freely, and furthermore, once you've gained it, it will never leave you" (p. 520). The at first crippling but ultimately empowering consequences of self-consciousness are at the heart of Heinrich von Kleist's essay *On Marionette Theater* which Pullman cites in the Acknowledgements as one of his three main sources in the trilogy.

True Values: Choose Life

Another way out of the paradoxical impasse is in recognizing that the high valuation of truth in the *katabasis* is by no means as out of kilter with the rest of the work as it may at first seem. As we've seen with Will's words to Lyra in the Land of the Dead, or Mrs. Coulter's encounter with the Regent, lies can be good, kind, and best while the truth can be deployed as a weapon intended to harm, manipulate, and annihilate. This is what Pullman is getting at when he chooses Blake's lines as the epigraph to

Chapter 11 of *The Amber Spyglass*: "A truth that's told with bad intent beats all the lies you can invent."

Truth is not, then, promoted—in the *katabasis* or elsewhere—for its own sake; it is not shown to be intrinsically valuable or good. It is instead a token or guarantee of something else: namely, a full life and an observant, appreciate liver of that life. "If they live in the world, they *should* see and touch and hear and love and learn things," says the harpy, and we sense Pullman close behind her (p. 334). Similarly, the ultimate crime of the Church is not the telling of lies in itself but the life-arresting consequences of those lies. The destruction of "the joys and truthfulness of life" is poignantly embodied in the martyr encountered in the Land of the Dead who explains how the promise of Heaven led to squander and desolation: "that's what led some of us to give our lives, and others to spend years in solitary prayer, while all the joy of life was going to waste around us, and we never knew" (*The Subtle Knife*, p. 283; *The Amber Spyglass*, p. 336). What's truly vaunted in this passage and in the trilogy overall is not truth *per se* but experience, gusto, joie de vivre. *Carpe diem*, remember well, and pass it on.

The Customer Comes First

Finally, we have to bear in mind the circumstances in which stories based on lived experiences and detailed personal observation come to the fore. We need to think about the communicative situation in which Lyra finds herself, and consider not only her motivation as speaker, but also the very particular requirements, needs and desires of her interlocutors (the dead).

What's going on here is best understood by comparing this particular situation with one just prior to the entry into the Land of the Dead. The travelers spend the night before they set out in a shack in the suburbs of the dead. Their hosts are still alive, waiting for their deaths to come and lead them onwards. For this audience Lyra offers a narrative (a more elaborate version of which will soon be brutally rejected by the harpy) interweaving lived experience with invention. It's an action-packed tale of high adventure which is utterly condemned and dismissed by the narrator who refers to it scathingly as "this nonsense" (*The Amber Spyglass*, p. 277). Writer and narrator rub shoulders here, since in "Writing Fantasy Realistically," Pullman speaks of "one of her Lyra-like fantasies, full of wild nonsense." But her interlocutors respond very differently, gazing at her enthralled. For those who've been reduced to an existence of waiting, entirely devoid of action and events, Lyra's story is precisely what they require. Lyra's lies take them away from the misery of their present circumstances without any of the debilitating consequences of the Church's inventions.

The self-same story addressed to those cut off from the world and gorged on a surfeit of evil is, on the other hand, woefully inadequate. Lyra here totally misjudges the needs and interests of her listeners. She will not make the same mistake again. Her brief is so much clearer when she meets the ghosts who tell her directly what it is they want to hear: "the things they remembered, the sun and the wind and the sky, and the things they'd forgotten, such as how to play" (p. 328).

In telling the ghosts "about the world," Lyra takes them back to their previous real, full existences and transports them from the Land of the Dead to the land of the living (p. 329). So if we compare these two moments, it becomes clear that truth satisfies the same escapist desires in the Land of the Dead as does fantasy in the land of the living. The promotion of truth at this particular moment in the story in no way implies a concurrent condemnation or disavowal of storytelling. Truth emerges instead as just one of the methods at the disposal of storytellers in order to move, to transport their listeners.

What is paramount, then, is the audience. Although it may seem that Pullman manipulates, misleads, and abuses his position of trust, the overall thrust of the story is actually quite the reverse. If the trilogy has received the critical acclaim and popular success which it has, it is surely precisely because Pullman, like Lyra, has understood the importance of thinking about, anticipating, and responding to, the very different needs of his very diverse audience.

11
His Dark Materials in a Post-Truth World

RICHARD LEAHY

Philip Pullman's *His Dark Materials,* and its sequel trilogy, *The Book of Dust,* raise questions surrounding the absolute authority of truth, and how this authority is evinced and upheld by those who wish to abuse it. Pullman brings into focus the reliability of truth, and how it may be reappropriated by those with malicious intent for nefarious purposes.

The *type* of truth that Pullman contends with, and the specific type that he appears to promote above all others, can provide valuable philosophical lessons into the nature of truth. In themes established in *His Dark Materials,* he attends to the nature of subjective truth, before considering how this functions in relation to authoritarian truths in *The Book of Dust* trilogy. Pullman's world has developed in parallel to our "real" world. Concepts of political post-truth and the morality of authority that were suggested in the earlier texts have been emphasized in the current political climate in which Pullman was writing *The Book of Dust.*

Truth, and Reading

So what, then, is truth? In what sense are we discussing it here? And how does it apply to *His Dark Materials?* Pullman seems simultaneously to both destroy the notion of a universal truth in his treatment of authority, religion and belief, while also saying that objective truths can be discovered through personal intimation and interpretation.

In his treatment of accepted and authoritarian truths—particularly through the Magisterium and their very divisive understanding of the innocence and experience of the human condition—and his treatment of objective truths (such as Lyra's alethiometer, the I Ching, and Dust itself), Pullman praises the self-discovery of interpretation. This is in turn mirrored in the composition of his work, and his own admission that "writing is despotic, reading is democratic."

Truth, if we consider it critically, relies on language. The correspondence theory of truth that has dominated western thought leans on the notion of language as representing and corresponding with actual reality. The three fundamental components of this classical theory of objective truth can be broken down as such; firstly, the priority of nature over language, secondly that truth corresponds with similarities, and that the third and most essential feature is that of the secondary and derivative character of the signs by which truth is symbolized and communicated.

This third essential feature of truth relates to the structuralist linguists of the mid-twentieth century, such as Roland Barthes, who argued that the signs by which we communicate truth (language and words) can themselves be *mythologized*. In other words, Barthes argues that truth occurs when we strip back the *sign* and consider its *signified* meaning.

In the work of Ferdinand de Saussure, language is split into its two component parts; sign and signifier. This roughly correlates to the idea that is intended to be expressed in an utterance, and the linguistic vehicle (word or phrase) that carries this idea. Together, Saussure argued that they form the *signified*—the token of language that holds meaning. Yet Barthes argued that this signified meaning is not added arbitrarily, but rather conditioned to perpetuate a hegemonic ideal of society—thereby affecting the value and validity of *truth*.

An example is the treatment of the "General Oblation Board" in *Northern Lights*. The organization is also known as the "Gobblers," a colloquial title in part inspired by the official abbreviation. It is an important example of where two different types of *truth* are represented by two very ideologically different signs. The "General Oblation Board" is so named due to the religious influence of the Magisterium, the term "Obla-tion" referring to a gift or offering to God. Conversely, those unaffected by the Magisterium's ideological language refer to them very differently, as they become the "Gobblers" that consume their children. Both of these statements are ultimately true, but they expose important questions about how the truth may be used or understood. This question of *interpretation* is vital to the type of truth Pullman espouses.

Understanding the Alethiometer

Truth, in Pullman's view, is not something to be trusted, but something to be discovered. We can see this in Lyra's alethiometer, and how it is treated in respect to *truth*. Lyra herself is, as her name suggests, a liar. She uses mistruths and false stories in order to escape consequences and negotiate the ebb of the narrative. Yet she's presented with an object that is claimed to "tell the truth." It does not predict or foretell, but simply states the *truth*. This is very different from a device that could only regurgitate facts—instead, the alethiometer implies the connection between uncovering the truth and telling stories. When discussing the origins of the alethiometer with Farder Coram, Lyra asks where the symbols that line its rim originated from, to which Coram responds:

> "Oh this was in the seventeenth century. Symbols and emblems were everywhere. Buildings and pictures were designed to be read like books. Everything stood for something else; if you had the right dictionary you could read Nature itself." (p. 173)

Coram's emblematic history suggests the importance Pullman places on *reading*. We should not accept the truth, but rather read into information in order *to discern* the truth. Coram implies the ideological influence of symbology and iconography as he identifies how buildings and pictures became designed to represent something other than their sole function. The idea that "Everything stood for something else" is highly significant, as it elucidates the notions of the structural linguists yet further. In this statement, we can see the breakdown of conventional notions of sign and signifier.

We move into the realms of Barthesian *myth* as Pullman breaks down the relationship between utterance and intent. This is, ultimately, how the alethiometer works—it mythologizes the relationship between *sign* and *signified* idea. Lyra tells herself a story based on the icon that she reads from the alethiometer and understands the truth *through* that story; it is an almost paradoxical idea of divining the truth through falsehoods and associated representations.

After meeting Mary Malone, Lyra attempts to use her Dust-detecting computer in a similar manner to how she uses the alethiometer. She thinks of the "candle (for understanding), the alpha and omega (for language), and the ant (for diligence)" (*The Subtle Knife*, p. 93).

Each of these images serves as a metaphor for what it represents, while also exposing the connections between the tenor and vehicle of the metaphor, and therefore the connection between sign and signified idea. The candle's connection with understanding is clear to see; in the phenomenological properties of the candle, we can see illumination, enlightenment, and a sense of individual purpose. Its quality of bringing light to darkness is what Lyra's understanding of its representation of understanding is based on. The ant that connotes diligence is similarly straightforward to comprehend—the ant represents an individual within a collective, while also implying subservience and passivity. The alpha and omega are a little more interesting. They represent language in this instance due to the fact that they are the first and last letters of the Greek alphabet, while also having significant religious connotations themselves.

The phrase "I am Alpha and Omega" is repeated in various derivations throughout the Book of Revelation, and has been taken by scholars to mean "I am both beginning and end." When taken in the context of *His Dark Materials,* a series that decries the authority of religion, Lyra's symbolic understanding carries much more weight. There is a sense of closure provided by the representative image of the Alpha and the Omega; knowledge, authority and truth are bookended by the opposing principals of beginning and end. The declarative nature of "I am Alpha and Omega" resounds with the desired authoritativeness of orthodox religion. This is only emphasized by the ant being the next symbol in the paradigmatic chain. It reinforces the notion that humanity is a slave to these imagined hierarchies of authority, and evokes Pullman's theme of innocence's journey to experience. There is nothing inherent that carries the meaning of these images, but rather, Lyra's own experiences and the collective understanding revolving around these images. There is a desire on Pullman's part to promote *illumination* and *enlightenment.*

Indeed, Mary Malone's Shadow-detecting computer is nicknamed *"The Cave,"* which is vitally important to Pullman's discourse surrounding accepting and interpreting truth. Mary acknowledges the origins of its name as she states: "Oh, sorry. The computer. We call it the Cave. Shadows on the walls of the Cave, you see, from Plato. That's our archaeologist again. He's an all-round intellectual" (p. 93). Plato's allegory attempts to compare the influence of education on our nature and the lack of it; the Cave suggests both the importance of self-discovered interpretation, and the dangers of assuming the truth of a reality.

Plato, through Socrates, describes a group of people who have been living chained to the wall of a cave. Inside the cave, the people watch a display of shadows caused by objects passing by a fire situated behind them. These shadows become the prisoners' reality; they cease questioning knowledge and reality, and instead accept an *image* of it. We can understand this in terms of the ideology of the Magisterium in *His Dark Materials;* people like Mrs. Coulter, as well as the doctors working at Bolvangar, are blinded by the shadows promoted by these authorities as truth, and are unable to move beyond the cave and see the reality of the situation.

The alethiometer, and other similar truth-telling devices, rely instead upon asserting the value of objective truths— instead of seeing the symbols as simply *signs,* like shadows on a cave wall, Lyra brings her own experience and understanding to the potential meanings. It is not strictly a type of universal truth, but rather, a self-discovered truth that flies in the face of the authoritatively asserted truths of the Magisterium and the Church. The Magisterium fears the alethiometer due to its ability to contradict to their own ideology; but they fear it not only for this contrast in truths, but in how they are discovered as well. Symbolically, the golden compass represents enlightenment and knowledge, and the renunciation of accepted truths in favor of critical thinking.

The Book of Dust and Contemporary Truths

These ideas are given yet more value in Pullman's updating of his original trilogy's themes in *The Book of Dust.* Within his more recent series, Pullman updates a number of thematic elements to more appropriately reflect this current age; comments on climate change, fascism, fake news, and post-truths are all evoked and emphasized in this twenty-first century reacquaintance with Lyra's (many) worlds.

The political schism in our contemporary culture is often framed as a contest between Left and Right, but it's really more about epistemology than politics. On one side we have those who value evidence and reason, and on the other side we have those who claim knowledge via emotion and drama. This sense of tribal epistemology may be witnessed all over the Western world, from debates surrounding the American presidency to issues of the EU in Europe. The idea of "good for our side" and "true" become blurred.

In *Northern Lights,* we can see the threatening authority of the Magisterium and their hegemony over knowledge— all scientific and philosophic discoveries have to be announced through them, as Lord Asriel states (p. 368). They decide the truth. In *The Secret Commonwealth,* this purporting of false truths is combined with a new method of reading the alethiometer which suggests the binary tribalism of the current political climate. Pierre Benaud, chief officer of the Consistorial Court of the Magisterium, attempts to find out more information about Lyra, but declines the offer of a Magisterium-endorsed Alethiometer reading:

> "Now, this other matter: the young woman. What do you know about her?
> "The Alethiometer—"
> "No, no, no. Old-fashioned, vague, too full of speculation. Give me facts, Marcel."
> "We have a new reader, who—"
> "Oh yes, I've heard of him. New method. Any better than the old one?"

"Times change, and understandings must change too. (*The Secret Commonwealth*, p. 9)

The Magisterium, in a manner that reflects dominant right-wing ideologies surrounding the power of "fact," disavow the trustworthiness of interpreting the Alethiometer. To them, it is too speculative. Indeed, *The Secret Commonwealth* establishes a division between the rationality of *fact,* and the much freer nature of the human imagination. Brande's *Hyperchoriasmians* acts as a symbol of the invasive and pervasive nature of fact and objective truth-based rhetoric.

Lyra is "spellbound, hypnotized" by the story, which leaves her "head ringing with the hammer-blows of the protagonist's denunciation of anything and everything that stood in the way of pure reason" (p. 76). Indeed, as Pantalaimon berates Lyra for losing her imagination, he argues "There's no room for them in the universe you want to believe in. How do you think the Alethiometer works? I suppose the symbols have got so many meanings you can read anything you want into them, so they don't mean anything at all, really" (p. 191).

Pullman establishes this mode of thinking as dominant among the young, which may be a reflection on the current pull of conservatism: "It had become fashionable to disparage any sort of excessive emotional reaction, or any attempt to read other meanings into something that happened, or any argument that couldn't be justified with logic" (pp. 76–77). This directly challenges the epistemological value of the Alethiometer—instead of using interpretive analysis to comprehend its symbols, it now simply represents logic, rationality and common sense—if such a thing even exists. Yet, espousing these concepts above all others limits creativity, imagination, and agency.

Pullman delineates the new method of interpreting the Alethiometer as he describes Lyra's experiments with it:

The classical method required the reader to frame a question by pointing each of the hands at a different symbol, and thus define precisely what it was they wanted to know. But with the new method, all three hands were pointed at one symbol, chosen by the reader. This was felt by classically trained readers to be grossly unorthodox and disrespectful of tradition, besides being unstable; instead of the steady and methodical enquiry made possible by the firmly based triangle of the three hands, the single anchor-hold of the new method allowed a wild and unpredictable chaos of meanings to emerge as the needle darted rapidly from place to place. (p. 154)

The fact that "all three hands were pointed at one symbol chosen by the reader" suggests that this is not a method that explores interpretation, but rather a method of divining the truth that is influenced by bias and prejudice. In essence, meaning has already been fixed. Lyra struggles with this method—many times after doing it she tells of her headaches and sickness. It does not seem natural to her. In this new method, "the answers come much more quickly, and you hardly need to read the books at all" (p. 139). This is reflective of political tribal epistemologies that emerge in the wake of populism. Tuukka Yia-Anttilla argues that populist rhetoric and ideology has a "tendency to valorize folk wisdom and 'common sense' while criticizing expertise" ("Populist Knowledge"). This is something witnessed throughout Pullman's texts; the Magisterium attempts to throttle Asriel's scientific research because it is deemed heretical; the tension between assumed beliefs and scholarly pursuits may be seen in Jordan College; as well as the "common-sense" views of Lyra's world we get from Brande and Simon Talbot in *The Secret Commonwealth,* who even go as far as to deny the existence of daemons.

Telling Them Stories

Also, within Pullman's second entry in *The Book of Dust* trilogy, we see a counterpoint to the Alethiometer in the *myriorama*. Given to Lyra by a mysterious man on the train to Antalya, the *myriorama* uses cards with different images on that can be rearranged in different successions, therefore telling stories. What is valuable about these cards, however, is what they leave out, and what the user's mind then fills in. Lyra begins to deny her common sense and rational new outlook, and revert back to the Lyra who believed in fantasy. As she places the cards out, she thinks "I could *choose* to believe in the secret commonwealth. I don't have to be skeptical about it. If free will exists, and I have it, I can choose that. I'll try one more" (p. 585). The solution to Lyra's crisis of imagination and rationality is, as at the end of *The Amber Spyglass,* to tell stories.

Pullman seems to find pleasure and reassurance in the act of *reading.* The very act of reading, by his own acknowledgment, goes against a pre-inscribed authoritative meaning:

> Now I'm not beginning like this in order to disclaim responsibility for what I've written; I'm doing it to remind all of us, myself as well as you, that my book doesn't have a single meaning, and that my relation to it is complex, and that my interpretation of what I wrote is likely to be as partial as anybody else's, and that anything I say about it has not much more authority than a reader's. Maybe a little bit more, if for no other reason than I know the text fairly closely; but no final authority. ("God and Dust," p. 434)

Acts of reading destroy centralized authority, due to the necessity of understanding both an overarching system (that of language), while at the same time bringing personal experience and understanding to a text. Indeed, this is reflected in the perceived etymology of the *myriorama.* Breaking the word down, we get two component parts; *myriad,* a Greek term denoting an indefinitely massive number, and *-orama,* a suffix most commonly found in diorama, which roughly means "to have a wide view of." This corresponds with another postmodern idea of Roland Barthes, that of "The Death of the Author"—he argued that no author ever truly has power over their work and that the power of interpretation lies with the reader. This appears to be what Pullman is also suggesting, as he not only tries to defeat the Authority, but also to question his own.

In the 2019 BBC/HBO adaptation of the series, Lyra describes reading the Alethiometer as like climbing down a ladder, unsure of your next step, but trusting that it will be there as you descend the rungs. This brings to mind the relational nature of language and truth. Language, as Barthes suggests, is a myth that we collectively believe in. Meaning is only found in relation to other meanings—words are like rungs on a ladder. Truth, then, is paradoxically everywhere and nowhere.

Pullman warns against the prescription of truth, and the perils of accepting hegemonic realities; in challenging God, and threatening Authority, he challenges his ownership over *his* texts. Yet he does so in a way that suggests the power of stories, and what these fictional realities can tell us about truth in our own. Indeed, Slavoj Žižek argues that in our own world, "we can now see what those who bemoan the 'death of truth' really deplore: the disintegration of one big Story more or less accepted by the majority, a story, which used to bring ideological stability to a society" ("Chaos, Europe, and Fake News").

Stories, like language, are relational and representative of societies and ideologies. As the Ghost says to Mary in *The Amber Spyglass,* "Tell them stories! That's what we didn't know. All this time and we never knew! But they need the truth. That's what nourishes them."

Again, there is a paradoxical idea here of telling stories and telling the truth. Yet if we consider this in more depth, it appears to be more interrelated to Pullman's debates about innocence and experience than may first appear. *Truth* is *experience.* The stories of the ghost's physical lives in the Land of the Dead may not be believed but they have been authentically lived. Stories allow us to organize experience and truth into engaging narratives.

Truth masquerades as authenticity, but stories embrace this ambiguity in a way that reflects the complex nature of the human self. We are neither good nor bad, consumed by both innocence and experience. Yet these falsehoods are what make us human, and what give us the power to *interpret, analyze, and criticize.*

In Pullman's own words: "Without stories, we wouldn't be human beings at all."

Part IV

---

*"Truly," he said,
"I am dead . . . I'm dead,
and I'm going to Hell . . ."
"Hush," said Lyra,
"we'll go together."*

12
Compassion in the Kingdom of Heaven

RACHEL ROBISON-GREENE

All sorts of beings occupy the many universes of *His Dark Materials*. These beings have different customs, cultures, and social practices. Perhaps the most noteworthy differences between different types of beings in the series are the metaphysical differences. Some beings have souls and others do not. Some beings are immortal and others aren't.

In the universe that we, the readers, occupy, we frequently use differences in traits and abilities among living things to guide us in making decisions regarding how things out to be treated. Some moral theorists, like Peter Singer, identify beings with interests as the kinds of beings that are deserving of moral consideration. He says:

> It would be nonsense to say that it was not in the interests of a stone to be kicked along the road by a schoolboy. A stone does not have interests because it cannot suffer. Nothing that we can do to it could possibly make any difference to its welfare . . . A mouse, for example, does have an interest in not being kicked along the road, because it will suffer if it is. ("All Animals Are Equal")

Other philosophers identify more lofty traits as requirements for personhood or membership in the moral community. Following Kant, some argue that autonomy, the capacity to reason, and the ability to provide and listen to reasons for action is necessary for thoroughgoing moral agency.

Still other thinkers in the history of philosophy have maintained that the fundamental difference between humans and other kinds of beings is that humans were created in God's image. There are different ways of understanding what, exactly, that means, but one thing it *might* mean is that human beings have immortal souls and other living beings do not. As a result, we have been granted dominion over the other living beings that exist on the planet, or so we're told in Genesis:

> And God said, Let us make man in our image, after our likeness: and let them have dominion over the fish of the sea, and over the fowl of the air, and over the cattle, and over all the earth, and over every creeping thing that creepeth upon the earth. (Genesis 1:26)

If what it means to be created after the likeness of God is to have an immortal soul, then perhaps we're justified in treating non-human animals like *things* for our consumption because they don't have souls.

Whatever standard gets employed, we tend to use standards like these to help us determine how to navigate the world we live in. We use them to determine which beings to grant legal rights, which beings to keep as pets, and which beings to eat for dinner. Arguably, in the universe we occupy, human beings do a terrible job at drawing these distinctions in coherent, consistent, and defensible ways. How much more difficult would making these sorts of decisions be in the world of Lyra and Pan—a set of universes in which all living creatures operate according to different metaphysical rules, a world in which *dust* is conscious? What kinds of features of matter are morally and practically relevant to decision making? Should we care more about the interests of Armored Bears than we do about foxes that tell mostly lies and speak only in the present tense?

Understanding and respecting the morally and existentially important features of other beings is part of living a good life, but understanding our *own* nature as best as we can also has value. The Oracle at Delphi imparted the wisdom *Know Thyself*. A philosophical life involves introspection, transparency, and honesty with yourself. When the self takes on an unusual structure, it's hard to know the way forward to self-knowledge. In *His Dark Materials*, there is no *single* structure of the self. On the face of it, this poses some problems for self-actualization and self-discovery—two of the primary purposes of the journey that Will and Lyra take together.

A Girl and Her Daemon

Rightly or wrongly, in our universe, many people behave as if there's a morally relevant difference between human beings and non-human animals. The metaphysics of Lyra's universe make this tricky—human and non-human animals are essentially linked. The relationship between Lyra and Pan is one of the most critical features of the series. Nevertheless, it's difficult to pin down. From the outset, the reader is left with the impression that daemons are, roughly, souls. The souls of Lyra's Oxford have metaphysical properties that are unique.

First, the souls are non-human animals. In children, the form that a daemon takes changes regularly. There's a lot of evidence throughout the series to suggest that changes in a daemon's form take place because children are in a unique position to engage in imaginative play. As Lyra darts around Oxford, her daemon takes on whatever shape is most convenient or exhilarating for the purposes of the game she's playing. As a person gets older, goes through puberty, and attains knowledge, their daemon settles on a fixed form that will in some sense either reflect or compliment the essence of its partner. As Lyra explains to Will:

> As you grow up you start thinking, well, that they might be this or they might be that . . . And usually they end up something that fits. I mean something like your real nature. Like if your daemon's a dog, that means you like doing what you're told, and knowing who's boss and following orders, and pleasing people who are in charge. A lot of servants are people whose demons are dogs. So it helps to know what you like and to find what you're good at. (*The Amber Spyglass*, p. 457)

Until the end of *The Amber Spyglass,* Will's soul is inside his body, but Lyra intuits that if his soul were an external daemon like her own, it would take the form of a cat. At the end of the story, this intuition is confirmed.

The idea that a human's daemon ultimately takes a form that suits its partner is consistent with the concept, frequently expressed throughout the series, that a person's daemon somehow *is that person*. Consider, for example, the part of the story when Lyra and Will cut into the world of the dead. To continue further, they must take a ship to where the ghosts are, but Pan is not permitted to come along.

> There was no need to speak. Will got in first, and then Lyra came forward to step down, too.
>   But the boatman held up his hand.
> "Not him," he said in a harsh whisper.
> "Not who?"
> "Not him."
> He extended a yellow-gray finger, pointing directly at Pantalaimon, whose red-brown stoat form immediately became ermine white.
> "But he *is* me!"
> "If you come, he must stay."
> "But we can't! We'll die!"
> "Isn't that what you want?"

This example highlights the unusual metaphysical nature of the relationship between a person and their daemon. Usually, when we ask questions about identity, we are asking about *numerical* identity. For example, when Lois Lane asks if Clark Kent is Superman, she is asking whether Kent and Superman are *one and the same person*. If she concludes that the answer is yes, she is also justified in believing what that conclusion entails—that when Superman flew her around the city, it was Kent flying her around the city as well. This is because part of what it is to be *identical* to a being is to occupy the same space in time as that being. Pan and Lyra clearly occupy different spaces in time. It's difficult, therefore, to make sense out of the claim that they are one and the same person.

In addition to occupying different spaces in time, Pan and Lyra also engage in different thoughts and actions. Pan wants to do things that Lyra doesn't want to do and vice versa. Pan might run away from a situation while Lyra holds firm. Through much of the last third of *The Amber Spyglass*,

Lyra and Will are in entirely different locations from their daemons. They have no idea where their daemons are, nor do they know what the daemons are thinking, feeling, or doing. This is a strange relationship to stand in to *oneself*.

Second, in most cases, daemons have a different gender, and, presumably, biological sex, from their human partner. One way to understand this is that beings in Lyra's universe have both a male and a female nature. The union between a human and their daemon, then, balances the male and female traits in a human person. Nevertheless, if Lyra and her daemon differ in this significant way, it's difficult to make sense out of the idea that she and Pan are *the same person*.

Further, it is possible, though not necessarily likely, that a human person can survive the process of intercision, that is, they can survive the process of being severed from their demon. In light of that, consider the following argument:

> *Premise One:* A person can't continue to exist without their essential features.
>
> *Premise Two:* A person can continue to exist without their daemon.
>
> *Conclusion:* Therefore, a daemon must not be an essential feature of a person.

This is an argument against understanding Pan as an essential component of Lyra. The books make a stronger claim than this. They claim that Pan *is* Lyra. We can construct a similar argument against this stronger position.

> *Premise One:* A person can't continue to exist when something *numerically identical* to them ceases to exist.
>
> *Premise Two:* A person can continue to exist without their daemon.
>
> *Conclusion:* Therefore, a person can't be *numerically identical* to their daemon.

One response to this line of thought might be that those beings that do manage to survive intercision are very different beings as a result of the process. Their features and capacities have changed in such significant ways that it might be appropriate to think of them as an entirely different person from the person they once were. Consider Lyra's observations about the nurses at Bolvangar:

> She was half expecting questions about where she had come from and how she had arrived, and she was preparing answers; but it wasn't only imagination the nurse lacked, it was curiosity as well. Bolvangar might have been on the outskirts of London, and children might have been arriving all the time, for all the interest Sister Clara seemed to show. Her pert neat little daemon trotted along at her heels just as brisk and blank as she was. (*The Golden Compass*, p. 238)

We later learn that the nurses at Bolvangar have had their daemons cut away, and though they often appear at the side of their former selves, they are now little more than docile pets.

Mrs. Coulter uses her research from Bolvangar to construct an army. When she visits Sir Charles in Will's world she discusses this development with him:

> But tell me about your curious bodyguards Marisa. I've never seen soldiers like that. Who are they?
>
> Men, that's all. But . . . they've undergone intercision. They have no daemons, so they have no fear and no imagination and no free will, and they'll fight till they're torn apart. (*The Subtle Knife*, p. 199)

When humans survive intercision, they lose their curiosity and their imagination. We can draw one of at least two conclusions.

First, it may be the case that curiosity and imagination exist when and only when a human form is connected to a daemon form.

Second, it could be the case that daemons are the part of the equation that is responsible for curiosity and imagination, so that without a daemon, a human no longer has those traits. The behavior of the nurse's daemon speaks against this second interpretation, since he too seems docile and to lack both curiosity and imagination.

Finally, at the end of the trilogy, we learn that daemons have a distinct purpose when it comes to the lives of human beings. Speaking to the children's daemons, Serafina Pekkala says:

> Those two have changed many things. We are all learning new ways, even witches. But one thing hasn't changed: you must help your humans, not hinder them. You must help them and guide them and encourage them toward wisdom. That's what daemons are for. (*The Amber Spyglass*, p. 473)

Again, this distinct purpose suggests uniqueness and distinction from the human part of the union between human and daemon. If Lyra and Pan were the same person, Pan couldn't do anything for Lyra that she couldn't do for herself. Is there a better way of understanding this relation?

Persons and Their Parts

One way around all of these troubles is to think of Lyra and Pan as a unified whole constructed out of parts that have different functions. This is not an uncommon position in the history of philosophy.

In *The Republic*, Plato offered an account of a soul with three parts. The appetitive soul is responsible for desire. The spirited part of the soul is responsible for passion. The rational soul is represented as a charioteer, guiding the other parts of the soul.

Aristotle's conception of the soul is fairly similar and is also comprised of three parts: vegetative, sensitive, and rational. The vegetative soul is capable of taking nutrition and growing. The sensitive soul is responsible for perception and mobility. The rational soul is responsible for rationality. Plants have only vegetative souls, non-human animals have vegetative souls and sensitive souls, and human beings have all three.

In the seventeenth century, René Descartes gave a dualist account of the human being. The mind-body union he describes is much like the relationship that exists between Pan and Lyra. Descartes argued that human beings are identical to their minds—their immaterial souls—but, in life, the material body and the immaterial soul are joined together in a union, each performing their own functions.

Upon death, however, the immaterial soul lives on, while the material body does not. Similarly, upon death, a daemon becomes dust, while Lyra's spirit goes on to the Land of the Dead (although this is no longer true at the point at which Lyra and Will free the dead forever by cutting a hole in that world, allowing them to escape.) Pan and Lyra are joined together as one being in life, but upon death they separate. The relationship that exists between Lyra and Pan seems to be dualist in nature, but in *The Amber Spyglass*, we are provided with the following surprising passage:

> "Could we really do that? Could we really go to the land of the dead? But—what part of us does that? Because daemons fade away when we die—I've seen them—and our bodies, well, they just stay in the grave and decay, don't they?"
>
> "Then there must be a third part. A different part."
>
> "You know," she said, full of excitement, "I think that must be true! Because I can think about my body and I can think about my daemon—so there must be another part, to do the thinking!"
>
> "Yes. And that's the ghost? (*The Amber Spyglass*, p. 166)

We suddenly learn that Lyra and Pan are not two parts that participate in a unified whole, but are, instead, two of *three* parts of a unified whole. Lyra's reflections on the very structure of her being are not just thrown in for a little added flavor. They are doing some work in Pullman's larger metaphor. Mary Malone (a.k.a. *the serpent*) explicitly mentions this element of the theological history of the Catholic Church:

> "You know," she said, "the Church—The Catholic Church that I used to belong to—wouldn't use the word *daemon*—but St. Paul talks about spirit *and* soul *and* body. So the idea of three parts in human nature isn't that strange." (*The Amber Spyglass*, p. 439)

Indeed, the idea that there are three parts of human nature isn't historically unusual at all. The more salient question, however, may be whether such an account is *defensible*.

Other Kinds of Beings

Like Lyra, we love to tell stories. Ideally we'd prefer those stories to be internally consistent, and we'd like them to *matter*. By contrast, the most significant story arcs in *His Dark Materials* don't ground meaning or value in the way we might expect. In our universe, stories about souls tend to be connected to stories about creation and stories about God in such a way that those stories help us find meaning in life.

If beings with souls are the children of God, and all and only children of God have the ultimate purpose of being with God forever after a life well lived, the question of meaning is settled by God's plan. In *His Dark Materials*, The Authority isn't the creator, he's just an incomprehensibly old angel who disintegrates into dust when released from his cage of crystal. Lord Asriel and Mrs. Coulter—not exactly paragons of virtue and strength, easily vanquish Metatron. The presence of a soul doesn't signal divine selection or lineage. It's simply a feature that some beings have and some beings don't.

Consider the Armored Bears. When Lyra first encounters Iorek Byrnison, he is despondent and useless without his armor. She inquires further into the nature of his misery:

> She said, "Why don't you just make some more armor out of this metal here, Iorek Byrnison?"
>
> "Because it's worthless. Look," he said, and, lifting the engine cover with one paw, he extended a claw on the other hand and ripped right through it like a can opener. "My armor is made of sky iron, made for me. A bear's armor is his soul, just as your daemon is your soul. You might as well take *him* away"—indicating Pantalaimon—"and replace him with a doll full of sawdust. That is the difference. Now, where is my armor?" (*The Golden Compass*, p. 196)

We learn later from Iorek that Armored Bears are mortal. They do not survive the deaths of their bodies. Iorek says:

> If you do not find a way out of the world of the dead, we shall not meet again because I have no ghost. My body will remain on earth, and then become part of it. But if it turns out that both you and I survive, then you will always be a welcome and honest visitor to Svalbard, and the same is true of Will. (*The Amber Spyglass*, p. 196)

We're left with the conclusion that Armored Bears have souls and their souls are their armor. The armor is inanimate. It doesn't contribute any conscious characteristics or traits to the bear that wears it. Nevertheless, each suit of armor is unique to a particular bear. When Iorek is distraught about his armor in *The Golden Compass*, he cannot simply buy or forge another suit. It must be *his* armor, *his* soul. The soul is not an immaterial, immortal part of Iorek that allows him to survive the destruction of his body. It is not his special genetic marker of divine lineage, it simply makes him stronger while he is alive and contributes to his sense of identity.

A sense of identity is frequently connected with personhood. The concept of personhood is frequently tied to the possession of a soul. As we've seen, some people connect rational traits to personhood, and personhood to souls.

Descartes considered the question of whether non-human animals were essentially just biological machines—mere automata. He concluded that they were through the use of two tests. First, he considered whether the being in question was capable of using language. Second, he asked if the behavior of the being in question arose entirely from the disposition of that being's organs. If the behavior can be explained purely in that way, then it is appropriate to think of that being as an automaton. The second test is an inquiry into whether a being's behavior is a self-conscious act of the will, or mere instinctual behavior instead.

Many beings without souls in the *His Dark Materials* universes pass Descartes's tests (assuming for the moment that his standards are appropriate, which they probably aren't). All sorts of creatures use language and seem to act freely. These beings all seem to be genuine *persons* in a way that stones are not. Mary Malone reflects on the nature of the mulefa:

> There were twenty or thirty huts, roughly grouped in a circle, made of—she had to shade her eyes against the sun to see—wooden beams covered with a kind of wattle-and-daub mixture on the walls and thatch on the roofs. Other wheeled creatures were working: some repairing a roof, others bringing brushwood for a fire.
>
> So they had a language, and they had fire, and they had society. And about then she found an adjustment being made in her mind as the word *creatures* became the word *people*. These

beings weren't human, but they were *people*, she told herself; it's not *them,* they're *us.* (*The Amber Spyglass*, p. 123)

Mary Malone comes to the realization that being a *person* isn't a matter of being shaped in a particular way, or having a certain orientation to one's own immortal soul. Instead, it is the common capacity to engage in certain kinds of behaviors. Armored Bears, Mulefa, Witches, and Gallivespians all share these traits in common.

Consciousness and Dust

The existence of the mysterious *Dust* drives much of the storyline in *His Dark Materials*. The Magisterium is obsessed with preventing dust from settling. Lord Asriel is willing to murder his daughter's best friend to understand dust better. Dust makes possible the operation of the golden compass, the subtle knife, the amber spyglass, and Mary Malone's computer in her research lab. One of the most striking revelations in the series is that Dust (dark matter in Mary's universe) is *conscious.*

If Dust is conscious and acts with intention, then it is difficult to resist a similar conclusion to the one that Mary drew about the Mulefa. We may not want to use the word *person*, since the concept seems to imply the existence of a concrete individual. When something is conscious and can form intentions, it is, at the very least *morally relevant*.

Indeed, there is evidence in the trilogy for an even more radical conclusion—that matter *itself* is conscious. Mary realizes, "Matter *loved* Dust. It didn't want to see it go. That was the meaning of this night, and it was Mary's meaning too" (*The Amber Spyglass*, p. 452).

Will's father advises will that Will and Lyra cannot spend their lives searching for the Kingdom of Heaven elsewhere. Instead, they each must build the Kingdom of Heaven *where they are*. Part of doing this will involve abandoning drawing distinctions between beings and focusing instead on practicing universal and unceasing empathy and compassion. If everything is conscious, no other behavior is warranted.[1]

---

[1] All references to *His Dark Materials* come from the 2002 Knopf trade paperback collection.

13
Faith and Circumcision

WAYNE YUEN

The scene in *The Golden Compass* where Lyra finds herself about to become one of the test subjects for the silver guillotine, a device that would forever separate her and her dæmon, Pantalaimon, may be the most frightening passage in the book.

The fear of a child losing her beloved animal companion at the hands of a powerful authority is heart-wrenching. Yet Pantalaimon is more than just a pet, he is metaphorically and literally Lyra's soul, and the silver guillotine serves as an obvious metaphor for circumcision (as well as being a metaphor for the atomic bomb).

Parents who circumcise their children aren't typically blamed for their acts, yet Mrs. Coulter seems to be morally accountable for her actions. Are we inconsistently blaming Mrs. Coulter, are we inconsistently failing to chide parents who circumcise, or is there a relevant difference between the two cases?

This issue is rooted in a deeper problem, Mrs. Coulter's actions and the actions of parents circumcising their children are the results of their faith. Is it morally permissible to act on beliefs without any evidence? Circumcision is defined as the removal of the foreskin, a sheath of skin that covers the glans, on a penis. This is usually performed on infants for religious purposes, for hygienic purposes, or both. But are these reasons good enough to justify the removal of part of a person's body?

Wayne Yuen

The Case Against Circumcision

In terms of hygiene, a foreskin is not particularly dirty, but rather it can trap dirt and bacteria, against the head of the penis. The removal of the foreskin makes keeping the penis clean easier. However, keeping the penis clean is not particularly difficult with a foreskin, you simply need to pull back the foreskin and clean the glans and foreskin on a regular basis. Teaching children to have good hygiene is part of raising a child, and this is simply one more piece of information that needs to be passed along to boys who are uncircumcised. The alternative is to simply forego educating the child, and remove the foreskin altogether. This is a rather odd solution to the problem of hygiene, and would be akin to removing every other tooth of a child so one would not have to teach the child to floss.

A slightly more profound reason for circumcision is that it may help prevent HIV infection. Although the research is not conclusive, the leading theory is that the foreskin contains less keratin than normal skin cells, making it easier to be infected by HIV, as well as creating a pocket between the glans and the foreskin for the virus to exist in longer and increase the chance of infection. However, there are much more effective ways of combating HIV infection than circumcision, namely condoms and other barriers that block HIV from being transmitted not only to males, but to females as well. Educating children that it is not only for their own safety but also for the safety of their partner, whom they ideally love and respect, that they practice safe sex is far more effective as a strategy against HIV infection.

But even if this is the case, you might be tempted to circumcise your child simply to prevent the off-chance of HIV infection or bacterial infection. Yet the risk of complications with any medical procedure should be taken into account as well. In the US, complications that arise with circumcision may be as low as .02 percent or as high as two percent. The most common complication would be excessive bleeding and infection. Staph infections, which are not at all uncommon in hospitals, have been reported in some cases (see the article by Nguyen et al.). The off-chance that a child will suffer a bacterial infection is repetitiously replaced with the off-chance that a child will suffer a bacterial infection.

Lord Asriel makes a similar comment about the oddness of this solution, when he recalls the precedence of castration: "the church wouldn't flinch at the idea of a little cut, you see. There was a precedent. And this would be so much more hygienic than the old methods, when they didn't have anesthetics or sterile bandages or proper nursing care. It would be gentle by comparison" (*The Golden Compass*, p. 374).

It may be that circumcision has improved over the years, but that doesn't make it any more necessary for it to be done. The American Academy of Pediatrics published a statement in 1999, and reaffirmed it in 2005 stating, "Existing scientific evidence demonstrates potential medical benefits of newborn male circumcision; however, these data are not sufficient to recommend routine neonatal circumcision" (Task Force on Circumcision, pp. 686–693). Without potential medical benefits and a host of potential harms, circumcision could be properly described as mutilation, a procedure that destroys a part of the body with virtually no benefit.

Tony Costa, who was a victim of the guillotine, became essentially a zombie when he was separated from his dæmon. Shortly after Lyra finds him and returns to her camp, Tony dies, apparently from the procedure. In 1998, a Cleveland Ohio boy died when a surgery was performed on the child to repair damage caused to the boy's urethra after a botched circumcision. The boy had an adverse reaction to the anesthesia and never regained consciousness. Had the boy not had the circumcision, he would have not needed the subsequent surgery which cost him his life (*Iowa Law Review*, pp. 1507–568).

Perhaps the most problematic aspect of circumcision is that it is done without consent of the patient. Proxy parental consent is used in place of the patient's consent because in all cases involving infants and children, they may not be rational enough to decide what is best for themselves. Most infants and children would probably refuse immunizations and going to the dentist, on the grounds that they didn't like it. However, as parents we intervene and say that this is better for them in the long run, a small amount of pain now to prevent a great deal of potential future pain. With circumcision, there is no great deal of future pain that is being prevented, only possible pain that could be prevented in other ways.

Worse, there is the potential loss of future pleasure as fore-skin contains many specialized nerve endings called stretch receptors that respond to being stretched, rolled, and pulled, the kinds of stimuli that sexual intercourse provides.

Believing in the Guillotine

However, it isn't for any of these reasons that Mrs. Coulter is cutting children with the silver guillotine. She's cutting them because she believes that the dust that settles and that prevents a person's dæmon from changing forms is original sin. If they can prevent that, by separating a person from their dæmon, then they could avoid original sin. For the most part, it is a religious belief that drives Mrs. Coulter and many others to cut. Many people also do it out of sheer tra-dition, but doing something because we've done it in the past is fallacious reasoning. Public executions, slavery, and drowning witches were done in the past as well, but this pro-vides little justification for us to do these things today.

Now in the course of the novels we learn that the dust is in fact not original sin, but let us place ourselves in Mrs. Coulter's position and suspend our knowledge of this. Is what Mrs. Coulter's doing reasonable? This is a much more interesting question, because it mirrors the question that re-ligious parents find themselves in today. In the Jewish tra-dition, circumcision is a covenant with God. Christian tradition grew out of the Jewish tradition, but there is no cir-cumcision requirement in the Bible for Christians. *Galatians* 5:6 states: "For in Christ Jesus neither circumcision nor un-circumcision carries any weight—the only thing that mat-ters is faith working through love."

According to the Jewish bible, known to Christians as the Old Testament, God promised the Jews:

"I will make you extremely fruitful. I will make nations of you, and kings will descend from you. I will confirm my covenant as a per-petual covenant between me and you. It will extend to your de-scendants after you throughout their generations. I will be your God and the God of your descendants after you. I will give the whole land of Canaan—the land where you are now residing—to you and your descendants after you as a permanent possession.

I will be their God." Then God said to Abraham, "As for you, you must keep the covenantal requirement I am imposing on you and your descendants after you throughout their generations. This is my requirement that you and your descendants after you must keep: Every male among you must be circumcised." (Genesis 17:6–10)

So whereas Mrs. Coulter is doing it to prevent sin, Jewish orthodoxy does it as a bargain with God for his favor. These are both very good goals to achieve, assuming a religious framework. An atheist would have very little justification for circumcising their children. But I would assume that even atheists would want to avoid sin, if they could do so.

How do we determine the reasonableness of such beliefs? One possibility is that we need not determine the reasonableness of the belief at all, but rather simply hold it in good faith that the belief is true. However, there are serious problems with holding beliefs based on faith alone, especially beliefs that affect others, like circumcision, or severing a person's connection with their dæmon.

William Kingdom Clifford in his essay titled "The Ethics of Belief" puts forth the following thought experiment: Imagine that you're an owner of a ship that is about to sail to the New World. You have some doubts about the seaworthiness of the ship, but you form a belief on faith that the ship will make it unharmed. The ship sets sail and sinks; everyone dies. It seems that the belief was an irresponsible belief. Even if the ship had made it across the ocean safely, the ship owner would have acted in an irresponsible manner. Clifford concludes: "It is wrong always, everywhere and for everyone to believe anything upon insufficient evidence." Instead what we must do is investigate our beliefs so that we can come upon sufficient evidence for accepting or rejecting our belief.

Investigation is precisely what Mrs. Coulter is attempting to do. She is investigating her belief about the connection between dust and original sin through experimentation. Severing the link between child and dæmon, and observing what happens to them, Mrs. Coulter hopes that she can learn to sever the link correctly, freeing people from sin and not turning them into zombies at the same time. It is the methodology of her investigation, the utilization of non-consensual persons, that one can find moral fault in, not her desire to learn the truth about Dust, or testing her hypothesis that it is original sin. Experimenting on children is fraught with moral problems, not the least of which is attempting to obtain informed rational consent from an agent who is not fully rational. In *The Golden Compass*, the children are kidnapped and experimented on against their will, compounding the wrongness of the scenario.

But let's imagine that Mrs. Coulter recruited willing volunteers and conducted the investigation morally. Let's further imagine that the guillotine is perfected so that children no longer become zombies after the procedure. In such a case, the arguments against circumcision seem minor, because the cut overwhelmingly works in the child's best interest, consequently it would be morally acceptable. Could there be other benefits that would make circumcision morally acceptable?

We've been thinking about male circumcision, since it is the most common. However, there is the equivalent procedure for females, clitoral circumcision. This should not be confused with female genital mutilation, which has had much media exposure in recent years. Clitoral circumcision is the more analogous procedure for women since it only removes the clitoral hood and not the clitoris itself or other parts of female genitalia like the labia in female genital mutilation. In America, clitoral circumcision was encouraged by physicians from the late nineteenth century up through the 1970s as a treatment for women who were unable to achieve orgasm through vaginal intercourse alone. Ten percent of women found that they were able to achieve orgasm more easily after clitoral circumcision. This may be a small percentage, but the number of women who would benefit from the procedure may be significantly higher due to the relatively low population of women who were actually circumcised in America, coupled with the cultural taboos surrounding sex, especially female sexuality, which would reduce the number of people who would seek medical treatment for sexual dysfunction.

For an act to be "mutilation," it would need to damage or destroy a part of the body in such a way that there would be no intended benefits of the damage. We normally wouldn't call amputation of a limb to save someone's life mutilation, but we would call cutting off a perfectly good foot for no particular benefit mutilation. So quite contrary to the popular notions of circumcision, male circumcision may be closer to a kind of mutilation, whereas female circumcision would not be mutilation at all, since there could be some demonstrable benefit. Likewise, in the trilogy, there is at least one other demonstrable benefit besides preserving the purity of the soul. Lyra has something akin to having the connection between Pantalaimon and herself severed (more specifically stretched) so that she could leave him behind uninjured in her journey through the land of the dead where Pantalaimon could not survive. However, both female circumcision cases and the stretching case of witches and shamans in the novels, are undertaken with informed consent, typically by adults.

If male circumcision were to mirror female circumcision more closely, where males would not be circumcised unless there was a demonstrable benefit and under the direction of the person being circumcised, then there would be little to fret about. One would simply need to ask them if they are happy with their foreskin. If they were, then they could continue to keep it. If they were not, they could be circumcised. However, those who have already been circumcised and are not happy about this cannot have their foreskins restored. (There are surgical foreskin "restoration" techniques and other techniques involving stretching existing skin, however none actually restore foreskin.) Additionally, the potential medical benefits of circumcision, could be acquired in the future before the man becomes sexually active and is in much better position to give his informed consent.

There's one more possibility that we must consider: We might have no control over our beliefs. David Hume argues that beliefs are nothing more than strong feelings that we have. Neither reason nor will would determine what we believe. I could not will myself to believe that an ordinary compass was actually an alethiometer. We might imagine that it's the case, but imagining something and truly believing something are very different things.

Most people have had the experience of trying to convince someone that something is correct, an attempt to change a belief. This is usually futile, until something, such as persuasive evidence or experience, is produced. Some kind of outside force, like encountering an actual panserbjørne, would be needed to change the belief that there are no panserbjørnes. But with our beliefs about the soul, there can be no evidence of this sort to radically change a person's beliefs. If this is the case, then Clifford's thesis that one is irresponsible in holding uninvestigated beliefs is incorrect, since we can only hold people responsible for things that they have genuine control over. It wouldn't make sense to chide someone morally for an accident and under this analysis all beliefs are accidental.

To judge people based on the beliefs they hold is problematic in another sense, in that there is no way for me to genuinely determine the kinds of beliefs you hold. I may be able to evaluate your actions but, as the saying goes, there is no thought police. It would be reasonable then, not to try to morally evaluate an agent's beliefs, but rather limit our judgment to actions.

Where's an Alethiometer when You Need One?

So how are we to judge the spiritual nature of the oblation that is circumcision? Lyra and Mrs. Coulter happen to be fortunate enough to meet with the divine beings themselves to find many of the fundamental answers that we can't. Ultimately, we can say that Mrs. Coulter is incorrect in her beliefs about Dust. Since we cannot really investigate the spiritual implications of a circumcision, then either we have to take it on faith that it is spiritually beneficial, or we reject it in favor of what we can investigate, the physical effects of circumcision. On this point, reasonable people can disagree about this particular issue with no real resolution.

Without an alethiometer, everybody is an equal authority on the care for our souls. Clifford's guidance here is clear, if we want to be fully responsible, we should reasonably suspend judgment on the spiritual implications of circumcision, since they lie beyond the possibility of knowledge. Note that this is not the same as denying the truth of the spiritual implications.

However, there's a relevant difference between circumcision and intercision, which is the likelihood and severity of harm. While there are many possible harms that may occur from circumcision, even death, the likelihood of these occurring is relatively small. Chances are circumcision will not adversely affect a child's life. Where circumcision may be a kind of physical mutilation of a relatively benign part of the body, intercision is a mutilation of the soul. Lyra has just cause to be suspicious of Mrs. Coulter, because the decisions she was making, although well-intentioned, were threatening Lyra's soul. On the matters that we can investigate, the stakes are much higher in *The Golden Compass* than in our world.

Similarly, since there is much less at stake in the case of circumcision, we should not judge it as severely irresponsible as Mrs. Coulter's actions in *The Golden Compass*. At worst, it's as irresponsible as exposing your child to chicken pox. Many people expose their children to chicken pox for the benefit of the child, which will assuredly lead to an amount of physical discomfort, and holds risks of more severe long-term complications and even death. There is also a reasonable alternative in a vaccination which is eighty-five percent effective, although this is not without debate either, but that is outside the scope of this paper.

The difference in severity does not mean that the two cases fall into different categories of moral evaluation, that is one being right and the other being wrong. The difference between a serial killer and a murderer is severity, but both are wrong. Yet some acts that are morally wrong but not severely wrong should be treated differently from acts that are severely wrong. It may be wrong to lie to someone, but judging someone to be morally corrupt over an inconsequential lie, like lying about one's weight or what their favorite color is, would be inappropriate. But the conclusion is hard to deny, if we think it's wrong to intercise Pantalaimon from Lyra, then for similar reasons, we should think it wrong to circumcise foreskins from their owners.

14
Does an Alethiometer Really Measure Truth?

Tomas Elliott

> And the Serpent said unto the woman, Ye shall not surely die: For God doth know that in the day ye eat thereof, then your eyes shall be opened, and your dæmons shall assume their true forms, and ye shall be as gods, knowing good and evil.
>
> —*Northern Lights*, p. 372

"So: what's Dust? And why's everyone so afraid of it?" (*Northern Lights*, p. 370).

This is among the questions that Lyra fires at Lord Asriel when she finally reaches his prison-home on Svalbard. As readers, we relish the challenge she poses him: we, like her, want answers; we also, like her, believe we've "got the right to know" (p. 369). It has, after all, taken Lyra almost two thousand miles and us almost four hundred pages to get here. It's time we knew the truth.

This desire for truth is at the heart of *His Dark Materials*. If the witches prophesy that Lyra's name is Eve, then it is because both their stories are about the acquisition of knowledge. Lyra's quest, however, severs the connection that Judaism and Christianity have made between knowing and sinning. At the same time, that quest also brings into question an idea shared by western religions, western philosophy and even western science: namely that truth and knowledge, in and of and for themselves, are of necessarily high value.

In Christianity, truth has tended to be synonymous with God; in Western science and philosophy, truth has often meant knowledge of the world and of the self. In all three, truth has primarily been thought of as good, even if in theological terms, it has been considered evil for us to try and access that truth, since that would betray our desire, which we share with Adam and Eve, to "be as gods."

What Lyra's story makes clear is that, in their search for truth, these various institutions of science, philosophy and religion have claimed that their version of truth is universal, when actually it's only partial, limited by a specific set of cultural and historical values. These institutions have tried to dictate the meaning of truth to all peoples in all places and at all times. According to the philosopher Jacques Derrida, this has constituted nothing more or less than "the most original and powerful ethnocentrism" of the West (p. 3).

By this, Derrida means that Western thought has always posited its own understanding of truth as superior to a range of other, alternative understandings. In turn, the West has variously denounced those other understandings as barbaric, childlike, savage, or worse. In my opinion, it's no accident that those are all adjectives that are applied to Lyra herself: she is a "thoughtless child," a "barbarian," "a coarse and greedy little savage" (*Northern Lights*, pp. 33, 35, 37).

To take another term that Western theology has often applied to others, and that summarises the Magisterium's fears about Lyra, we should say that Lyra is, in every sense of the word, a heretic. From Greek *hairetikos*, meaning somebody capable of choosing, Lyra is the one who has to "make a choice" about what she herself thinks regarding the nature of good and evil and the meaning of Dust. It is in this act of choosing that Lyra rewrites the tragedy of Eve's original sin, her choice to take the apple, as a story of salvation. Lyra sets truth free from the stranglehold placed on it by the institutions of religion, science, and philosophy within which, over many centuries and across multiple universes, it has ossified into doctrine.

The Fall into Knowledge

This is clear even from the very first scene of *Northern Lights*, which begins within the imposing stone walls of Jordan College, a center where knowledge is housed. In fact, it begins in that establishment's most exclusive, inner sanctuary: the Retiring Room, a place which "only Scholars and their guests" are allowed to enter, "and never females" (p. 4); that is, a place where truth is guarded.

Lyra, innocently, displaying the natural curiosity of a young child, steps across the threshold of this space, and in so doing, enters into understanding. She learns about things she was never supposed to learn: Dust, the Aurora, the Master's attempted murder of Lord Asriel. Like Eve in the garden of Eden, Lyra in the Retiring Room commits a transgression: she enters a forbidden space and attains forbidden knowledge. What she does not realize at this point, but will do by the trilogy's end, is that while she had always been told that the limits placed on her access to knowledge had been for her own benefit (that the policing of truth, much like the policing of the entrance to the Retiring Room itself, was right and proper and good), in fact those limits had only ever been placed there in service of the interests of power.

In *Northern Lights*, this culminates in a re-evaluation, provided by Pantalaimon, of everything he and Lyra had thought they knew about Dust. In the moments following Lord Asriel's severing of Roger from his dæmon (an act that is half scientific experiment, half religious sacrifice in the style of Abraham and Isaac), Pantalaimon offers Lyra a new hypothesis to replace the so-called truths that they had always been taught:

> "If they all think Dust is bad, it must be good . . . We've heard them all talk about Dust, and they're so afraid of it, and you know what? We believed them, even though we could see what they were doing was wicked and evil and wrong . . . We thought Dust must be bad too, because they were grown-up and they said so. But what if it isn't? What if it's—"
>
> She said breathlessly, "Yeah! What if it's really *good . . . ?*" (pp. 397–98)

This moment is a celebration of new understanding. A young woman and her dæmon hesitate on the edge of a previously undiscovered country of truth. Importantly, just as this truth does not take the form of a religious revelation, neither is it a kind of scientific discovery: Lyra doesn't care whether Rusakov particles prove the existence of Dust; she cares about the consequences of that discovery for her friend, Roger. Lord Asriel, on the other hand, is emblematic of the quest for scientific knowledge for its own sake, a knowledge that he seeks to wield as power. He wants to understand the natural world in order to control it (think of Lyra's revelation when she witnesses him connect his apparatus to the Aurora: "he was *controlling* it . . . or leading power down from it" (p. 392). Lord Asriel uses scientific truth to tear the very fabric of the universe apart, regardless of whether a child has to die in service of his aims. This is the dream he tries to sell to Mrs Coulter: "You and I could take the universe to pieces and put it together again, Marisa!" (p. 396).

In contrast to this urge for knowledge as power, however, the knowledge that Lyra and Pantalaimon gain is moral. They acquire an ethical understanding that supersedes the search for scientific or religious truth. Having witnessed both science and religion being put to use to justify the severing of children from their dæmons in Bolvangar, and now having seen Lord Asriel cast Roger's life aside in order to construct his bridge to the stars, Lyra and Pantalaimon learn to mistrust these so-called authorities and to think for themselves. In a sense, Lyra's journey in *Northern Lights* teaches her and Pantalaimon that neither Lord Asriel's science nor Mrs. Coulter's religion will be enough to save them.

Incidentally, Lyra's journey also recapitulates that of Mary Malone, who describes her relationship to science and religion in precisely similar terms. Mary notes that, when she was a nun, she was told what she should think about the nature of good and evil. In her words, it was "whatever the church taught me to think" (*The Amber Spyglass*, p. 470). As a scientist, she then remarks, she "had to think about other things altogether," so she didn't need to worry about morality (p. 470). Mary's journey is one of realizing that she has to continue to think about good and evil even as a scientist, which leads her to a perpetual questioning of authority: she stops believing that there is "a power of good and a power of evil" that exist "outside us," and she comes "to believe that good and evil are names for what people do" (pp. 470–71).

This is a transformation from an understanding of moral truth as either pre-ordained (in broad terms, as it is for western religions), or as irrelevant (in broad terms, as it is for western science), towards an understanding of morality as a constant process of figuring out truths that can only ever be partial and dependent on context. In Mary's terms: "All we can say is that this is a good deed, because it helps someone, or that's an evil one, because it hurts them. People are too complicated to have simple labels." To this statement, Lyra simply replies with a firm "Yes" (p. 471). Just like Mary, Lyra also forsakes all faith in the doctrines of science and religion and undertakes her own journey in search of truth.

It's fitting that Lyra's guide for this journey should be an alethiometer: a "symbol reader," as Farder Coram explains, "from *aletheia*, which means truth . . . a truth-measure" (*Northern Lights*, p. 126). The alethiometer poses a powerful threat to the church's hold on truth, but it also challenges the authority of Western science. It does this in two ways. First, it democratizes knowledge. With the alethiometer, Lyra can learn on her own. She has no need of a teacher. She doesn't even need the books of learning. Second, and perhaps even more importantly, in terms of its technological design, the alethiometer undermines the reliance in western theology and philosophy on a connection between truth and the spoken word. The alethiometer provides access to knowledge, but it does not do so through words; it does so through symbols. This is significant, as we shall see, as it untethers truth from its reliance on what is known as *mimesis*, a Greek word meaning simply representation or copying (it has the same root as words like "mimicry" and "miming"). The alethiometer offers a non-mimetic path to truth.

This makes it a radical object. To understand just how radical, we can turn to the work of Jacques Derrida, whose project, in some ways, is reflected in Lyra's own. Derrida strove to untangle knowledge and truth from the powerful institutions that guarded them. He took aim at religious authorities, universities, scientists, even his own philosophical project. As Michael Payne points out, Derrida viewed the quest for truth as a highly ethical task. Moreover, he specifically challenged the relationship between truth, mimesis, and the word. Derrida's quest, in its scope and ambition, rivalled that of Will and Lyra, who take on perhaps the most fiercely guarded site of truth in western history: "the throne and monarchy of God" (*Paradise Lost*, Book I, line 42).

Tomas Elliott

The Symbol Reader

Why is it important that Lyra can read the alethiometer alone? To answer this, we have to understand the alethiometer's place in a history of science and philosophy that crosses between her world and ours. In *Northern Lights*, we learn that the alethiometer was invented in the early seventeenth century (p. 173). Originally a kind of astrological compass, it was designed as an early mechanism for measuring the planets. It was soon discovered, however, that its needle responded to something else: consciousness, comprised of elementary particles, or Dust. The alethiometer offered knowledge or truth, but a truth that could only be understood if you learned to read the symbols on its dial and interpret their potentially limitless meanings.

The six alethiometers that were made were almost immediately outlawed and seized by the Magisterium as objects of occult divination. From another perspective, though, we could say that they were seized because they threatened to introduce a revolution in scientific thought. In terms of the history of empiricist science (the science of observation and experiment), the development of the alethiometer is structurally similar to the creation of the telescope and the microscope in our world, both of which were also developed in the early seventeenth century. Like the alethiometer, those new technologies launched new ways of seeing the world and, accordingly, new modes of understanding.

Along with these new technologies came a slew of new ideas. One of the most radical of these ran as follows: if individuals (assuming they had access to telescopes) could now get a close-up view of the stars all by themselves, then, in a quite literal way, they no longer needed priests to describe the heavens to them. The telescope, therefore, was in many ways a symbol of self-reliance. Like the alethiometer, it democratized knowledge. It built knowledge from the ground up, rather than delivering it from the top down. With both the alethiometer and the telescope, it is the investigator who counts, the person willing, as Lyra does time and time again, to "frame the question".

From a philosophical perspective, this is what Jacques Derrida and many other philosophers have referred to as the hallmark of "the great rationalisms of the seventeenth century," all of which involved an insistence on the importance of subjectivity and self-hood in the generation of knowledge (*Of Grammatology*, p. 17). Nowhere is this new emphasis better encapsulated than in the philosophy of René Descartes, who in his 1637 book, *Discourse on Method*, claimed that the individual required only themselves alone in order to generate proof of their existence. As he put it in his famous phrase: "*I* think, therefore *I* am" (Part 4, paragraph 1).

On one level, this phrase suggests a profound break with religious authority. In the wake of this statement, commonly referred to as Descartes' *cogito* (Latin for "I think"), the philosopher is able to claim that they have knowledge of themselves not because God has told them they exist, but simply because they themselves know that they are thinking. Derrida defines this as the process by which, in the seventeenth century, "the determination of presence is constituted as self-presence" (p. 17). By this, Derrida simply means that with Descartes, the idea of *being present* somewhere (which could be redefined as just knowing that you're alive) is transformed into *being present to oneself*. In other words: you don't need anyone else, least of all God, to tell you that you exist.

For Derrida, however, it is this emphasis on the idea of *presence* that demonstrates that there is actually more of a continuity than a break between Descartes and the theological and philosophical thinkers who had preceded him. Presence, Derrida claims, has been one of the most highly valued ideas in western culture. In Judaeo-Christian theology, for example, presence meant being close to God. In western philosophy, the meaning of presence has taken many forms, but it has always been valued more highly than whatever is conceived as its opposite. One example of this is the idea that an original thing is always more present and more real than a copy or a representation of that thing, the most famous account of which is found in Plato's *Republic*.

In this book, the philosopher Socrates claims that every object that exists in the world is merely a representation of a more perfect, ideal form of that object. Specifically, Plato claims that such representations are simply "imitations," an English term that translates his Greek word, "*mimesis*"

(597b–e). For Plato, an imitation is "far removed from the truth," much farther removed than the thing it imitates (598c).

Related to this idea that the original is "truer" and "better" than the copy is the idea that speech is "truer" and "better" than writing. This is because, in some sense, the written word can be thought of as simply a representation or copy of speech. Speech, it is assumed, is purer, more immediate, more present than writing, whereas writing is merely a "secondary and instrumental function: the translator of a full and fully *present* speech" (p. 8).

In the Beginning Was the Word

Derrida charts an entire philosophical history in which speech is posited as primary to writing. He extends his argument back not only to Plato, but also to Aristotle, for whom writing is a secondary mediator of an already mediating speech. Derrida points to Aristotle's claim that "spoken words are the symbols of mental experience and written words are the symbols of spoken words" (*On Interpretation*, I, 16a3). Writing, therefore, is doubly late to the party: people had thoughts, then they learned to speak their thoughts out loud, then finally they learnt to write those thoughts down. In this way, Derrida argues, Aristotle, like Plato, "debases writing considered as mediation of mediation" (p. 13). Furthermore, ranging over more than two thousand years of philosophical thought, Derrida notes that this idea is equally prevalent in the work of more recent philosophers, such as that of the eighteenth-century author Jean-Jacques Rousseau, who claimed that "writing is only the representation of speech" (p. 29).

For all of Plato, Aristotle and Rousseau, then, writing is simply a form of copying, a representation that spoils pure and present speech. To get to the truth, these authors seem to imply, we simply need to strip away these layers of mediation to achieve a truer and more perfect form of *mimesis*.

This prejudice for speech over writing is even contained in the Greek word for "word" itself: *logos*. More specifically than "word," *logos* means "spoken word" or "speech." It is derived from the Greek verb *legein*, meaning "to speak" or "tell."

At the same time, though, it can also mean "reason" and "understanding," and refers to whatever is able to be known. In Greek philosophy, therefore, speaking and knowing are intimately connected to one another: if you know something, you should be able to say what it is. This idea is also taken up in Christianity, where it gets expressed in the opening line of John's Gospel, which reads: "In the beginning was the word, and the word was with God, and the word was God" (John 1:1). The Greek version of the last part of this sentence claims that God, *theos*, is "rational truth," but also "speech," or "word": *theos* is *logos*.

Derrida argues that this connection between speech, reason, understanding, God and truth has gone on to underwrite a prejudice that has informed a range of writers in the western philosophical and theological traditions. It is perhaps best embodied in the work of Georg Wilhelm Friedrich Hegel. Hegel agreed with both Aristotle's and Plato's view that writing is a copy of speech, but he differed from them by distinguishing between different forms of writing.

Hegel argued that, while writing is always a copy, the western form of writing (what Hegel calls "alphabetic script") is nonetheless better than other forms of writing because it is closer in its method of representation to the patterns of speech themselves. This is because most western forms of writing are phonetic; they attempt to replicate the way in which a word sounds when it is spoken. By contrast, Hegel argued that other non-phonetic forms of writing, such as Egyptian hieroglyphs or Chinese characters, were worse than western forms (more backwards, savage, or childish) because they did not and do not endeavour to represent speech at all; they are non-mimetic, non-imitative.

This leads Hegel to claim (and it is this that makes the ethnocentrism or racism of his idea clear) that "alphabetic script is in itself and for itself the most intelligent" form of writing (*Of Grammatology*, p. 3). For Hegel, western writing was more godly than non-western writing because, in replicating the sounds of speech, it remained closer to the ideas of "god" and *logos*.

Jacques Derrida refers to this idea as the "logocentrism" of western philosophy, which simply means the tendency to privilege the idea of the *logos* as the highest form of reason or understanding. Importantly, Derrida argues, this "logo-centrism" is actually a kind of "phonocentrism;" it is simply a way of claiming that western writing is somehow more advanced or "more intelligent" than other forms (p. 3). In other words, the western idea of reason and understanding (*logos*) has always depended on privileging phonetic writing over non-phonetic writing. Therefore, Derrida argues, truth as *logos* is simply a mechanism for preserving the belief system and the power base of the West. Non-phonetic, non-representative, non-mimetic forms of writing have accordingly always been denigrated in order to shore up the authority of western philosophies, cultures and religions.

The Measure of Truth

The alethiometer, however, challenges this authority. It provides access to truth and understanding through symbols, and in so doing deprivileges the western emphasis on the phonetic word as a mechanism for representing pure and present speech.

One of the most in-depth descriptions of this method occurs in Lyra's meeting with Dr. Lanselius, the Witch-Consul at Trollesund. Dr. Lanselius asks Lyra a question: what are the intentions of the Tartars with regards to Kamchatka? To find out, Lyra turns the alethiometer's hands to "the camel, which meant Asia, which meant Tartars; to the cornucopia, for Kamchatka, where there were gold mines; and to the ant, which meant activity, which meant purpose and intention." In response, the needle of the alethiometer swings to "the dolphin, the helmet, the baby and the anchor" (*Northern Lights*, p. 174). Lyra interprets this as meaning that the Tartars are going to "pretend to attack" Kamchatka, but that they won't actually go through with it. When asked for an explanation of this interpretation, Lyra says:

> The dolphin, one of its deep-down meanings is playing, sort of like being playful . . . And the helmet means war, and both together they mean pretend to go to war but not be serious. And the baby means—it means difficult—it'd be too hard for them to attack it, and the anchor says why, because they'd be stretched out as tight as an anchor rope. (*Northern Lights*, pp. 174–75)

Immediately, we can see that this process largely undermines the idea of truth as *mimesis* or representation: the camel does not stand for Tartars because Tartars look like camels. Rather, the alethiometer's relationship to truth is one of association. Its meanings are metaphorical, metonymic, even literary: helmets are used for war, so war is one of the meanings of the helmet; war does not resemble, copy, look or even sound like a helmet.

To be clear, however, the alethiometer is not a radical instrument simply because it relies on symbols. Non-phonetic forms of writing are not inherently more freeing than phonetic forms of writing. The point about the alethiometer is that it does not define in advance the relationship between truth and the medium of expression in which that truth takes shape. It requires constant reflection on the part of the questioner. In a sense, reading the alethiometer is a constant process of *choosing* how to define its symbols, of striving towards truth. It requires the application of an active interpreter.

It is, in this sense, somewhat characteristic of an approach to truth that Derrida, among others, has highlighted as contrasting with the idea of truth as *mimesis*. This, fittingly, is truth understood as *aletheia*. As mentioned, this is where the alethiometer gets its name, but while Farder Coram is right that *aletheia* means "truth," it means truth only in a specific sense. It is derived from the Greek prefix *a-*, meaning "not" or "un-," and *lethe*, meaning forgetfulness and oblivion: *a* + *lethe* means "unforgetting." Furthermore, *lethe* also has connotations of death, since in Greek cosmology, all those who travelled to the underworld had to pass through the river Lethe, the river of forgetfulness. The unconcealing of truth, therefore, would mean the process of coming back from Lethe, of remembering something that had seemed to pass into oblivion. When truth is understood as *aletheia*, truthfulness becomes less a measure of how closely a copy replicates an original, or of how closely (western, phonetic) writing approximates speech, reason, presence and God. Rather, *aletheia* is truth as a perpetual quest to remember what you didn't even know you had forgotten, to unravel what, in a sense, you had always just assumed to be true.

This ultimately brings us closer to an understanding of how the alethiometer works as a guide for Lyra in her search for truth. Lyra, of course, undertakes a literal journey into and out of the underworld; she crosses the river Lethe and saves the dead from the prison in which they languish, forgotten by the world. Perhaps we can understand this voyage as a quest for truth as much as a quest for freedom. Put more strongly, perhaps we can understand it as a quest for the very freedom of truth itself.

With the alethiometer, Lyra saves the dead from the so-called authorities who have sought to define the meaning of truth. She saves Roger, the emblem of this neglected dead, a helpless victim sacrificed by science and abandoned by religion. Therefore, insofar as the alethiometer is a "truth-measure," it is one that allows Lyra not merely to ascend to a truth already laid out for her by others, but rather to undergo truth as a perilous fight for freedom.

The alethiometer doesn't offer us complete and timeless understanding of truth, and it certainly doesn't insist on the western, mimetic model of rational truth, understood as *logos*. Rather, it is a constant reminder of the need to challenge whosoever tries to lay claim to truth in the service of a quest for power.

Bibliography

American Academy of Pediatrics. 1999. Circumcision Policy Statement. *Pediatrics* 103:3 (March).

Aristotle. 1991. *History of Animals: Books 7–10*. Harvard University Press.

———. 2001. On Interpretation. In McKeon 2001.

Bassham, Gregory, and Jerry L. Walls, eds. 2005. *The Chronicles of Narnia and Philosophy: The Lion, the Witch, and the Worldview*. Open Court.

BBC Radio Four. Seagull Urban Myths: Fact or Fiction? <www.bbc.co.uk/programmes/articles/15TM4CDpDGHSq08n WHF3h89/seagull-urban-myths-fact-or-fiction>.

Beauvoir, Simone de. 2011 [1949]. *The Second Sex*. Vintage.

Birks, Johnny. 2017. *Pine Martens*. Whittet.

Cavendish, Margaret. 1994 [1666]. *The Blazing World and Other Writings*. Penguin.

———. 2016 [1666]. *A Description of a New World Called the Blazing-World*. Project Gutenberg <http://www.gutenberg.org/files/51783/51783-h/51783-h.htm>.

———. 2001. *Observations Upon Experimental Philosophy*. Cambridge University Press.

Charlesworth, J.H., ed. 1983. *The Old Testament Pseudepigrapha*. Two volumes. Doubleday.

Clifford, William Kingdom. 1999. *The Ethics of Belief and Other Essays*. Prometheus.

Dennett, Daniel. 1992. The Self as a Narrative Centre of Gravity. In Kessel, Cole, and Johnson 1992.

Derrida, Jacques. 2016. *Of Grammatology*. John Hopkins University Press.

Bibliography

Descartes, René. 1998. *Discourse on Method*. Hackett.
Durante, Chris. 2013. A Philosophical Identity Crisis. *Philosophy Now* 97.
Epicurus. 2019. *The Philosophy of Epicurus*. Dover.
Falconer, Rachel. 2009. *The Crossover Novel: Contemporary Children's Fiction and Its Adult Readership*. Routledge.
Farmer, S.D. 2004. *Power Animals*. Hay House.
Freitas, Donna. 2007. God in the Dust: What Catholics Attacking 'The Golden Compass' Are Really Afraid Of. *Boston Globe* (25th November).
Frost, Laurie. 2019. *The Definitive Guide to Philip Pullman's His Dark Materials*. Scholastic.
Gallagher, Shaun, ed. 2011. *The Oxford Handbook of the Self*. Oxford University Press.
Giannelli, Matthew R. 2000. Circumcision and the American Academy of Pediatrics: Should Scientific Misconduct Result in Trade Association Liability? *Iowa Law Review* 85:4 (May).
Giles, J. 1993. The No-Self Theory: Hume, Buddhism, and Personal Identity. *Philosophy East and West* 43:2 (April).
Greene, Richard, and Rachel Robison-Greene. 2009. *The Golden Compass and Philosophy: God Bites the Dust*. Open Court.
Kessel, F.S., P.M. Cole, and D.L. Johnson, eds. 1992. *Self and Consciousness: Multiple Perspectives*. Lawrence Erlbaum.
Kierkegaard, Søren 1946. *A Kierkegaard Anthology*. Random House.
Lund-Molfese, Nicholas C. 2003. What Is Mutilation? *The American Journal of Bioethics* 3.2.
Lewis, David K. 2001 [1986]. *On the Plurality of Worlds*. Wiley-Blackwell.
McCarthy, J. 2007. *Dennett and Ricoeur on the Narrative Self*. Prometheus.
McKeon, Richard, ed. 2001. *The Basic Works of Aristotle*. Modern Library.
Meacham, Steve. 2003. The Shed Where God Died. *Sydney Morning Herald Online* (13th December).
Milton, John. *Paradise Lost*. Edited by Alastair Fowler. Pearson Longman, 2007.
Nguyen, D.M., Elizabeth Bancroft, Laurene Mascola, and Ramon Guevara. 2007. Risk Factors for Neonatal Methicillinresistant Staphylococcus Aureus Infection in a Well-Infant Nursery. *Infection Control and Hospital Epidemiology* 28:4 (April).
Nietzsche, Friedrich. 1977. *The Portable Nietzsche*. Penguin.
———. 2008. *Beyond Good and Evil: Prelude to a Philosophy of the Future*. Oxford University Press.
O'Brien, Flann. 1968. *The Third Policeman*. Dalkey.
Palmer, J. 2001. *Animal Wisdom: The Definitive Guide to Myth, Folklore, and Medicine Power of Animals*. Thorsons.

Parsons, Wendy, and Catriona Nicholson. 1999. Talking to Philip Pullman: An Interview. *The Lion and the Unicorn* 23:1.

Payne, Michael. 1993. *Reading Theory: An Introduction to Lacan, Derrida, and Kristeva*. Blackwell.

Peirce, Charles Sanders. 1955. *Philosophical Writings of Peirce*. Dover.

Pellauer, David, and Bernard Dauenhauer. 2016. Paul Ricoeur. In *The Stanford Encyclopedia of Philosophy* <https://plato.stanford.edu/archives/win2016/entries/ricoeur>.

Plato. 1992. *Republic*. Hackett.

Pullman, Philip. 1995. *Northern Lights*. Scholastic.

———. 1996. *The Golden Compass*, Knopf.

———. *The Subtle Knife*. Scholastic, 1997.

———. 1997. *The Subtle Knife*. Knopf.

———. 2000. *The Amber Spyglass*. Knopf.

———. 2002. Writing Fantasy Realistically. Address to Sea of Faith Annual Conference <https://www.sofn.org.uk/conferences/pullman2002.html>.

———. 2003. *Lyra's Oxford*. Knopf.

———. 2008. *Once Upon a Time in the North*. Knopf.

———. 2010. *The Good Man Jesus and the Scoundrel Christ*. Canongate.

———. 2017. *La Belle Sauvage*. Knopf.

———. 2018. *Daemon Voices: On Stories and Storytelling*. Knopf.

———. 2019. *The Secret Commonwealth*. Penguin.

———. 2019. *The Secret Commonwealth*. Knopf.

Regan, Tom, and Peter Singer, eds. 1989 [1976]. *Animal Rights and Human Obligations*. Prentice Hall.

Ricoeur, Paul. 1984–88 [1983]. *Time and Narrative*. Three volumes. University of Chicago Press.

———. 2016. *Hermeneutics and the Human Sciences: Essays on Language, Action, and Interpretation*. Cambridge University Press.

Rudd, A. 2009. In Defence of Narrative. *European Journal of Philosophy* 17:1.

Schechtman, Marya. 2011. The Narrative Self. In Gallagher 2011.

Simek, Rudolf. 1993 [1984]. *Dictionary of Northern Mythology*. D.S. Brewer.

Singer, Peter. 1974. All Animals are Equal. *Philosophic Exchange* 5:1. Reprinted in Regan and Singer 1989.

Snow Leopard Network. Snow Leopard Toolkit: The Tributary Fund <www.snowleopardnetwork.org/GrantFinalReports/Higginsfinal12.pdf>.

Thornsson, O., ed. 2005. *The Sagas of Icelanders*. Penguin.

Bibliography

Traviss, K. 2005. I Got to Get Me One of Those: Why Daemons Might Make the World a Better Place. In Yeffeth 2005.

Vere, Pete, and Sandra Miesel. 2008. *Pied Piper of Atheism: Philip Pullman and Children's Fantasy*. Ignatius.

Warne, S.P. 2002. Primates Face to Face: Conservation Implications of Human-Nonhuman Primate Interconnections. *Anthrozoös* 15:2.

Webber, Sara, and Toby L. Schonfeld. 2003. Cutting History, Cutting Culture: Female Circumcision in the United States. *American Journal of Bioethics* 3.2.

Yeffeth, Glenn, ed. 2005. *Navigating The Golden Compass: Religion, Science, and Daemonology in Philip Pullman's His Dark Materials*. Benbella.

Yia-Anttilla, Tuukka. 2018. Populist Knowledge: 'Post-Truth' Repertoires of Contesting Epistemic Authorities. *European Journal of Cultural and Political Sociology* 5:4.

Žižek, Slavoj. 2018. Three Variations on Trump: Chaos, Europe, and Fake News. *The Philosophical Salon* (29th July).

The Authorities

RANDALL E. AUXIER lives in a forgotten corner of New Denmark called Carbondale, where he teaches experimental theology to young witches from the Shawnee Forest Clan. In return for esoteric instruction, they pretend to be ordinary undergraduates at Southern Illinois University. This past year he led them on a field trip to the Tori degli Angeles, and lost only a few to the specters. In spite of his years, his dæmon hasn't settled yet, although her favored sleeping form is as a gigantic housecat.

RACHEL MEGAN BARKER has been exploring philosophy in both academia and in life for the past eleven years. She's also a published poet, and a political writer and activist—working on bringing down the Magisterium. She has yet to do anything as exciting as riding an armored bear, but she has been to Iceland.

TOMAS ELLIOTT is a PhD candidate in Comparative Literature and Literary Theory at the University of Pennsylvania. Once a student at a poor imitation of Jordan in a poor imitation of Lyra's Oxford, his travels took him west, not north, in search of a professorship in experimental theology. He's still looking, but has loved teaching about the multiple worlds of literature, film and philosophy along the way.

ABROL FAIRWEATHER received his Ph.D. in Philosophy from UC Santa Barbara, and has published in the areas of virtue epistemology, and the philosophy of emotion. His personal interests are focused on his wonderful daughter Barbara, ridiculously hot Bikram yoga classes, and an occasional leap into the cool abyss.

RICHARD GREENE is Professor of Philosophy and Director of the Richards Richards Institute for Ethics at Weber State University. He is the past Director of the Intercollegiate Ethics Bowl. He is the author of *Spoiler Alert! (It's a Book about the Philosophy of Spoilers)* (2019), and has edited seventeen books on philosophy and popular culture. He co-hosts the popular podcast I Think, Therefore I Fan. Richard's dæmon takes the form of a ukulele.

RICHARD LEAHY is a Lecturer in English Literature at the University of Chester, where he specializes in Victorian literature, gothic fiction, and science fiction. His PhD focused on the influence of Artificial Light (electric, not anbaric) in nineteenth-century literature, which was later adapted into his first book, *Literary Illumination* (2019). Richard's daemon would be a chocolate labrador, because they're both smart yet stupid, and have very similar hair.

JIMMY LEONARD is an English teacher and author of the fantasy novel *The Evangelist in Hell* (2017). Since earning degrees from the University of Michigan and Oakland University, his research career has been much like Mary Malone's: speculative, underfunded, and often requiring travel to another world.

RACHEL ROBISON-GREENE is an Assistant Professor of Philosophy at Utah State University. She received her PhD in Philosophy from the University of Massachusetts, Amherst. She is the editor of *The Handmaid's Tale and Philosophy: A Womb of One's Own* (2018), along with many other books on philosophy and culture. She co-hosts the popular podcast I Think, Therefore I Fan. Like Lyra, Rachel has had a lot of problems with Authority.

NINA SEALE is a writer and wildlife conservationist currently working for the international wildlife charity Synchronicity Earth. She has had many adventures, from being a safari guide in South Africa to sleeping in the canopy of a Bornean rainforest, and is currently finishing her first novel. Since she first read *His Dark Materials*, she has prized any Lyra-like qualities she has found in herself, such as bravery (like that time she infiltrated a lion pride and tricked the lion king), loyalty (like that time she rescued her friend from the clutches of a golden monkey), and determination (like that time she went to the Land of the Dead to demand Stieg Larsson finish the Millennium series). But not lying. Never lying.

KIERA VACLAVIK is Professor of Children's Literature and Childhood Culture at Queen Mary University of London and has worked extensively on one of Lyra's literary forebears, Lewis Carroll's Alice, especially in relation to fashion and dress. That's to say that she has developed a particular interest in all manner of materials . . . dark, light, sequined, and polka dot. Because her name should be spelt with a 'y' and because she has a beautiful and complicated relationship with a brilliant and worthy Will, she fancies herself as a bit of a Lyra—aspiring always to the deft and dexterous deployment of very good words.

PETER WEST is a PhD candidate and adjunct assistant professor in philosophy at Trinity College Dublin. He specializes in early modern philosophy, especially the work of George Berkeley and Margaret Cavendish. His daemon is a small, scruffy dog who encourages him to spend less time on twitter and more time in the park. Like the Gyptians, Peter hails from the Fens and spent a year in Oxford, frequenting the pub Malcolm Polstead's parents once owned.

WAYNE YUEN teaches at Ohlone College in Fremont, California, and has edited and contributed to several volumes of the Popular Culture and Philosophy series. He has three daemons who frequently cough up hair balls, but intercision is off the table.

Index

THE
PRINCESS
BRIDE
AND PHILOSOPHY
INCONCEIVABLE!

EDITED BY RICHARD GREENE AND
RACHEL ROBISON-GREENE

This book has not been prepared, authorized,
or endorsed by the creators or producers of
The Princess Bride

ALSO FROM OPEN COURT

The Princess Bride and Philosophy
Inconceivable!

Edited by Richard Greene and Rachel Robison-Greene

VOLUME 98 IN THE OPEN COURT SERIES,
POPULAR CULTURE AND PHILOSOPHY®

The Princess Bride is our favorite story in all the world. But until now, no one has unlocked the profound secrets of this wise and witty adventure tale.

If you've ever wondered why men of action shouldn't lie, how the Battle of Wits could have turned out differently, what a rotten miracle would look like and whether it would amount to malpractice, or how Westley could have killed a lot of innocent people and still be a good guy, then *The Princess Bride and Philosophy* has all the answers.

And if you've never wondered about these things, we'll go through your clothes and look for loose change.

"This is an inconceivably enjoyable collection of essays discussing philosophical themes from The Princess Bride. *What are the ethics of revenge? When are promises obligatory? Are things truly inconceivable if they actually occur? What would morons like Plato, Aristotle, and Socrates think of* The Princess Bride? *There's something in this collection for every philosophically reflective fan of the movie."*

— ERIC J. SILVERMAN, philosophy professor and author of *The Prudence of Love*

AVAILABLE FROM BOOKSTORES OR ONLINE BOOKSELLERS

For more information on Open Court books, in printed or e-book format, go to www.opencourtbooks.com.